THE SECRET ROOM
OF MORGATE HOUSE

Novels by Elissa Grandower

THE SECRET ROOM OF MORGATE HOUSE
THE SUMMER AT RAVEN'S ROOST
SEAVIEW MANOR

The Secret Room of Morgate House

ELISSA GRANDOWER

Doubleday & Company, Inc.
GARDEN CITY, NEW YORK
1977

Gr

Library of Congress Cataloging in Publication Data

Grandower, Elissa.
The secret room of Morgate House.

I. Title.
PZ4.G757Sf   [PS3557.R255]   813'.5'4
ISBN: 0-385-12452-X
Library of Congress Catalog Card Number 77-788879

10-78,

Jesten's
5.91

THE SECRET ROOM
OF MORGATE HOUSE

CHAPTER ONE

Fatigue and hunger made her feel lightheaded; otherwise, Leslie Marsh thought she was all right. When she squatted to pin the hem of Doris Wiggins' dress and had to stay down too long, however, the clock, the gilt mirror, and the striped wallpaper started spinning. Then everything was black and she could hear Miss Wiggins' running footsteps and her fading voice calling, "Mama, Mama, come quickly."

Leslie didn't recover until she had been jostled and lifted onto the satin sofa in front of the tall curtained parlor windows and she opened her eyes to see the gray hair and concerned face of Mrs. Wiggins close above her own. "Good heavens, child," Mrs. Wiggins was saying, patting her hand. "Are you all right?"

"Yes'm, thank you," Leslie said, embarrassed at the trouble she had caused and trying to sit up.

"No, no, lie still." Mrs. Wiggins looked assessingly at Leslie's wan cheeks and great dark eyes. "Did you have any lunch, child?"

"No'm, I wasn't hungry," Leslie answered, feeling uneasy at lying on that beautiful sofa in her poor, coarse clothes.

"Not hungry? Ridiculous."

"No, really. I didn't have time and—"

"Lie still, child. That's what sofas are for. Dorrie, run tell maid to fetch a big bowl of that black bean soup right away."

Leslie managed to raise herself weakly. She tried not to cry. "Oh, please, Mrs. Wiggins. I'm all right, really, and I've got to finish hemming the dress and get home. Mama is sick and it's getting very late—"

"Good heavens," Mrs. Wiggins said, turning to the grandfather's clock. "It's twenty after five and dark as a hoot owl outside."

"Yes'm," Leslie said, trying to shake off the dizziness. "And I've got to finish the hemming—"

"Nonsense. You'll do no such thing. Dorrie doesn't need the dress till Friday night. You've got tomorrow and Thursday for that. I'm going to help you into the kitchen and sit you down to a big bowl of hot soup and a roast beef sandwich. You've been getting thinner and thinner these last months and we can't have that. A young girl like you has got to keep up her strength. Let me see, how much do we owe you? Two dollars at the moment, I believe."

"Except I haven't finished the dress yet."

"I'm sure you won't mind a little money in advance. Here, now, let me help you to the kitchen. You're still rocky on your feet. And don't you ever go without lunch again, you hear? Let this teach you a lesson."

It was ten minutes of six when Leslie slipped out the back door of the gracious Wiggins house, warmed by the heat of the soup and the feel of two silver dollars in her purse. She started quickly through the fog for home, a slender figure, black in the night, half walking, half running, her frayed wrap around her shoulders, a black shawl over her head, clutched tight around her face against the cold, moist air. There was no snow on the ground, but the weather was raw. Mist formed white halos around the gaslights, the streets were muddy and rutted, and the wet on the sidewalks soaked through her thin leather soles and chilled her feet.

A horsecar at the corner was taking on passengers, but she passed it by. Leslie was accustomed to traveling on foot, given all but the vilest of weather. The horsecar would take precious pennies and she could cover the two miles across town to her doorstep faster than the horse.

It was half-past six when she crossed the last street and came to the large roominghouse that marked her home. Christmas was less than three weeks away and the nearby shop windows were already gay with holiday decorations. Mr. Parsons, hanging a wreath on the door of his grocery, said, "Don't you ever stop running?" as she passed, but she was too breathless to do more than wave.

Then Leslie was hurrying along the walk to the rear door of the house and up the narrow back-hall stairway to the second floor. Old Mrs. Bodwell, who lived in the parlor and owned the house, only let the roomers on the first floor, who were all relatives, use the front door. The others she did not want to see nor hear.

In the upper hall a lone gas jet revealed the doors to four apartments, the bathroom, and the stairs to the top floor. Leslie's apartment was the first door on the left, beyond the adjacent doors to the bath and opposite apartment, and she hurried to it quickly. Her mother had needed help using the chamber pot that morning and had refused more than a cup of tea for breakfast. Leslie had had Dr. Nichols in on Saturday. He had looked very somber and had left two medicines to be taken every four hours, but the medicines didn't seem to be helping.

The door was unlocked and Leslie entered quickly. The apartment was one large room, containing a kerosene stove, couch, two windows, three straight chairs and a table in the forward area, and two cots, a bureau and a rear window at the back.

The room was dark and the glow of the gas jet threw a shaft of light diagonally into the corner where her mother's bed stood, dim and mussed and indistinct.

"Mama?" Leslie threw the door wide and moved to shift her shadow. The bed was empty.

"Mama?"

She heard a sound in the front area and wheeled, but it was dark and she could only make out vague shapes, the baskets of laundry on the floor, the tub of washing on the table, the clothes on the lines that had been stretched across the room. Those were the clothes that Leslie had hung the night before. And the ironing board was up and standing. Leslie had not got that out. Then there was the form on the floor, trying to speak.

"Mama!" Leslie knelt beside the frail woman in the tattered nightgown who lay there and gathered her into her arms. "What are you doing, Mama?"

Her mother tried to talk, but all she could say was, "Iron."

"Iron? Mama, how long have you been here? Oh, Mama!" Leslie held her mother tight, rocked her and wept. Then she said, "You're cold. You're icy cold. Why did you get out of bed?"

She rose and, with strength she didn't know she had, lifted the frail older woman in her arms and carried her back, laying her

3

gently on her cot, tucking her in, while her tears dropped onto the sheets and blankets. She stroked the woman's brow and spoke soft, muffled, soothing words.

"Stove," her mother said.

"Stove?"

"Turn off," her mother whispered weakly.

Leslie looked to check the stove. "Yes," she said. "You turned it off." She went for matches and quickly lighted the two kerosene lamps. They brought a warm glow to the otherwise shabby room and, in the light, the story was told. The hotiron was on the stove, the ironing board was up, and a half-ironed shirt lay atop it. Her mother, against all orders, had struggled out of bed, tried to heat the iron and get done the work she had been doing for the thirteen years of her widowhood. She had failed, but she had managed to turn off the stove. Leslie felt the iron and it was cold. There was no telling how long her mother had lain on the floor in her thin nightgown.

"I'll fix you a hotiron for your feet," Leslie said. "And hot tea." But before she could light the stove, her mother was seized with a fit of consumptive coughing, the dry, hollow sound that made Leslie's blood run cold. She ran back and propped her mother with pillows. The coughing subsided after a bit, but the half-conscious woman's breathing rattled and she looked so near death that Leslie was frightened. "I'm going to get Dr. Nichols again," she said. "I'll be back as soon as I can."

Leslie, who had not yet removed her wrap, snatched up her scarf and flew down the stairs again. Why, she thought frantically to herself, did she have to faint and have soup at the Wigginses'. It had cost her half an hour.

The doctor lived eight blocks away and she ran nearly the whole distance, splashing through the mud of the unpaved streets, running across on cobblestones where she could. A few carriages bounced along, their horses clip-clopping, their wheels grinding on the stones or sloshing through the mud, and Leslie wished she could leap aboard one of the light, quick ones, and urge its driver to deliver her to the doctor's with all speed.

Nevertheless, she was nearly as quick in reaching her destination as all but the fastest carriages would have been, and she was soon banging the large knocker on the doctor's front door, mentally urging him into action and catching her own breath of wet night air that smelled of coal soot.

The maid opened the door and Leslie said, "Tell the doctor he must come quickly. It's my mother—the consumption." The maid turned without a word and Leslie came quickly through the door, closing it with the weight of her body, leaning against it, panting and looking around at the furnishings and décor of the large, shabby, but comfortable house.

Then the doctor appeared, his dinner napkin in his hand, a gray, sober, kindly man. "Hello, Leslie, have some hot beef stew with us while Jack and Roger hitch up Daisy. You must be cold and tired after your trip."

"It's Mama," Leslie said and told him about her seizure.

He nodded gently and led her to the dining room, where Mrs. Nichols and the two little girls were eating and the two chairs of the older boys were empty. Dr. Nichols put Leslie in one, removing the plate, and called to the maid for more stew. "Mrs. Marsh is in a bad way," he told his wife, grabbing a few last bites while standing. "I think I'd better be prepared to stay awhile." He went for his bag.

The boys were quick and by the time Leslie had cleaned her plate and caught her breath, they were back and the doctor was ready. Leslie said her thank yous and followed him through the kitchen and out to the yard where Daisy stood in front of the barn, hitched to the buggy. The doctor helped Leslie up onto the seat and climbed after her. "Fast now, Daisy," he clucked to the horse and started her out the drive.

The horse picked up a quick trot in the street and Leslie told Dr. Nichols the details. Mother was worse than Saturday, far too sick to leave the bed, yet she had struggled to set up the ironing board and get the iron hot.

"She should have had more sense," the doctor said, shaking his head.

"I know, but that's the way she is. She doesn't want me doing my own work and then doing the washing and ironing too."

"She should stop taking in washing when she's sick."

"But people depend on her for their weekly wash. If she stopped, they wouldn't come back to her again."

"It doesn't matter. Your mother isn't ever going to be able to take in wash again, and you can't do her work and yours and take care of her at the same time. You'll get sick yourself."

"I'm all right. It's Mama I'm worried about. Now I'm afraid to leave her alone."

"She shouldn't be left alone, Leslie. Not any more. Somebody's got to stay with her all the time."

Leslie bowed her head and large tears dropped from her eyes. "We don't have any friends who can stay with her," she said in a low voice. "And we can't afford to pay anyone. I'd stay, but I have to support us."

"Don't you have any relatives?"

She shook her head and firmed her chin.

"Not anyone in the world?"

"She has a brother in Illinois," Leslie answered, "but she hasn't seen him since she was a little girl. He left home when he was sixteen and he's never been back. He's kind of a black sheep, I guess you'd call him."

"But you hear from him? You know where he is?"

Leslie nodded. "Sometimes he'd write to Mama and he'd send her some money. Then there'd be years when we wouldn't hear a word and we'd think he was dead. Then we'd get a letter again. Mama thinks he wouldn't write when he was down on his luck, only when he was flush."

"When did you last hear from him?"

"In September. The last two years he's sent Mama a birthday letter and a hundred dollars."

"A hundred dollars?"

"It's all gone, though. With Mama being sick this past year we were behind in our bills."

"I mean that's an enormous sum for a birthday present!"

"Oh, he's apparently very well off right now."

"Hasn't your mother written him of her situation?"

6

Leslie shook her head vigorously. "Oh, no. Mama only says that I'm getting work as a dressmaker and doing well. She wouldn't dream of telling him she had to take in washing after my father died. She's too proud. And she'd never beg. Besides, he got married a year ago—to a widow with a son as old as I am—and he's got responsibilities of his own."

Dr. Nichols clucked to the horse and turned a corner. "What about your father's family? Surely there must be someone—?"

Leslie shook her head. "They're from the South," she said. "He came up here to study medicine and fell in love with my mother. They had a girl picked out for him down there and a practice all waiting, but he wanted Mama instead and he knew it would not be wise for him to take her down there, so he stayed up here. Then the war came, which made matters worse, and he died in the epidemic in 1863. He caught the fever treating those who had it, and we sent word to his family but we never heard back, so we don't know if they ever got our message or whatever happened to any of them. They lived in Atlanta, so we expect their home got burned."

"Paul Marsh?" Dr. Nichols said. "He was your father? I knew him—not well—but we were contemporaries. I remember when he died. Thirteen years ago. I didn't make the connection."

"I know," Leslie said. "One doesn't expect a woman who scrubs floors and takes in wash to have been married to a doctor."

"I'm sorry," Dr. Nichols said quickly. "I didn't mean—"

"Oh, it's all right. It couldn't be helped. Doctors don't make much money either, at least my father didn't. You have to treat the sick even if they can't pay."

"And your father's death left you without resource," the doctor said, shaking his head, "—not even his family."

"But we've managed—up until now."

"But you can't manage now. You've got to have help. Have you nothing?"

"I have two silver dollars in my purse, and there's a little change in the drawer of the table." Then she said, "Oh, yes, I have a gold nugget that weighs five ounces, on a gold chain to go around my neck. My uncle sent it to my mother for me when I was born. He got it in California in forty-nine."

The doctor pulled up the buggy in front of the shops. "You wouldn't get anything like fair value selling it around here," he said, climbing out and helping the young girl. "And the little you'd get wouldn't last. There's only one thing you can do. You've got to write your uncle for money—tell him the situation and ask for help."

"Mama would never stand for it."

The doctor hitched the horse and retrieved his bag. "Your mother isn't to know about it. *You're* going to write the letter—and tonight. Time is short."

They went down the walk to the back and Leslie bit her lip as the doctor opened and held the door. She said, "There isn't anything you can do for her?"

"There isn't much any doctor can do for any patient," he answered, "except keep them warm, rested and comfortable. You give them morphine if the pain gets too bad, and about the only other thing you can do is pray."

CHAPTER TWO

Mr. Savin, who had the room opposite, heard her on the stairs and opened his door. "Out kinda late, ain'tcha," he grinned through the tobacco-stained grizzle of his beard. He was the worst of the tenants, more than one of whom worked to catch her alone in the hall, and all of whom were men, except for a straight-up, tight-lipped schoolteacher on the third floor who spoke to no one.

Leslie went past without a word and the man, discovering the doctor behind her, disappeared again. She entered her own room and hurried quickly to her mother's side. The old woman's eyes were closed and her breath came in strangled gasps.

"Dr. Nichols is here, Mama," Leslie said, grasping the pale, thin hand. "You're cold. Let me make you a hotiron and some tea." She hurried to the little two-burner stove and struck a match while the doctor went to the bed.

While she waited for the water and the iron, and the doctor sat with her mother, Leslie put the washtub on the floor and settled at the table with pen and writing paper to compose a letter to her uncle. In the table drawer was the letter he had sent in September and she took that out to reread. It was short, written in the broad scrawl of one who was not used to writing and, as the scratches in the inky lines showed, one not used to holding a pen. It was a blunt and forthright letter, wishing Mary a happy birthday, announcing the enclosure of a little remembrance (that large and beautiful check for one hundred dollars) and a brief recitation of his year. He had married at Christmas, acquiring not only a wife but a fully grown stepson in the bargain. He had, further, become a man of property for the first time, buying a house in a tiny town twenty miles west of Chicago, and it looked as if, at long last, he was going to settle down and become respectable. The return address on the envelope was "Walter Barrett, Box 100, Fletcher, Illinois."

Leslie had read the long thank-you letter her mother had written in reply. It was appreciative, cheery and newsy. The news had been about Leslie and her supposed skill as a dressmaker. She had been working as a seamstress for a fine dressmaker since she was thirteen and, upon the other woman's death, shortly after Leslie's graduation from high school—with honors, her mother had made sure to mention—Leslie had put her experience to profitable use and was able to earn a living from her trade, though she would not turn twenty-one until the twenty-eighth of next January.

Omitted from the letter was any mention of the hardships and privation Leslie and her mother had endured since the death of

9

her father. The house and her father's meager savings were spent on his final illness and, upon his death, her mother, untrained in anything but the domestic virtues necessary to wife and mother-hood, had nowhere to turn but the domestic chores of scrubbing, scouring, washing and ironing. Burdened with a daughter, she couldn't even hire herself out as a live-in domestic, not without putting Leslie in an orphanage, which she would not do.

No word of their troubles had ever been communicated to Uncle Walter. But then, no word of what Uncle Walter had suffered had come to them. What had he been undergoing those years when he didn't send letters and money? And how much money did he actually have when he had it? There was the five-ounce gold nugget that came when Leslie was born, and there were other years when money would arrive with brief letters that said all was well, that he was prospecting, or that he was in mining, or oil. But the addresses kept changing and he kept moving. Now he had finally married and bought a house. But he was three years older than her mother. He was into his fifties. Was he set-tling down because he had a lot of money, or was he getting tired? Was the hundred dollars he sent an amount he could ill afford, proffered for show? Or was there a lot more where that came from?

Leslie feared the former and she felt uncomfortable putting pen to paper. Never had she had communication with him before. The letters were always to and from her mother. For the first time, then, she would be writing, and her communication would be a request for money. It was painful.

Behind her, her mother started coughing again, so weakly that Leslie's heart sank. She started scribbling quickly then. "Dear Uncle Walter, Mother is too sick to write. She has consumption and all goes ill—"

She penned the words rapidly, then rose to get water from the stove. She put a second iron on that flame then, so that she could alternately wrap the two in towels for her mother's feet. She brewed tea quickly and took it to the doctor, who was holding his fingers on her mother's wrist and listening to her chest. "Set it on the bureau, Leslie," he said. "She's not ready for it now."

Leslie obeyed. "How about a hotiron for her feet?"

He kept his ear to the old woman's chest and did not answer.

Leslie returned to the stove and picked up the first iron with a hot pad, wrapping it in a small towel from the rack by the door. When she brought it back, Dr. Nichols raised his head. "No," he said gently, lifting a negative hand. "It's no use."

"Is she still—"

"She's gone, Leslie," he said and rose, preparing for her response. "You must be brave."

Leslie stood silent, her head bowed, and tears fell. "She's better out of it," she said softly, then moved past the doctor to her mother's side. "Mama," she said, getting down on her knees beside the still form and taking her hand. "Sweet peace. May it be your gift. You knew so little of it here."

She stroked her mother's brow and then kissed it and rose, tears wet on her cheeks. "Thank you for coming, Doctor," she said. "You were very kind."

Dr. Nichols shook his head. "I did nothing," he said. "No one could. There comes a time. That's all we know."

"You made it easier for her. You could give her your strength where I have none to give."

Leslie turned away and the doctor went to draw the sheet over her mother's face. The half-finished letter lay on the table and Leslie stood over it, letting a tear fall on its surface. She lifted her gaze from that to the two baskets of washing still to be done and delivered. One should have been taken back that day, the other on the morrow. Above the baskets, spanning the room, clothes hung on the taut lines, sagging them with their weight. A part of one line was empty, its contents on the ironing board. It had been Mary Marsh's last effort. She could not bear to have her daughter doing the work of two. Mary had not been able to get them ironed, but the job still needed to be done. The wash had to be done too, and the stove took forever to heat up water. It would be a long, long night, and there was two days' work still to do on Doris Wiggins' gown for the ball on Friday night.

Dr. Nichols came close, stopping behind her so he would not see her tears. "Leslie, it's for the best. Some say fresh air and sunshine can sometimes effect a cure, but I don't believe it. She could never have got better."

"I know," Leslie said dully. "I know it's for the best. It's hard, even so."

There was a silence and then the doctor said, awkwardly and with embarrassment, "Do you have any plans?"

Leslie didn't lift her eyes. "You mean, what I shall do? No. I haven't thought."

"I meant—" There was that hesitation again. "Your mother." He went on, a little more strongly. "Is there a cemetery plot?"

Leslie hadn't thought about that at all. She shook her head. "We have none."

"Do you have any wishes? About your mother?"

Leslie turned. "I wish the best for her, but I suppose you're saying that I can only have what I can pay for."

Dr. Nichols nodded. "Only that."

Leslie shook her head. "I have just the two silver dollars and the gold nugget." She undid one of the buttons on her shirtwaist and plunged her hand inside, withdrawing a small lump of gold dangling from a chain around her neck.

Dr. Nichols didn't even examine it. "I'm afraid Connecticut funeral parlors want cash, not nuggets."

"The beds, the table and chairs are mine. They could go."

The doctor shook his head.

"There's the washing. I will get twenty-five cents for each of those loads."

"It will not be enough. And without a plot—"

"But what am I to do?" Leslie said desperately.

"You have no friends? What about your mother's customers? What about your landlady?"

"I could not ask her customers for anything except that they let me do her work. As for Mrs. Bodwell, I can only pray she does not dispossess me now that my mother has died in her house."

Dr. Nichols sighed. "If there's no one else, I suppose I can take care of things for you," he said.

"You mean, make arrangements for a funeral?"

He nodded. "I'd rather you did, if you possibly could, but if you can't, I can."

"Oh, Doctor, I'd be so grateful. I might not be able to pay you right away, but—"

"There would be no charge," the doctor said and moved to the door. "Leave her for the night. Try to get some sleep. I'll make the arrangements and see you in the morning." Then he went out, not looking at either Leslie or her mother.

"Yes, I'll try," Leslie said as she locked the door behind. Then she surveyed the two baskets of wash to be done. The clothes on the line were dry. They'd be easy. What was very hard was trying to iron wet clothes. The iron cooled so fast, one needed ten extra irons on the stove, not just one. But one was all Leslie had, and the laundry had to be delivered on the morrow.

She unwrapped the iron she had prepared for her mother, but it needed reheating. She put it back on the stove, as well as a kettle of water for the first wash.

And while that was heating, she thought to herself, she could wash and bathe her mother, brush and comb her hair, and get her into her best dress.

CHAPTER THREE

Dawn was breaking and it was seven o'clock when Leslie finished the washing and ironing. She had reached the stage now where she was totally numb and unfeeling. The food was all gone, there was nothing in the cabinet but tea and three slices of dry bread. Leslie didn't care. She wasn't hungry, she wasn't cold. She could

13

even look at her mother's body, dressed up as prettily as Leslie could make her, with the sheet up to her chin, without any feeling of loss. She didn't even have any awareness of feeling tired.

Leslie put the ironing board away and pushed open the window curtains. It was the morning of Wednesday, the sixth of December 1876. Nineteen days until Christmas.

She turned from the window and looked at the worn, thin face of her mother. Glory be that she hadn't suffered longer. She had had no strength. That was why she couldn't stand long against the disease. For thirteen years she had struggled to support and maintain her daughter. Now Leslie was grown, a month shy of twenty-one. The job had been done. Young Leslie was presumably equipped with the necessary minimums required to go forth and survive in an alien world.

Leslie sank down on her creaky bed. There were so many things to be done: The washing had to be delivered, Doris Wiggins' dress had to be finished.

And her mother? Dr. Nichols would come and take care of things. She did not know quite what that meant, but the fact he would be present gave her comfort. She could let go a little, relax and rely on him.

She stretched out without undressing and tried to sleep. She was too tired to wonder what life was about and why it should come out that way, but she was too keyed up by the tragedy to gain repose.

Eventually Leslie did doze for a bit but she awoke again at eight, not at all refreshed. She lay there for a moment, staring at the ceiling, then the stained wallpaper beside her, as recollection brought back pain. Doing nothing made it worse, and she found herself forced to her feet by the need to keep going.

She avoided the figure on the next bed and wandered into the middle of the room. The up-ended kerosene jug in the stove was almost empty, the rent was a month in arrears and Mrs. Bodwell was not indulgent. She had two dollars change to her name, nothing but tea and bread in the larder, and a long, busy day ahead.

For a moment, as she stood there, Leslie was seized with despair. What was it all for, now that her mother was gone? Her mother was in a happier land, but Leslie was now alone in the world, without even companionship to ease her own travails.

She fought down tears of self-pity. Crying would avail her nothing, and more than ever she had to be strong. She washed her thin, pale face in warm water and bathed her weary eyes. She combed her long, dark hair and reset it in a bun while brewing tea and toasting bread, then ate by the window that looked out upon the vacant lot next door. The day was gray and cheerless, the sky leaden and gloomy. At least there was no ice and no rain.

She was just finishing when she heard a clumping in the hall outside, the tread of heavy feet, the bumping of something against the walls. A husky male voice said, "Is this the place," and another answered that it was.

There came a hard rapping on the door, and Leslie opened it to find herself face to face with two burly, unshaven men with a large pine box standing between them. "This where the body is?" the first man said. His face was round, his lips thick, and he worked the stub of a smoking cigar between them.

Leslie, dwarfed by the size of him, nodded and stepped back.

"I guess this is for you." He thrust a small envelope into her hand and entered, helping with the box and followed by his partner. The partner was older, smaller, with gray hair and a beard. He gave Leslie only a glance as he worked his end through the door. "Easy now," he said. "Where do we go?"

Leslie, ripping open the envelope, found a short note inside. "My dear Leslie," it said, "I've been called on an emergency and can't be with you. The bearer, however, will take care of your mother. Leave everything in his hands. I'm sorry. R. C. Nichols."

At the bed, the first man turned, a change coming over his burly face. "This your mother, girl?"

Leslie nodded and fought back sudden tears.

"I'm sorry," the big man said in softer tones. "I'll tell ya. Whyn't you wait out in the hall for a minute?"

Leslie obediently went outside and drew the door closed. She was glad not to have to watch, and she moved to the far end so she wouldn't have to hear.

After a bit, the two men came out of the room again, tipping

15

the pine box to get it into the hall. It was heavier now and the smaller, older man used two hands and didn't close the door. Leslie returned to them. "Where are you taking her?"

The big man with the smelly cigar said, "To be buried."

"Where?"

"—Cemetery, the far side of town."

"Will there be a minister?"

The man shook his head and moved to the head of the stairs, feeling with his foot for the first step. "Just the two of us, miss. It's the town cemetery. They don't go in none for frills."

"Could I go? —Be there when she's buried?"

The big man was halfway down the stairs, telling his helper not to push. "If you want," he said. "You know how to get there?"

"Could I ride with you?"

"We only got a wagon, ma'am. It's not a fitting hearse."

"It's all right," Leslie said. "Wait, I'll get my coat."

It was a rude, open wagon, drawn by two horses. The big man was already in the seat with the reins in his hand, and the old man was in the wagon beside the box, hooking up the back. He looked very displeased.

The big man threw away his cigar and patted the seat beside him. "You can get up here with me, miss," he offered.

"Where will your friend sit?"

"He can ride in the back."

Leslie shook her head. She did not want to dispossess the sour-faced man, and she did not want to make conversation with the driver. She insisted, instead, on riding in the back herself, and the old man lowered the gate for her and helped her up. He still didn't speak but his expression was less hostile. He climbed up onto the seat beside his companion and the horses were slapped into motion by the reins.

For Leslie there was no place to sit except upon the box, and there she silently rode through the city to its farther outskirts, a somber figure in a black dress and black cape, with her dark shawl over her head.

The cemetery was an open field adjacent to a large multistoned cemetery that was well manicured. The field wherein Leslie's mother was to lie, however, contained no markers. There was a dirt road through untended grass and, a short distance in, a mound of dirt stuck with two shovels, hiding a shallow hole.

It was into this hole that the two men lowered the box, and it had been cut so close to size that there was scarce three inches' clearance around, or more than two on top. Then the old man seized a shovel.

Leslie said, "Would it be all right to pray?"

"If you like," the big man said, and motioned to the other to wait. The old man, a shovelful of dirt in his hands, made a face, but paused while Leslie and the big man bowed their heads and Leslie recited the Twenty-third Psalm. Then the two men got to work filling in the hole, the excess dirt forming a small mound above it.

She rode back in the wagon with the men to the center of town, which was as far as they went, and she walked home from there. The weather was turning colder now and the men had talked about snow.

She bought food at the market and made herself some lunch. Then she delivered the laundry and the ironing, saying that she would pick up again next week. Though dressmaking paid more than washing and ironing, it was less steady and she was not yet in enough demand to make it a full-time career. For the time being, she would have to continue as a laundress.

After she had made her deliveries, she walked the mile and a half to the center of town again. Change was jingling in her purse now, quite a bit in fact, despite what she had paid out for food, for she had collected from the customers. It gave her a good feeling, something to counteract the ache of her mother's death, but she knew the sense of well-being was an illusion. What money she had must last a week, and there would be a rent payment as well, unless she wanted to be out on the streets come Christmas Day. No, she had to husband her resources sparingly. But she had it all planned. She knew exactly what she had to do and how to do it.

In the center of town she went into the Western Union office

17

and wrote out a telegram. She addressed it to Walter Barrett, Box 100, Fletcher, Illinois, copying the information from the unfinished letter she carried in her purse. Then she wrote: "MARY BARRETT MARSH DIED YESTERDAY STOP FUNERAL TODAY STOP LESLIE MARSH."

She paid for the wire from her purse, then went three doors down to a pawnshop. There, she took the gold nugget and chain from around her neck, let the impressed pawnbroker discover that it was really gold, took the money he lent her on it and the accompanying ticket and went to a nearby florist shop.

From there she rode a horsecar out to the rude cemetery where her mother's body lay, knelt beside the freshly turned grave to put a bouquet of yellow roses on the mound of dirt and pray.

Then she took the horsecar and went back to the Wigginses' to work on Doris Wiggins' gown.

CHAPTER FOUR

For the next two weeks, Leslie was too busy to grieve. Even had she the time, she was too numb, too tired, too worn. The money she got for the gold nugget more than paid the rent and the doctor. She had honored all her other debts, restored the pantry with staples, and got Miss Wiggins' gown ready in time for the ball. Miss Wiggins had looked lovely in it and she and her mother were most pleased. In fact, as a result, two other women had had her appear for interviews and the results were most promising. Then, by working all day both Sundays, Leslie got ahead a little on the washing and ironing so that she would be available at any time should the new dressmaking assignments come through.

But, oh, she was tired. She was so rushed and exhausted she didn't even have time to think. She fell into bed at night and couldn't remember her head hitting the pillow. And when she arose, it was to wash, put some food into her, and get to work.

In time, particularly when the pace slowed a little, she would come to feel the loneliness of her lot, would miss the companionship of her mother—not the dying mother of the last few months, but the mother she knew in better days, the mother who insisted that Leslie finish school before plunging full time into helping maintain them, the mother who smiled and listened all the while she worked, uncomplainingly, to keep them alive.

All around her, as Leslie passed through the town, Christmas decorations proliferated. Carols were being sung on street corners and alms were being collected for the poor. Leslie even contributed a few of her pennies to the poor boxes, unaware that, in the eyes of most, she would have qualified as one of those receiving the benefits.

She had no one to buy presents for, no one to send cards to. There was no one to give her a gift or send her a card. Leslie blotted the thought of Christmas out of her mind. It would be a tragic day for her when it finally arrived. That would be the time, her instincts told her, the grief and loneliness would finally come to rest upon her shoulders, and she didn't know how she would endure it.

It was on Wednesday, the twentieth of December, two weeks after she had placed her bouquet of flowers upon her mother's grave, that Leslie came home for supper with a bag of groceries. She had been all afternoon cutting and fitting a dress pattern to the dressmaker's form in the Rideout home. Mrs. Rideout was impatient with holding still and having pieces of cloth cut and fitted to her body. The adjustable form, shaped by Leslie to Mrs. Rideout's measurements, stood in her place, and Leslie had worked diligently measuring, cutting and sewing the fabric. Unlike washing and ironing, it was work that Leslie enjoyed. There was a challenge to making clothes, and there was something to show for the effort. It wasn't like cleaning and scrubbing or repairing, where all one did was restore things to a former condition. This was creative. One could stand off and view it afterward and realize it was a permanent token of oneself. And it wasn't only cutting and fitting any longer. Leslie had reached the point of skill where she could depart from the patterns—with approval of the customer, of course—and try innovations. "Mrs. so-and-so, this pattern is lovely and the material is just right to do it justice, but what would you think if, instead of this kind of cuff, we just—" And the women listened. And more often than not, they would raise their eyebrows and say, "Why, Leslie, I think that is a capital idea. Why don't you try it!"

Mr. Savin came out of his room as Leslie turned the corner of the stairs. She shuddered at the sight of him. He was going to block her path and she sensed trouble.

It had been six years before, when the onset of womanhood had struck her, that her mother had explained to her certain facts and realities of life to which, theretofore, Leslie had given no thought. She accepted that boys were boys and girls were girls without ever wondering why. From her mother she now learned what the differences were for and what dangers to women resulted from those differences. She also learned the proscribed methods for avoiding and averting danger, as well as proper methods of coping when danger had to be faced.

Right then, Mr. Savin appeared to be a danger she would have to face, but he was too small and wizened to be as threatening as some of the other men in the building. Besides that, Leslie had put on eight pounds in two weeks and was a good deal more buxom and strong than before. Give her another fortnight and she would no longer be the wasted, frail creature of the past but a robust, vigorous and well-developed young adult, strong and determined. Even now, though burdened by her groceries, she could look the man in the eye without fear.

"Yes, Mr. Savin?" she said, approaching the head of the stairs, speaking to him in a firm tone.

He grinned and fawned a little. "I have not expressed my sympathy for your poor mother's passing."

"Thank you, Mr. Savin." Leslie stared at him boldly and

gained the hallway. Now the bags in her arms were a protection. "My mother thought well of you," she added.

Mr. Savin smiled. He followed as Leslie edged past. "I meant to give you this," he said, having no further recourse. He was holding out an envelope.

"Oh?" Leslie turned and frowned.

"It was in the mail—a letter. It was in the box."

Leslie's frown was so forbidding that Mr. Savin only stuffed it in the top of one of her bags. "I thought I would save you the trip down the stairs," he said. "I was getting my own." Mr. Savin paused. How strong Miss Marsh had become since her mother's death. The frail and beautiful child seemed no longer timid and vulnerable.

Leslie said, in even tones, "Thank you, Mr. Savin. I am glad to be saved the trip."

Then she was fitting her key into her door and Mr. Savin had no choice but to depart. He had delivered her letter, but it had given him no lever.

Inside the room, Leslie deposited the groceries on the table, struck a match to light the nearest lamp, and kicked the door shut. She plucked out the letter and held it under the lamp. It bore her name and address, and on the back was written, in elegant script: "Barrett, Box 100, Fletcher, Illinois." Her uncle had received her telegram and was replying.

Leslie slit the envelope with the bread knife and opened the paper inside. Again the script was the clean, neat, professional kind that secretaries used and it served as testimony to her uncle's wealth. "My dear Leslie," it said, "you can imagine what a shock it was to receive your telegram reporting the death of my dearest sister Mary. Words cannot convey to you the sadness that afflicts me. Though your mother and I have not seen each other for many years, she has always been close to my heart.

"Though I grieve for her, my thoughts are of you. I understand you have been doing very well as a dressmaker. My wife needs a dressmaker badly. Nobody in Illinois knows how to sew a straight line. Would you consider coming out to live with us and helping my wife with her clothes? I ask you not only because you are my niece and my nearest blood relative, but because you could be such a help to us, especially to my wife with your dressmaking.

"I have a large house with plenty of rooms. The work would not be tedious, you would live in comfort and luxury. I do not know what your wages are there in the East, but, in addition to your room and board and other expenses, I would pay you five dollars a week.

"If you will send a telegram saying you will come, I shall send you train tickets and fifty dollars for expenses. My wife and I look forward to your presence. We want and need you. Please say yes.

"Sincerely, Your Uncle Walter."

Underneath that, in the familiar scrawl, was his signature.

Leslie read the words over and over again, her heart leaping. A home to live in, relatives around, the finest of materials to work with, and a free hand to invent and devise and create! All that and the huge sum of five dollars a week besides!

CHAPTER FIVE

It snowed hard the next morning, but Leslie Marsh was out in it bright and early, tramping through the deepening layer of white, down to the Western Union office again. It took more of the money she had gained through pawning her nugget to pay for the wire, and Leslie was thankful she had something on hand for the unexpected expenditure. How awful had the offer come through and found her without the funds to answer back!

On the telegram pad she wrote: "THANK YOU FOR

OFFER STOP WOULD LOVE TO ACCEPT STOP WILL WAIT FOR TICKETS AND MONEY—LESLIE." It was a long telegram and cost extra, but Leslie was lighthearted this morning and could even tell herself, when she paid the telegrapher, "It's only money!"

She walked home, thoroughly enjoying the snow, thinking how lovely it would make everything look for Christmas. Her own Christmas could be spent in solitude, but it would not be in despair. She would go around to all her customers immediately and give them notice that she expected to be leaving town shortly after New Year's, so they would have as much time as possible to make other arrangements. Then she would brighten her own Christmas by baking herself a cake. And maybe a cake for Mrs. Wiggins, who had been so nice.

Leslie did bake herself and Mrs. Wiggins a Christmas cake. She decorated her room with crepe-paper streamers and popcorn balls. She even found, at Mr. Pemberton's shop, a small, scraggly Christmas tree that was within her means, but which he wouldn't let her pay for because he said it would hurt his reputation to sell it. She set up the tree on her table on Christmas Eve and hung it with candy canes and colored angels and cherubs and stars she cut out of construction paper. It wasn't anywhere near as nice as the one she and Mama had had the year before, but it was festive and fitting for the occasion. Nevertheless, though it was snowing again and everything outside looked absolutely perfect, and even though she could hear carolers in the streets, and even though she had this wonderful job with her Uncle Walter to solve her future problems, Leslie couldn't quite get her heart into Christmas this year.

The loneliness didn't really hit her, though, until she arose the next morning. It was half-past seven and light outside. The cake she had decorated so carefully stood on the table beside the tree. It really was beautiful and she knew how good it would taste, but there was no one to share it with. The little tree, which struggled so manfully to be gay and cheerful, and upon which she had lavished so much effort, did look as nice as it could, but there was no one to enjoy the results of her labors.

23

Leslie busied herself with her morning ablutions, then brushed her dark hair till it shone, pinned it prettily, and donned her best frock. Then she prepared herself a special breakfast of sausage and pancakes with maple syrup. She hadn't had that breakfast since the previous Christmas.

It did not help. She tried to concentrate on how good everything was; that she looked her best; that her dress, made over from a discarded party frock of Doris Wiggins, was most becoming. But all she could think was, "Oh, Mama, of all the days in the year when somebody needs somebody—!"

She finished her special breakfast, washed the dishes and put them away, and looked at the clock on the shelf above the stove. It wasn't yet nine, and a whole day stretched out ahead. She was caught up on all her work, she had fulfilled all her obligations, and there was nothing to do. All the stores were closed, all other people were snug in their own homes sharing Christmas happiness, and Leslie was alone.

She thought of church, but the only church she had ever known, back when her father was alive and her mother didn't work every day in the week, did not have Christmas Day services, and she would not feel right trying another.

She could get out of the room—she knew she would have to do that. She could walk aimlessly to escape the horror of her abode, but it was a doomed day. Leslie didn't know how she would get through it.

She was startled by a knock and went to the door, without an idea who in the world was there. When she pulled it open, there stood Mrs. Wiggins and young Doris, enhancing the dingy hall with their Christmas finery.

Mrs. Wiggins said, "How are you, my dear? Could we come in for a moment?" She was carrying a small package wrapped in Christmas gaiety. "For you, dear," she said. "We hate to see you go and couldn't let you depart without some remembrance."

An amazed Leslie had them sit down while she opened it. It was a lovely woman's purse with a check inside. Leslie looked at the amount and blinked. "But, Mrs. Wiggins—"

"That money is to be spent in only one way, child," Mrs.

Wiggins admonished. "It is for a sewing box. You are going West to continue as a dressmaker, and you need the proper equipment. Mind you, I intended to present you with a sewing box, but Doris reminded me how burdensome it would be for you to transport to Chicago. She's right, and the thing to do is for you to buy it there, instead. But that is what the money's for."

"Oh, my goodness," said Leslie, "but this—this would buy such a handsome set."

"A very good set—for a very good dressmaker. The best deserves the best. And while we're here, we want to thank you again for the delicious cake. You cook as well as you sew."

Mrs. Wiggins and her daughter stayed long enough to have a piece of Leslie's Christmas cake. It wasn't cake time, of course, so Leslie wrapped them a section for their Christmas dinner.

It gave her a much less lonely feeling after Mrs. Wiggins and Doris had hurried back to their own family, and Leslie smiled with pleasure at the experience and thought about shopping for a dressmaker's kit in Chicago.

There was another knock and, to Leslie's astonishment, Mrs. Rideout was at the door. She was brusque and to the point. She regretted Leslie's departure and did want to leave a memento. She gave Leslie a gift-wrapped box, patted her on the head, and departed. That Mrs. Rideout, who was inclined not to bother about things, should make the trip, let alone come into the shabby building in which Leslie lived, was quite astonishing. So, too, was her gift, a silk-lined fur muff for the cold western winter.

Then Mrs. Wilson and her four small children came to the door with a farewell card, molasses cookies, and pine-needle sachets the children had made. Leslie and her mother had been doing the Wilsons' wash for the past three years.

Other of Leslie's and her mother's customers appeared as well, each with a token for the departing girl, until she was quite overwhelmed.

Leslie had thought she would flee her lonely room that day, but she never did. By suppertime every one of her customers had come by with a token of affection and remembrance, and not only was the cake she had made all gone, but so was a second she had baked as a replacement.

Leslie cooked herself a simple evening meal and ate it at a table crowded with a display of gifts. "Oh, Mama," she said as she looked around at what had befallen her that day, "if only you could have seen it! There hasn't been a Christmas like this since Father was alive."

CHAPTER SIX

The train tickets from New York to Chicago and fifty dollars for expenses arrived in the morning post on the fourth of January 1877. It was a Thursday, and Leslie went to the Kosco Stables that afternoon to make travel arrangements. There were three stages a day leaving for New York, she was told, but since it was a ten-hour trip in winter weather over icy, rutted, frozen roads, if she wanted to arrive in New York before dark and without reservations, she had best take the early morning coach. If she wished to write ahead and assure herself of accommodations, Mr. Kosco had a list of recommended inns and hotels for ladies that would assure her freedom from obnoxious strangers. Mr. Kosco also had a complete list of train schedules out of New York, including trips to far-off Chicago. It would take close to a day and a half to make such a trip, and trains, of course, were for sitting not sleeping. However, seats on the Chicago trains were spacious, pillows could be rented, and there were periodic station stops where lunch counters were available for the purchase of food. Mr. Kosco, in an aside, because he was very knowledgeable, did suggest to Miss Marsh that she bring along some food of her own. The nutritional value of the food at the counters, the fact that it was almost impossible to get served and to eat in the ten minutes of allotted time, and the struggle to get a spot at a counter—plus certain other needs that a traveler might encounter—did make him want to warn a tender young thing like Miss Marsh that the more food for the trip she could supply herself, the better off she would be.

Leslie listened and heeded and decided to make reservations—for a small fee, Mr. Kosco would make them for her—at a modest but respectable New York hotel run by the stage company and adjacent to its terminal. Thereupon, she booked passage on the Monday-morning coach, which was the first available, with hotel reservations to be confirmed. As for trains for Chicago, they left at ten in the morning, and no reservations were needed. One just got there early and boarded when they opened the gates.

Leslie, armed with this information, was able to spend the next two days packing what things she would take and disposing of the rest. The furniture she got Mrs. Bodwell to buy for two dollars, and she was pleased at her shrewdness, for she would gladly have given it away rather than try to sell or store it. Better to be rid of it. Leslie knew not when, if ever, she would return to her Connecticut homestead. It held nothing but sad memories, and she wanted to close the door on the past.

Thus it was that Leslie Marsh, a slender but no longer frail girl, approaching her twenty-first birthday, packed two bags and a lunch basket, redeemed her gold nugget from the pawnbroker with money from her uncle, closed the door on the shabby quarters that had housed her and her mother for more years than she wanted to remember, took a hansom cab to Mr. Kosco's stage-coach depot, and embarked on a new career and a new life. Leslie Marsh had never been ten miles from town before. Now she was going to a distant part of the country so far west that it bordered Indian territory.

At times she viewed her future with uneasiness, for it would be strange and different from anything she had known. Then she would remember there was an anchor there, a connection to the past. Uncle Walter, black sheep that he supposedly was, was still family. He had been generous to her mother, to the younger sister he hadn't seen since he was sixteen. Surely, then, she was in safe hands. Leslie boarded her first stagecoach that Monday, January 8, certain she had nothing to fear.

The trip to New York took the whole day. The roads were icy and wheel-tracked, making it hard for the horses, and the weather was so cold that even though Leslie spent every rest stop close to the stove, she could not thaw out before it was time to climb into the poorly heated coach once more and proceed to the next stop. Others passengers boarded and left; the coach was sometimes crowded, sometimes nearly empty. Two others besides herself went all the way into the sprawling, smoking, densely packed, bustling and dirty city of New York.

Once they reached the streets of the city, Leslie gaped and stared. The roadways were so wide, the traffic so heavy! It was already dark but the streets were crowded with horses and wagons of every description, the sidewalks alive with people. It was early evening and never had Leslie seen such hordes. They flooded the thoroughfares on their way home from work.

The stage came to its destination on Forty-second Street—a large, wooden, four-storied hotel adjacent to the terminal and not far from the railroad station. This was where Leslie and the final passengers disembarked and registered while the horses and carriage were taken to the stables in the rear. The hotel was large but not grand. The carpet on the lobby floor was worn and ragged, the air was little heated, and the clerks at the desk were warmly dressed. It was, however, so much warmer inside than it had been in the coach that Leslie felt as if she were stepping into a welcome oven.

The hotel, however, proved no oasis. Her room on the third floor was no warmer than the lobby. The blankets on the bed were insufficient, the food was indifferent, the service slow, the accommodations shabby.

For Leslie, however, the fare was better than her usual, and she accepted the rigors of the journey without complaint. This, she concluded, was what anyone who wanted to go from one place to another had to endure.

Her train was to leave from New York's vast railroad yard at ten in the morning, and Leslie, agog with excitement and chilled by her lack of blankets, slept only fitfully in the hotel the night before. Long ere the first hint of dawn she was awake, huddled in all her warm clothing, sitting in a chair by the window, wrapped in the thin blankets. She was too keyed up to sleep and she peered through her dirty pane of glass at the roofs of the nearby buildings as the light began to grow and she could make out her surroundings. Chicago was another big city, she mused, and she sought to learn all she could about big cities by studying New York. Thus she wouldn't appear too ignorant and provincial when she came before her Uncle Walter. Uncle Walter, she reflected, had been almost everywhere and done almost everything. Uncle Walter had been rich and poor, East and West, North and South, better and worse, probably even good and bad. Now he could even boast of having been unmarried and married.

Leslie was packed and ready when the breakfast call came, and she filled herself with bacon and greasy eggs, finding little to complain about since she had no other public food to measure her meal against except what was served at the stagecoach stopovers, and no fare could be worse than that. Home cooking, she decided, was what you got at home. It wasn't what one received in restaurants.

The train was puffing and building up steam when she got to the platform. It was the first train she had ever seen, and the size of the engine and the size of the wooden coaches awed her. Why, one could put three or four stagecoaches in one railroad car.

The great train did not leave the station until ten minutes past the hour. Then it blew whistles, chugged, puffed, spun wheels, and slowly got into motion. Leslie, beside the window, listened and watched, soaking up the experience, breathless and excited. The coach she was in was moving rather more rapidly now, slipping silently except for the rattle of switches beneath the wheels, the subtle rumble of the engine's vibrations, and the lonesome shriek of the whistle. There were so many tracks, Leslie thought as they left the yard—so many idle cars, extra engines and equipment. Traveling, she thought, was the most exciting experience in the world.

Once out of the yards and speeding across the countryside, Leslie's coach developed a rhythm. It had a beat as it clicked over the rails, and Leslie was exhilarated by the passing scenery. She couldn't believe a human being could travel so rapidly. Until the invention of steam engines, she thought as she watched the trees and houses flash by, no human had ever experienced that same blur of speed, the inability to do more than blink at the passing homes. And when, as happened once or twice, her train passed another train moving in the opposite direction, that speed was so blinding it made her head spin.

Nevertheless, as the hours passed, the experience of travel lost its sheen of newness and Leslie became accustomed to the rattles and bumps of the coach, to the vendors who hawked wares and food and drink through the cars. Only the varying scenery continued to interest her, but even that began to pall toward midafternoon.

There were periodic rest stops, the same as with the stagecoaches, but they were only for ten minutes, and the crowded counters, when a trainload of people descended upon them in frantic haste, were almost dangerous to a young girl. Leslie had the feeling she could be trampled to death in the rush.

She had, however, listened well to Mr. Kosco, and her lunch basket contained water, bread, lettuce, and some bologna she had sliced. These she kept refrigerated by storing them out on the platform of the railroad car. In fact, the weather was so cold that she had to alternate bringing the basket inside and putting it back out so her food wouldn't freeze.

For entertainment, Leslie had brought along a book. She had to abandon it, however, for she found the car bounced and swayed too much to let her read. There was nothing, therefore, to do but watch the passing landscape.

A hawker boarded the train at the last stop before nightfall.

He had a basket full of pillows which he was renting for the night. Leslie had already found that the seats were so hard and uncomfortable that sleep would be impossible, so she splurged the few pennies necessary to rent such a pillow and, before midnight, in the darkened coach, she had fallen fast asleep. And she slept solidly until a station stop at ten the next morning, having dreamed all night long about Chicago and her Uncle Walter.

CHAPTER SEVEN

Leslie's train did not get into the huge Chicago station until late afternoon on Wednesday, the day after she left New York. Icy weather had slowed its passage, and Leslie was well weary of the trip by the time the city was reached.

The train lurched to a stop, expelling steam, while, around it, myriads of people in heavy winter gear—men with ice on their beards, women with great fur collars—moved forward. There was noise and shouts. Trains came from New York all the time now, but the novelty was still fresh, and excitement inevitably bubbled at greeting people who had ridden all the way from that famed, august metropolis eight hundred miles east on the Atlantic Ocean. New York had glamor. New York had sophistication. New York had *savoir-faire* and culture and class. Chicago was provincial in comparison. It was a western city, dusty, vigorous: Mecca for the herds of cattle come for auction and the butcher's axe. Chicagoans were farm boys alongside the city folk of New York, and they knew it.

Leslie, looking out her window, peered at the waiting throng, wondering which among them was her uncle. Would he be big and fat with the pounds of luxury, or thin, like her mother, with the remnants of the hard times he had known? Would he be bearded or clean-shaven? Would his hair be black, as her mother remembered it, or grizzled and gray from his fifty-one years of life? Would his face be tanned and wrinkled from the western winds and desert suns, or soft and smooth from sitting behind desks, giving orders to others? Would his hands be gnarled and rough, or soft and manicured? How did black sheep look after thirty-five years?

Leslie retrieved her suitcases and waited until the other passengers had passed before moving them down to the door and onto the debarking platform outside. She returned for her lunch basket next, then stood on the platform in the frigid air, four steps above the ground, where she could both see and be seen.

It wasn't Uncle Walter who caught her eye, however; it was the stout, brassy woman with the orange hair and elegant furs, pushing toward her through the crowd. The woman had a forceful way, a concentration on objective that was not to be deflected by obstructing people, and she approached in a near straight line, her eyes unwaveringly on Leslie's face. "You're Leslie," she boomed in a raucous voice that carried above the din.

Leslie nodded.

"I knew it!" the orange-haired woman called. She had the pipes of a saloon singer, though Leslie, never having been in a saloon, would not have so described them. "I'm Queenie, your Uncle Walter's wife!" The woman pushed closer, and now Leslie saw that she was not alone. A man was following, well behind, a tall, lean and smiling gentleman, wearing a handsome black overcoat with a black lamb's-wool collar. And behind him was another man, this one of Leslie's age, wearing a gray overcoat with the same black lamb's-wool collar and a gray top hat. He carried a black cane with a silver head and, from that distance, Leslie thought he was the handsomest man she had ever seen.

Leslie came down the platform steps as Queenie got to her. The large, solid woman, her face well plied with powder and rouge, grabbed Leslie in a bear hug and bussed her grandly on the cheek. "Welcome to God's country," she boomed. "What a sight for sore eyes you are!"

"Well, thank you," Leslie said shyly, "—Aunt—Queenie?"

"Oh, never mind that aunt stuff," the other woman said. "Just call me Queenie. That's what m'friends call me, and the same should go for relatives too, eh?" and thereupon she gave Leslie an elbow in the ribs that nearly knocked her over.

"Yes," Leslie said, "I guess so—er—Queenie." She looked up then as the tall, older man appeared beside the flaming-haired woman. "Uncle Walter?" Leslie said.

Uncle Walter, tall, lean and grinning, came forward. "My child," he said gently. "After all these years!" He took her hands, and his own were soft. His hair was only beginning to gray and his face was relatively unlined. He was far from the wrinkled, grizzled creature she had expected. "It's so good to have you with us," he said, beaming. "You're all the relative I have left." He looked at Queenie and laughed. "Not counting my new bride, of course."

Then the handsome young man was with them, bowing and being introduced. "Meet your step-cousin, dearie," Queenie was saying. "This is my son, George Trowbridge. Isn't he a handsome thing?"

Queenie giggled with pride, but there was no denying that she spoke the truth. George was dark-haired, tall—at least six feet—with an inch to spare over Uncle Walter. With his dark eyes, dark brows and full lips, he was a fetching figure, a little soft in the jowls and round in the stomach perhaps, with a slight, sulky twist to the mouth, but nonetheless a gorgeous male. And, Leslie noted, he wore the most elegant and expensive clothes she had ever seen.

They took her bags and brought her through the station, and Queenie, who had appropriated Leslie, explained that they would not be going home that night. Fletcher was an outpost town, she said, on the rail line running to Missouri and Kansas. There was a train a day in and out, with a weekly through train to those Far West terminals.

Fletcher was, nevertheless, up-to-date, Queenie stressed, not at all reliant upon the Sears, Roebuck catalogue. It had shops that sold nearly anything one could ask for; its finest restaurant could equal all but the best Chicago had to offer; every modern convenience was available—post office, Western Union telegraph, train and coach service, secretaries and office help, two banks, a number of other financial institutions, a judge, a sheriff and six deputies. Most of the people in Fletcher, Queenie said, never had cause to go to Chicago.

However, Queenie explained, since they were in the big city, they would take advantage of the occasion. The plan was to spend the night—rooms were already reserved—and take the late-afternoon train to Fletcher the next day. Meantime, they would spend their time shopping for material for the clothes Leslie would make, for the patterns, and whatever else a dressmaker would need. Queenie was not familiar with the field, and that would be Leslie's choice.

Leslie couldn't have been more pleased, for in addition to the opportunities it afforded for equipping herself for Queenie's needs, it would enable her to buy the cherished sewing basket that was Mrs. Wiggins' gift. How pleased Mrs. Wiggins would be when she heard the details about her contribution to Leslie's new life.

"D'ya think you'll have any trouble fitting me?" Queenie asked, pausing outside the station to pose and do a full turn. "I trust you can sew for someone with my figure?"

"Oh, yes," Leslie was quick to reply. "I shouldn't have any trouble at all." She was conscious that her handsome step-cousin was ever close, listening intently to what was said.

"I'm afraid such talk must be boring to you," Leslie remarked, trying to engage him in conversation.

"Fascinating is the word," George answered. "And did anyone tell you that you are very beautiful?"

Leslie flushed. No one ever had told her she was very beautiful. She had never even thought about it before. There had been no time, and certainly there had been no one to notice. She was sure Mr. Savin didn't leer at her because she was beautiful, only because she was young.

"You are very kind," Leslie said and looked away.

34

The hotel was The Emporium, a large, ornate, four-floored structure just across the broad frozen street, and George helped Leslie over its slippery width with gentle care, holding her so close she could feel his body against her arm.

Nor did he let her go even after they entered the rich, paneled lobby with its red-carpeted floor and broad runners to protect it from the sand and grit of the travelers. Uncle Walter signed them in and bellhops took their bags up the flight of stairs to their first-floor rooms. Through it all, George held Leslie's arm, nor did he let her go until they reached the suite that she and Queenie would share. Leslie found herself tingling at the experience. She had never been attended to by a man before.

The room was spacious and well-appointed, and Leslie was hard put not to go around touching and admiring everything. It was almost like being in Mrs. Wiggins' or Mrs. Rideout's house.

"Don't unpack more than you need," Queenie told her, then said that she should wear something nice to the restaurant that evening. That removed all choice, for the only nice thing Leslie had was Doris Wiggins' made-over frock.

She got it out and Queenie said, yes, that would do very well and looked it over for a label. Finding none, she said, "Did you make this, girl?"

"Yes, I did, though I'm afraid the material is better than the style."

"Nonsense," Queenie answered. "The dress is better than the material. No question of that. The cut and flair of the styling are becoming. You are even better than I expected."

Queenie was sincerely impressed and much of Leslie's nervousness evaporated. She felt a little more at home with these strangers.

CHAPTER EIGHT

It seemed to Leslie that the Chicago visit was over before it began. So much happened that it was a kaleidoscope of events, of richness, luxury, charm, new colors, new smells, new experiences, new sensations, new people. They ate in the most unbelievable restaurant that Wednesday evening. Never had Leslie seen such beautiful gowns, never had she seen so many jewels. Never had she tasted such savory dishes, such succulent steak. Never had she had so much wine. It was almost enough to set her head to spinning.

And her new family! Could anybody be as handsome and attentive as George? Could anybody be as entertaining as Uncle Walter? He had an endless supply of funny stories and amusing remarks. There was Queenie, so interested in her new niece. What with the wine and the concerned interest of those around her, Leslie found herself revealing the nature of the life she and her mother had led, the terrible poverty that had afflicted them. Queenie patted her arm and told her it was a bad dream, that nothing like that would ever happen again. Her new life, Queenie promised, would rival that of a fairy princess. They would all see to it. "Isn't that right, George?" Queenie had said, and George, whose interest in Leslie seemed to exceed his interest in his meal, said a heartfelt, "Very right!"

Then, after that when Queenie and Uncle Walter went back to the hotel and she, herself, was ready to drop, nothing would do but that George take her for a ride through the park in a hansom cab. They wrapped themselves in the heavy blankets and snuggled close while the driver took them at a slow trot through the snowy wastes. George put his arm around her as they rode, but Leslie did not know it until they arrived back at the hotel, for she had fallen fast asleep.

The next day, almost till train time, was spent with Queenie, going to store after store. There was so much to buy—some serviceable clothes for Leslie, new material for Queenie's wardrobe-to-be, patterns by the dozen of all the latest styles for all manner and kinds of garments, and of course the sewing basket to be bought with Mrs. Wiggins' money. Leslie found just the thing, so extravagant yet so perfect. She did not have money enough, but Queenie willingly advanced her the difference, and Leslie returned to the hotel clutching it to her bosom like a chest of treasure.

Uncle Walter checked them out of their rooms and they took the Fletcher train at five o'clock. It was the only one of the day and would stay in the Fletcher station overnight, leaving with Chicago-bound passengers at nine-thirty the next morning. The trip was forty-five minutes and the coal stove in their car kept the passengers uncomfortably warm despite the near-zero temperature outside.

Then they were disembarking in the frigid town of Fletcher. The black of night was bitter, but lamps glowed comfortingly in town-house windows and the gaslights were lit. Close by was the green-and-gold sign of the Chevalier Restaurant & Hotel, the lamps in its long row of windows warm and inviting. A farther inn was across the tracks, its big red-and-gold sign unreadable in the dimness. The street was silent except for the snort of an unseen horse; a passerby was silhouetted by windows in the distance, and Leslie, waiting with Queenie for George and Uncle Walter to pick up the horse and sleigh from the adjacent stables, could sense that Fletcher was a warm and cozy town.

George and Uncle Walter arrived, Leslie and Queenie were helped into the sleigh, and off they went behind a mare named Brindle along an icy road away from the lights, into darkness.

"Less than a mile to go," Queenie told Leslie as they left the town behind and the lights grew fewer, the white fields larger. Ahead of them, Brindle sniffed the air and sensed it too. Her pace quickened.

"Half a mile to go," Queenie next said as they passed a snow-bound house with lighted windows. "We're next."

Brindle, stepping lightly but carefully, moved nimbly on the frozen surface without sliding. Queenie and Leslie were alone in the sleigh, for George sat beside Uncle Walter in the driver's seat.

"Who lives there?" Leslie asked as the house retreated behind them.

"I don't know. Name of Cranston, I think. Nobody we bother with."

Leslie thought it odd not even to know one's neighbors. She said, "Do you have many friends in town?"

"George does. Not your Uncle Walter and me. He's away a lot seeing to his oil fields and his mines. We don't have time to socialize. Besides, there's nobody worth socializing with."

Leslie wondered why Queenie and Uncle Walter had moved to Fletcher if there was nobody there they wanted to know, but dared not ask. Around her were patches of woodland, black against the night, but for the most part the landscape was open fields of snow which glowed a faint white under the stars. It was an unknown world she was entering, and despite the magnitude of her welcome, the extravagant dinner and the zealous attention, she felt a growing unease.

On this day everyone seemed too businesslike. George had been dutifully attentive, and Queenie had spent the day with her, but it was as if, with the welcome over, Leslie could now be taken for granted and paid no heed. Uncle Walter, who had been so delightful the night before, had hardly said two words to her today. She had told of her life and now was eager to hear about his, to learn what he had done in the years he'd been gone. At lunch his conversation had been chit-chat, and on the train he had read the paper. Leslie had even undone a button on her shirt-waist to show him the gold nugget that dangled always over her heart, hoping to lead him to tell her where he got it. Instead, he didn't even remember he'd given it to her, let alone where or when he'd come by it. "Long ago. Out in the gold fields, I guess," was his response, and he'd picked up the paper again.

Now he was up on the seat handling the reins. She wished he'd let George do that while he sat beside her and eased her entry into this frosty, white, and strange new world. She needed an anchor in the form of a relative, and she was given, instead, an orange-haired mentor.

They rounded a bend and, far ahead, a tiny dot of light appeared. "That's your new home," Queenie said proudly. "Biggest house in Fletcher and next to last on the road."

"Where does the road go?"

"Another mile to the last house. Lasky's farm. He raises cattle and vegetables and gives us everything we want."

"*Gives* it to you?"

"And money besides. Your Uncle Walter lets him farm some of our property."

"You have a lot of property?"

"Three hundred acres goes with the house. The Morgates who built it weren't farmers, but they knew how to get money from the farmers."

The house drew nearer and, as more lights became visible, it began to loom large. It was set well back from the road and rose two stories and attic above the flat, rolling countryside.

The carriage turned into a broad driveway that had been plowed along the far side of the house out to a barn adjacent to the servants' wing out back. A silo stood farther back, and there was an abandoned chicken coop and outbuildings across the drive from the house. The house itself was square and boxlike with wide clapboards, a sizable porch, and a mansard roof. A post lantern out back showed it to be a dark brown—the color, like the shape, providing a sense of strength and solidity.

A path through deep snow had been shoveled along the front of the house from driveway to porch steps, and it was opposite that that Uncle Walter stopped the sleigh. The lantern on the sleigh had signaled arrival to those inside, and no sooner had Brindle come to a halt and stomped her dainty feet than the front door opened and three men came hurrying out. One moved quickly to take the young mare's reins, another approached the luggage rack to which the suitcases were strapped, and the third sought to assist the men from their perches.

George needed no aid, but sprang to the ground to push aside blankets and help Leslie and his mother out of the sleigh. "Get the servants lined up, Lambert," he said to the man assisting his stepfather. "And have tea ready. You, Swift," he went on, addressing the groom who held the mare, "give her a good rubbing down and make sure she's warm. I don't know what kind of care she got in the stable."

The groom assured him that he would take good care of the horse and, when the foursome had disembarked and the footman had got all the luggage off, led Brindle toward the barn.

Lambert meanwhile had gone ahead, and when the family entered the spacious front hall a gathering of servants, three of them on the broad staircase, had assembled.

George did the honors, presenting Miss Leslie Marsh, niece of Mr. Barrett, to the staff. The staff was, to Leslie, surprisingly large. Besides Paul Lambert, the head butler, Swift, who cared for the horses, and Harry Best, the footman struggling with the luggage, there was a cook, a scullery maid, a personal maid for Mrs. Barrett, a parlormaid, and two chambermaids. Lambert bowed, the girls curtsied, and Leslie, more than a little overwhelmed, said she hoped she would be forgiven but it would take her a little time to know them all by name.

Tea was ready in the library and the party repaired to a comfortable room through sliding doors on the left. Lambert had called it the library, but though there were many shelves to indicate its purpose, there were no books, and the vacant surfaces were used for the display of bric-a-brac.

The tea was warming after the ride, and there were cookies as well, but the snack was brief, for dinner was in the offing and a little time was needed to prepare.

Queenie summoned Lambert and was told that Best had taken the bags to the proper rooms and they were being unpacked. "Have Mabel show Miss Marsh to her room," she said and turned to Leslie. "Go with Lambert, honey. He'll have Mabel show you around. Then get yourself changed and we'll have dinner at eight."

Lambert led Leslie up the curving stairs to an overlooking passage where closed doors hid strange rooms and branching corridors disappeared around corners. He led her along the railinged route to the opposite side of the stairwell and a door at the end. "This will be your room, ma'am," he told her and showed her inside.

A small interior hall opened into a spacious front bedroom with windows facing south and east. As in the library, a small coal stove, with a hod and shovel beside it, was piped into the fireplace, making the room amply warm. The bed was against the opposite wall, there was a bureau and a vanity, a wardrobe, a washstand with the necessary basin and water pitcher, and a luggage rack at the foot of the bed, upon which lay one of Leslie's suitcases, while the chambermaid, named Mabel, put its contents away.

Lambert departed, leaving instructions for Mabel to acquaint Miss Marsh with the ways of the house. Mabel explained as she unpacked: She or Fanny, the other chambermaid, would bring in a kettle of hot water at seven-thirty in the morning and build up the fire. Breakfast was in the breakfast room at eight. Lunch was at noon, and dinner at seven in the dining room. There was a bathroom at the end of the rear hall with a tub and sink that pumped hot water from a tank in the scullery below. From the bathroom window Miss Marsh would be able to see the family privy out behind the servants' quarters, shielded by bushes and fences. The chamber pot was under the bed.

Mabel, finishing, took Leslie's suitcases and lunch basket off to storage while Leslie changed for dinner.

Dinner was another sumptuous meal, as rich and tasty as in the restaurant, but even more bountiful. There were thick slabs of roast beef, mashed potatoes, buckets of gravy, onions, preserved string beans, pickled beets, fresh baked bread. For dessert, there was apple pie, two kinds of cake and a pudding to choose from. Leslie, who had been undernourished and gaunt during her mother's final illness, thought that if this type of feast were the rule in Uncle Walter's house, she would soon have to worry about getting fat.

The dining room, in the northeast corner of the house, was a lovely room, Leslie thought. It had cream-colored wainscoting and blue wallpaper with a design of white figures. The snow-white tablecloth and napery, the polished silver, gleaming crystal, the blue of the china that matched the wallpaper, were almost as stimulating to the appetite as the aroma of the delicious food.

41

The adjacent living room, which was twice the size and faced east and south, was overwhelming with its giant fireplace, huge mirrors, and ornate white-and-gold motif. The satin upholstery, marble-topped tables, and great gold frames were far richer even than the Wiggins place, but Leslie did not feel as much at home there as she did in the smaller, less dazzling dining room.

Again there was wine and Leslie sipped it sparingly. Conversation sparkled, led by Uncle Walter, who seemed bent on charming his new niece out of her senses. The only trouble was, he would never be serious. She wanted so much to learn all about his background and his work, to get fully acquainted with her long-lost relative, but she could not pin him down. And if she asked a direct question, Queenie would interrupt and brush it aside with a vague, general answer, dismissing the matter as trivial and boring to the others present. All Leslie could discover was that her uncle's holdings were in Colorado and that they included copper, silver and lead mines, and oil wells that were just coming in.

How he had acquired them and how he managed them, and why from so far away, were questions she wished to have answered, but she would have to wait for a time when she could get him alone.

How Uncle Walter managed them from Fletcher, however, was one question that did get answered, and to her dismay. As dinner was ending, Uncle Walter remarked that he would have to get busy packing.

"Packing?" Leslie asked.

"Gotta get the train tomorrow," her uncle said, not quite meeting her eye. "Gotta go visit my holdings."

"You mean," Leslie said, distraught, "you're going away?"

Uncle Walter looked uncomfortable. "Couldn't tell you before, my dear. We wanted you out here as fast as we could get you. You understand that? But business is business and I can't just sit in Fletcher all the time. The money won't come in if I don't go out and get it." He chuckled at his remark, though Leslie didn't.

Leslie nodded unhappily. She had just arrived in a new and foreign world with only her uncle to lean on. Now he would leave her stranded with strangers. She had no roots any more and she needed someone to cling to—at least until she could get herself oriented. "How long will you be gone?" she asked dismally.

"Two weeks ought to do it."

Leslie's heart sank. Two weeks seemed an eternity. "That long?"

"Takes a long time to get there," Queenie put in. "And a long time back."

Leslie nodded. Then, because she knew nothing about the Far West and was worried, she said, "That's Indian country, isn't it?"

"Indian country?" Uncle Walter glanced at Queenie.

"I mean," Leslie said, "isn't it dangerous out there?"

Queenie, who sat opposite Uncle Walter, reached over to pat Leslie's hand. "You don't have to worry about that any longer, my dear. Colorado became a state on August first."

CHAPTER NINE

Leslie was already awake when Mabel knocked on her door at seven-thirty and came in to stoke and recoal the fire and leave a kettle of hot water on the stovetop. Leslie threw back the covers, sat up and slipped her feet into the woolen slippers she'd brought with her. Back in Connecticut her room was icy in the morning, but here, with the windows tight-shut, the fire banked but alive, she didn't need all the blankets she'd been given. The water in her pitcher hadn't frozen, the room was cool but not cold.

Leslie performed her ablutions at the washstand, shed her

nightgown without shivering, and got into her clothes. Her undergarments were especially delightful, for she had warmed them over the top of the stove while washing.

The breakfast room was new to Leslie, lying between the library and kitchen with double windows on the west side of the house overlooking the driveway, coop and barn and, between them, rolling snow-covered fields that led to far-off woods.

On the menu was grapefruit out of season, shipped by train from Florida, hot oatmeal, bacon and eggs, toast and coffee, with pancakes and Vermont maple syrup if she wanted. Breakfast at Uncle Walter's was a national showcase. Railroads supplied the little town of Fletcher with all the East and South had to offer.

Uncle Walter made light jokes over the meal, pretending the parting was of no import. Queenie wore a matronly air of watchfulness, and George, the handsome youth across the table, said nothing. It had become known that he, as well as Uncle Walter, would be taking the nine-thirty train to Chicago, but he avoided discussing the reasons as carefully as he avoided Leslie's glance. Leslie was aware, however, that George's gaze was directed at her all the time she was not looking back, and though she did not know the reason, she found the experience pleasantly disconcerting.

Then the meal was concluded and the men got into overcoats while Swift brought the sleigh around. Uncle Walter kissed Queenie goodbye and acted as if he wanted to make it lingering, but Queenie kept it short. George then kissed her on the cheek. Leslie, waiting nearby, was given a token peck by her departing uncle, and she resisted the impulse to clutch him, to make him feel real and lasting.

Then the men were out on the porch, slamming the door behind them, and the women watched through the windows as they trekked to the sleigh, climbed in and waved Swift to be off. The sleigh moved out into the road and turned left, almost hidden behind the heaps of snow the road plows had raised. They were gone and Leslie was alone with Queenie, wishing more than anything in the world that the men were back, that she did not have to be left with this woman.

44

There was no help for it and Leslie put on her best face. Queenie was, after all, the reason for her presence. Fitting Queenie out in proper attire was her job. If she could lose herself in that, all would be well.

For the following hour, however, Queenie was unavailable. She retired to her room with Glenda, her personal maid, as soon as the sleigh had disappeared. "Make yourself comfortable," was her admonition to Leslie. "We'll tend to the dressmaking business when I'm ready."

Leslie, left to her own devices, did the obvious thing. She explored her new domicile. What did the house and grounds contain?

Bundling herself into warm clothing, she ventured out the kitchen door onto a small enclosed porch that bordered the servants' quarters, faced the drive, and looked out onto the great barn to the right, the silo behind, and the coop to the left. She went down the pair of steps onto the plowed and rutted ice of the yard. A path between the jutting servants' quarters and the barn marked the well-trod route to the privies beyond. The barn itself had the door ajar and Leslie, entering, found horse stalls on her right, carriage stalls on her left, a haymow around the corner beyond them, and a ladder to a hayloft over the horses. There was a layer of straw over the dirt of the floor, a rear door that opened north beyond the servants' quarters, and the warm smell of hay and manure inside.

Leslie, exploring and enjoying the realms of the stable, did not venture into the silo or empty coop. Instead, she returned to the house. It was an enormous residence and she had still to find her way about.

The first floor was easy. The kitchen occupied the northwest corner, its entrance from the porch. Included there were the scullery and pantry and, through the pantry, the door to the servants' wing. Opposite that, in the other corner, was the servants' staircase to the second floor, and the stairs to the cellar.

A hallway led to the dining room on the east, a south door led to the breakfast room. South of that was the library, and east was the L of the living room behind the front hall and stairs.

The second floor was harder to get used to, for there were more rooms and they all opened into enclosed corridors. Leslie at first found herself getting lost. Three doors were close at hand at the head of the curving main stairs. Two were in a little alcove, the one on the right leading to the master bedroom where Queenie and Uncle Walter slept, the one straight ahead leading to George's room.

The third door faced her own at the other end of the railinged passage and opened into a small spare room overlooking the drive. There was a sewing table there and, to Leslie's delight, a sewing machine. Mrs. Wiggins had had a sewing machine and Leslie had learned how to use it. It was the only other one she had ever seen.

Leslie went close to examine it, turning the wheel to make the needle plunge. It was new, obviously bought for her, and the thought made her tingle. She mattered to somebody.

Leslie left the room glowing with anticipation. Making clothes for Queenie would be fun with a machine like that. She could hardly wait to begin.

The next room Leslie tried was in the center of the second floor and had corridors all around it. It was a huge, windowless storage closet with a skylight in the ceiling and was empty except for a scattering of suitcases, including her own.

She crossed over and tried the doors on her side of the house. There were two, close together near the head of the kitchen staircase, and they opened into unused bedrooms. Then, around a jog in the corridor, facing the back, was the bathroom with its hot and cold running water.

Leslie passed that by and followed the corridor into uncharted territory. And there, at its end, where it turned left around the dining-room staircase, she found a final door. But unlike the other doors in the house, this door was locked. Unlike the other doors in the house, which were cream-colored against dark wallpaper, this door was painted brown so that, far from the nearest gas jets, it would all but pass unnoticed.

Leslie, puzzled, twisted the knob this way and that, but the door was not stuck, it was most definitely locked.

46

What was the purpose of shutting off this segment of the house? Leslie wondered. The room, as best she could judge, was over the kitchen and scullery. And now, as she looked about her, she saw that there was an unlighted gas jet close at hand. This could have been one of the brightest corners of the upstairs hall, but a deliberate effort had been made to isolate it, to cut it off from the rest of the house.

Leslie shivered and suddenly felt as isolated as the room. There were people about. Queenie and her maid were around corridor corners at the front of the house. She had heard servants in the kitchen when she passed the stairs by the bathroom. But now she was alone and all was still. She shivered again and realized that this back corner of the house was not only dark, it was cold. There was a draft of icy air around her ankles. Leslie knelt and put her hand against the crack at the bottom of the door. The razor-thin stream of air that came through was as frigid as the air that came through the front door when George and Uncle Walter had left.

As Leslie rose, Mabel appeared at the other end of the corridor, a stack of towels on her arm, and entered the bathroom. Leslie intercepted her when she came out, startling the young maid, who had not known she was there.

"What's in that room, Mabel?"

"What room, miss?"

"That room. Where I'm pointing."

Mabel walked down to it slowly and regarded its brown panels. "Why, I don't know, miss."

"You haven't ever cleaned it? You haven't ever had to enter it?"

Mabel said, uneasily, "Miss, I didn't know it was there. I paid it no attention."

"But you're a chambermaid. You ought to know every room in this house. Why is it you haven't cleaned this room?"

Mabel was showing real fright now. "Miss, I never been told to."

"Never? How long have you worked here?"

"Only a month, miss. Less than that. I don't know anything

about this house, miss. I didn't know the door was there. I don't know why it's locked."

At that moment, Glenda appeared at the end of the opposite corridor. "Oh, there you are," she said sternly to Leslie. "Mrs. Barrett is looking for you. She's ready for you to start making her some clothes."

CHAPTER TEN

The balance of the morning was spent giving Queenie a fitting. With all the new materials and dress patterns to work from, it was an exciting and challenging event. Even the Wiggins family had not laid in such an array of colors and materials at one time. Enough material was on hand to keep Leslie hard at work for a month, and there would be enough clothes at the end to fill out a modest wardrobe.

If Leslie had intended to ask Queenie about the locked room, she thought better of it. There was something aggressively cheerful about Queenie's manner that morning that did not invite questions. Moreover, the pains that had been taken to discourage notice of the room indicated that questions were not welcome. If Uncle Walter were around, that would be one thing. She would have dared to ask him. With Queenie she did not feel sufficiently at ease. Friendly as the large woman tried to be, there was something brittle about her manner, as if the friendliness were a mask and hostility lay beneath.

So Leslie paid attention to her trade, answering Queenie's questions, trying to compensate for the fact that Queenie would not hold still, coping with the growingly obvious fact that Queenie had never had a fitting before in her life. The room was alive with full-length mirrors. They were on all the walls, sometimes two or three on the same wall. In addition, three were on wheels, and it meant that no matter where Leslie looked, Queenie's stout figure and increasingly impatient face were in sight. The ample woman obeyed instructions with little grace and, as noon approached, asked how long it would take to fit one dress, whereupon, of course, Leslie could make all the rest from that.

"Oh, no, Queenie," Leslie said. "Each dress has to be fitted separately."

"Stuff and nonsense. Why?"

"They're different styles. They're different patterns. The pieces are going to have to be cut differently. And even if we used the same pattern, the way it's sewed makes a difference. I couldn't be sure of sewing it the same way every time. It would have to be checked."

"There must be some way of saving me all this fuss and bother. You can't tell me every woman who wants to have a seamstress has to spend half her time standing around with pieces of cloth draped over her."

"There are dressmaker's forms," Leslie told her, and then, because Queenie had obviously never heard of them, had to explain what they were.

"Well, that's fine," Queenie said. "I'll get one of those right away and you can work on that hereafter."

"I can do that for a rough mock-up," Leslie answered, "but I would never complete a dress except on the woman who's going to wear it. There is no fit substitute for the woman herself."

"Well, we'll see about that. Now let's get me out of this stuff. It's time for lunch."

Leslie, to her surprise, had lunch by herself. It seemed that Queenie was accustomed to having hers in her bedroom suite. Nor did she appear after lunch, and Leslie was left without any instructions as to how she was to occupy her afternoon. She wished more than ever that Uncle Walter had not gone away. She was not yet adjusted and, without him and with nothing to do, she felt lonely.

Then she spoke sharply to herself. What right did she have to complain? She was the luckiest girl in the world. She was living

49

in a great house, the niece of a rich man, enjoying luxuries beyond her wildest dreams. She had the best sewing box a seamstress could desire, a brand-new sewing machine, bolts and bolts of material, and a free hand to do with it as she pleased. What did it matter if she lived half a mile from the nearest neighbor, if her uncle went on a business trip, if her step-aunt might not be as fond of her as she pretended to be, if there was a strange locked room at the back of the house? Did not the richest and handsomest man in the world occupy the bedroom next to hers? How many girls wouldn't give everything they owned to be in her shoes?

Leslie went back to the sewing room and spent the rest of the afternoon hard at work.

CHAPTER ELEVEN

George came back on the late-afternoon train and arrived home at half-past six, just in time to dress for dinner.

Though they heard him in the downstairs hall, the first Leslie and Queenie saw of him was when he joined them in the living room a few minutes before the dinner call. "How well you look," he said to his mother, smiling crookedly and kissing her hand. "And how fine you look, my beauty," he said to Leslie, eyeing her with a good deal more appreciation, as he kissed her hand as well. There was an animal quality about him, a sensuous way that made her tingle at his touch, but in ways she wasn't sure she liked. He was too handsome, too soft, too spoiled. He knew too much. Something about the way he looked at and responded to women made her uneasy. He had wealth and looks, an irresistible combination. It gave him power, and he knew it and knew how to use it. It was this that made Leslie unsure of why she tingled.

"Did you see my uncle safely off?" she asked, trying to withdraw her hand unobtrusively from his.

"That I did, and then, of course, took care of certain of his business matters. We work closely together, as you can imagine."

Leslie would have liked to learn about those business matters, but George's attention seemed to be more on her than on the subject of his discourse.

Then dinner was announced and George took her arm as well as Queenie's as they moved to the table and were seated, with George at the head. Over the meal, Leslie tried to assuage her curiosity about her uncle's business, but with no better success. George put her off with vague answers which, at times, seemed almost contradictory and left her less knowledgeable than before. It was irritating. The men in the West seemed to believe women lacked either the interest or the brains to understand men's affairs. She found it frustrating to be constantly put off with explanations that Uncle Walter had some mines and some oil wells in Colorado and he had to go visit them periodically while George took care of affairs at home. What affairs? How much land was involved? George admitted there was an office in Chicago and there were some women secretaries, but he wouldn't tell her anything else. All he did was chide her for wanting to know about the women in his life and how many there were. This very effectively stopped Leslie from asking further questions.

Leslie bit her lip and wondered how to persuade George and her uncle that she was not, after all, a stupid little goose who asked questions about subjects beyond her comprehension because she had been taught that was the way to interest young men. She wanted to make them realize she was very much interested, not only in the family business affairs but all aspects of the new culture she was now a part of. She wished Queenie would give her support. Queenie was no idiot and George treated her with respect, even if she was a woman. Why couldn't Queenie see that Leslie had a good head too? But Queenie sided with George. She interrupted Leslie's questions with irrelevant chit-chat of her own, and Leslie, for the time being, could get no-where.

George put an end to serious conversation midway through the meal. "After a hard day of work," he said, "a man should find dinner conversation untaxing. It's time for fun."

With that, Queenie heartily agreed.

"In fact," George went on, smiling directly at Leslie, "enough of talk about the work I did during the day. What's important is what we're going to do tonight."

"We? Tonight?"

"Tonight we celebrate your arrival in Fletcher in proper style. Tonight I take you into town and we go dancing."

Leslie blinked and her breath caught in a gasp, so total was her surprise. And behind the surprise were sudden fears, the first of which was blurted out: "You mean—your mother—chaper-one—"

Queenie roared. "Chaperone? Wherever are you from? You don't need a chaperone—leastways me! We don't bother with that eastern fol-de-rol out here."

The second fear came forth. "But I don't dance." She was trembling. "I don't know how to. I've never danced in my life."

"We'll teach you," George said as if that settled the matter. "Right after dinner. It won't take a minute."

"I'll teach you myself," Queenie broke in. "That's all there is to it. Do you good to get out of the house, and it's right good of George to see to it. You're looking a mite peaked and your eyes are getting squinty from all the sewing you've been doing."

"But," Leslie said, drawing upon her last fear to support the panic that seized her, "I don't have anything to wear."

"Nonsense," Queenie countered. "There's the dress you wore to the restaurant Wednesday night."

Leslie could not demur further, but she finished her meal view-ing the evening ahead with dismay. Cinderella would be going out with Prince Charming, but not as a princess.

Queenie took her onto the bare floor of the living room "L" after dinner and, counting in singsong tones, showed Leslie how to place her hand upon a man's shoulder and let him take her other hand, how to let his hand upon her waist guide her where he wished her to go, and how to move her feet in rhythm in ways that would keep them in step with his feet and not under them.

Leslie, concentrating carefully, quickly discovered that the secret of dancing did not have to be passed from generation to generation through tribal rites. It could be acquired by anyone of reasonable intelligence and co-ordination in an amazingly short space of time. It was not long before Queenie was saying, "Now you've got it. Just remember how to place your hands and which foot you move back first. The rest will take care of itself."

Thereafter, Leslie went up to dress and came down to find George, in his beautifully tailored coat, his black hair showing the trace of a wave, looking devastatingly handsome, the slight, sulky twist of his mouth adding a touch of danger and excitement to his appearance. Oh, the girls would fall at his feet. He had that touch of recklessness about him, the heedlessness and arrogance, a spoiled quality that went with his looks, that had probably been put there by girls. Leslie could feel the effects herself and could not resist the surge of pride at being seen with such a strong, dashing, masterful man.

He stood by while Queenie helped her on with her things. Then they were outside with Queenie standing behind in the door and Swift holding Brindle beside the path to the drive. The groom tucked them in, gave George the reins and they were off, the steel runners of the sleigh squeaking against the packed snow of the road. Above, the stars were myriad, winking with sharp, icy brightness, and, beside, there was the pressure of George's body, snuggling close. Though he hardly spoke and looked at her but little, George liked her nearness. Leslie could get the vibrations and they sent shivers through her. She could not believe that this dark and handsome man could care two figs about her. She was so plain and inexperienced, so without talents, without the proper clothes, so untutored and untrained. Why, she was certain to disgrace them both on the dance floor. Yet here she

53

was, riding beside him in a stark but romantic situation that was beyond her most fanciful dreams. It was enough to make a girl's head spin.

Before she knew it, the loneliness of the road was replaced by the bustle and noise of other sleighs and the snorting of stomping horses. The town was about them now, and everywhere there were people. For Leslie the evening was already late, but in Fletcher it seemed scarcely to have begun.

The green-and-gold sign of the Chevalier Hotel appeared across from the dark, empty railroad station. Beyond, on the next corner and across the tracks, dim in the gaslights, was the red-and-gold sign she had seen before.

George, moody and silent on the ride, grew brighter as the liveliness of the town enveloped them. "Here," he said. "We'll park the sleigh here—give Edward the horses behind the tavern."

They disembarked and the groom named Edward appeared in the narrow stable yard into which they had turned, to take the reins and hold Brindle steady.

George led the way through a side door and Leslie found herself in an ale room nearly completely filled by men, nearly completely blue from the smoke of their pipes.

"Hey, lass," one of the men said, leaning back to impede her progress and rub against her body.

George, leading the way, turned and kicked the man's chair so hard it came out from under him and he crashed to the floor.

"Scum," George muttered, taking Leslie's arm and guiding her through the raucous room. There was laughter at the fate of George's victim, whistles and remarks directed at Leslie. She followed as close to George as she could, her face crimson.

Then they were in a larger room which, though noisy, was less boisterous than the previous one. Here the tables had checked cloths, couples abounded, and waiters wore shirtsleeves and white aprons. There was an orchestra on a platform at one end with a dancing area in front, and the couples cavorting there gave Leslie no reason to fear her own inadequacy. Nobody cared what they looked like, they were intent on having fun. Leslie's expectation that she would dance in a Chicago-like ballroom, like Cinderella at the palace, flew broken-winged away. The handsome prince had, instead, come to the scullery.

George found a table on the side, pushed two extra chairs away and seated her. Her disappointment must have shown, for he took the chair adjacent and said above the noise, "This is the best dance orchestra in town."

Leslie nodded. She knew she should be appreciative, but she couldn't help voicing her disappointment. "I thought it would be —like a Chicago hotel."

"In Fletcher?" George laughed. "We don't have any hotels worth talking about."

"What about the one across the tracks, with the red-and-gold sign?"

George laughed uproariously. "The Red Star? Well," he said, "I guess you could call that a hotel all right. They rent rooms, but it's not a place a nice girl should ever want to go."

Leslie understood what that meant and she turned away, flushing red again. A waiter appeared in response to George's snapping fingers and Leslie was spared the embarrassment of a reply. George asked what she would drink, and Leslie, not having any idea, left it to him.

"Two ryes with beer chasers," he ordered and, when the waiter had departed, rose beside her with a smile and said, "Now let's see what my mother taught you."

CHAPTER TWELVE

The décor, the outfits, the raucous orchestra and cavorting couples all made the tavern the antithesis of everything Leslie had expected dances to be. The plump, ungainly women here did not wear the kind of gown Leslie had prepared for Doris Wiggins, nor behave as she had imagined Doris would behave. Only George seemed dressed for the formal occasion she had thought she would attend.

If she no longer worried what the others would think of her, however, she did worry about the impression she would make on her escort. He was the man of distinction, of expertise, of experience and *savoir-faire*. He was the one who, for some strange reason, had chosen to squire her for the evening and she felt a nervous obligation to fulfill his expectations as, she was sure, the other ladies inevitably did.

Once in George's arms, however, her fears abated and she found that dancing was easy. He had a way of holding a girl, of leading her, of indicating by the pressure of a hand or the twist of his body, where she was to turn next and how her feet should move. Though there was little room, and the others on the floor kept bumping them, George made the most of the available space, and after two numbers Leslie was starting to enjoy herself. And by the time the orchestra retired for an intermission, she didn't want to stop.

They returned to the table and Leslie discovered at their places a stein of beer and a small glass of rye. Leslie had never had anything stronger than wine before and she did not know how to handle this new experience. She sat down to watch George's management of the two glasses, deciding she should do what he did.

What he did, however, made her blink. He lifted the small glass, said, "Here's looking at you," then downed the contents in one quick swallow. He gagged a little, took some of the beer, shook his head and smiled. He moved his chair closer and his knee touched hers under the table. "Now you," he said.

Leslie tensed at the touch. She knew it should have excited her, but now his nearness made her nervous. She felt as skittery as a fawn and she didn't know why.

Leslie stared at the tiny glass with the brown liquid in it, and the prospect of drinking it filled her with as much dread as walking on broken glass. Yet he wanted her to have the drink.

She picked it up slowly and he leaned so close she could smell the rye on his breath. "That's right," he whispered. "Now down the hatch."

Leslie brought the drink closer and its aroma was enough to make her reel. She was sure she couldn't do with it what George had done. She lifted it slowly instead and let it wet her lips and tongue. It was a burning fluid. She would have choked to death had she tried to down it at a gulp.

George took her free hand in both of his. "That's not the way, sweetheart," he said. "You have to gulp it and then drink the beer."

The act was beyond her and she probed for an escape. He was suffocatingly close to her now, his chair beside hers, his knee against hers, his hands on hers. She did not know what was the matter with her. This handsome man was showing an interest in her and she wanted him to desist.

"Show me again," she said desperately and pushed the glass into his hand.

The tactic worked. He accepted it with a laugh, but one hand still covered hers and the pressure of his knee was stronger.

"Look now," he said and bade her lean nearer. "You open your mouth and open your throat. That's the key to it. You have to open your throat. It doesn't stay in your mouth, it just goes on through. It's not even supposed to touch your tongue. Watch."

He gave her a second demonstration, without a gasp this time, put the thick glass down smartly and drank another third of the beer. "You see, there's nothing to it."

He ordered another round and, while they waited, took her onto the dance floor again. Leslie found it not as pleasant as the first time. George was holding her tightly now, so close that their thighs brushed and he was nearly putting his cheek against her hair.

Leslie closed her eyes and told herself she should be enjoying her escort's amorous inclinations. She was on her way to capturing the most eligible bachelor in the Chicago area. Certainly, he was far above her wildest flights of fancy, few as they had been.

But it was too soon. She could not get interested in a young

57

man so quickly. She had been too conservatively brought up. If the relationship were allowed to grow naturally, she was sure she could become interested. If only he would stop forcing things so fast.

They returned to the table and the new drinks were there. George looked heartened and again sat in close beside her. "How old are you, Leslie?" he whispered, his lips close to her ear.

"Twenty."

George took her hand in his. "Twenty," he breathed. "How could a girl get to be as beautiful as you in only twenty years?"

The improbable recollection of Mr. Savin came to Leslie's mind and, for the moment, she responded as she would have to Mr. Savin. "By taking care of my sick mother."

George studied her for a moment—coolly, she thought. "For how long will you be twenty?"

"You mean this beautiful?" Leslie couldn't resist being flip, lest the scene become maudlin. "Only until the twenty-eighth of this month. Then the coach becomes a pumpkin again."

"You should not laugh," George said soberly, pressing her hand in both of his. "You are the most beautiful girl Fletcher has ever seen."

Leslie looked around at the middle-aged couples occupying the other tables and anticking on the dance floor, and she was tempted to make a caustic comment. Instead, she laughed lightly. "If what you say is true," she answered, "I pity all the young girls in Fletcher. Why have they not all killed themselves?"

George let that one pass. "The twenty-eighth?" he said. "That's two weeks from Sunday. There's only sixteen more days, then. You have to learn how to drink in sixteen more days."

"Why?"

"You can't reach your majority and not know how to take a drink. Try it."

George was hovering close, caressing her wrist and palm, and the whiskey on his breath came strong when he spoke. George was trying hard to teach her how to bolt a shot of rye and follow it with a beer chaser. It was a procedure, however, that Leslie was determined she would not acquire.

"Could I practice first?" she asked, and when George asked of what her practice would consist, she explained that she'd like one of those small glasses and a pitcher of water. She would practice with that until she got it right.

George regarded the request as reasonable, and another glass and a pitcher of water were supplied. Leslie filled the glass with the clear water and held it up. "Now show me again exactly how you do it." When George hesitated, she said, "Oh, dear me, I forgot. I'm holding the glass. You'll want to use water, of course. Rye would be a—little too strong—"

George let go her hand and sat up straighter. "Rye too strong? You can't believe that."

"Not the first time, no. But you've had two, and almost the whole of a glass of beer besides. Don't you think you should demonstrate with water?"

George, of course, was not about to oblige. He would demonstrate his skill with the real stuff while Leslie drank water.

"Watch me," George said, and tossed his drink off. He didn't gasp, gulp, or do anything. After a moment, he reached for his mug of beer and finished it. "All right, now let's see you."

Leslie tried. It was her plan not to succeed, but even if it were the opposite, she found herself unable to do more than gulp half of the water.

"I'm sorry," she said. "I messed it up. Maybe you'd better show me again."

George was willing, but it had to be the real thing. He picked up Leslie's glass.

Now she felt real concern. "Are you sure you should?"

George tossed it off before replying. Then he set the glass down and said, "Y'shee? Nushing to it." He put an arm around her and pulled her close. His knee was trying to pry her own apart. "Did anybody tell you you're bu-ful?"

Leslie disengaged herself gently, but firmly. "You should sit up straighter," she said. "Are you all right?"

"A'course I'm all right. You're bu-ful." He was groping for her again.

"The music's starting. Don't you think we should dance?"

"You dance," George said. "I'll sit thish one out."

"All right," Leslie rose and left him there, taking refuge in a corner near the kitchen. She had reduced his amatory advances to governable control, but she did have to worry about getting home.

She went back to the table. "Hello."

He looked up at her, blinking before recognition broke through. "Hullo, Bu-ful."

"Do you know how to manage the horse?"

"'Course I do."

"Because I'm feeling ill. Do you think you could get me home before I get sick?"

"It's early."

"Or do you know someone else who could take me home if you—aren't able to do it?"

"Whad'ya mean, if I can't do it?"

"I mean you've had a lot to drink, more than anybody I've ever seen before. Most people would not be able to stand up if they'd drunk as much as you have."

"I'm not mos' people."

"You mean you could stand up and manage a horse and get us home?"

"'Course I can. I can hold my liquor."

"And pay the bill, and everything?"

He nodded. "Wash me."

He pulled himself to his feet and, though she had to steady him, he did get his balance. He summoned the waiter and weaved a little producing his billfold. He didn't really know what he paid, but it was the correct amount, for Leslie was at hand, giving him subtle support and keeping a hard eye on the waiter's handling of the money. One who grows up in poverty learns never to be casual about money.

George held her arm tightly when they went outside, but Leslie didn't mind. It wasn't for love, it was for support.

The sleigh was brought around, the stableman helped them aboard, and Leslie made sure the blankets were well snugged around their legs and laps. She knew nothing about handling

60

horses, but George could manage Brindle in his sleep and started her off for home.

It was the horse who took them back, however, for George had gone to sleep almost as soon as they got under way, the reins still lying in his half-closed hands. As for Leslie, she was left to ponder the quirks of fate that found her a thousand miles from the only life she had ever known, riding in a sleigh beside a strange man she had scarcely heard of before and never thought she'd meet.

When they approached the great house, Leslie worried lest Brindle go on past, but Brindle knew her way and turned unerringly into the drive toward the lantern post near the barn and the lights in the servants' quarters, coming to a quiet halt beside the kitchen porch.

Swift came out the door, buttoning up his heavy jacket as Leslie shook George and said, "We're home."

George's head only slumped a little more to the side.

She shook him again, but in vain. Swift was beside her now, helping her out. "He seems to be asleep," she said.

"Yes, ma'am. You get inside and I'll take care of Mr. Trowbridge."

Leslie watched as Swift took her place and tried to shake the big man awake. George stirred but did not rouse. "It's all right, miss," Swift said, stepping back out of the sleigh. "You go on inside. I'll get Harry Best to help me."

"That's all right, I'll wait with him," Leslie said. "But get help quickly. I think Brindle should not stand too long in the cold."

"As you wish, miss."

"Does this happen often?" Leslie inquired as he passed her to mount the porch.

"Miss, I do not know. I've only been here a month."

He went inside and Leslie was left standing in the icy drive, frowning. Swift was the second servant she'd talked to who had only been in service a month. It made her wonder how long the others had been with the family.

She climbed into the sleigh beside George again, pulling the heavy robe around her. George was snoring softly. He'd been working all day, riding the train to Chicago and back, then entertaining her in the evening, letting her persuade him to drink more than he should. She couldn't really blame him.

It was bitter in the night air and the post light was flickering in a growing breeze. She knew she could leave George and go in where it was warm. Swift and Best would take care of him and put Brindle in the stable. Nevertheless, Leslie felt that loyalty required her to wait with George until he was safely inside.

She turned to look around at the house. Except for the kitchen, the bottom half on her side was dark. Above, there was a light in the front bedroom where Queenie was still awake. Leslie could not yet understand the hours these Westerners kept. It was nearing midnight.

Her gaze swept the rest of the second floor, and all the windows were dark. The two next to Queenie's were in the sewing room. And the rest of the windows—the ones that were over the kitchen? Leslie remembered and a small chill went through her. Those windows belonged to the locked room. She fastened her gaze upon them, a tingling sensation playing around her spine. And then she saw something that made her blink and stare. That first window—it was not like the others. The lower sash stood raised at least a foot. No wonder such a cold draft of air knifed out from under the locked door of the secret room. One of the windows was open.

Leslie could not more than notice the strangeness of the fact before Swift reappeared with a bundling Best at his heels. Leslie let Swift help her from the sleigh again and told him that Mr. Trowbridge appeared to be unwakable. "Be careful with him," she admonished, then turned to Best. "Best, do you know where Mr. Trowbridge's room is?"

"Yes'm, I think so, ma'am."

"Then, you can see that he gets to bed without any trouble?"

"Oh yes, ma'am."

"Good." Then she asked the question she wanted. "How long have you been with the family, Best?"

"Since a week before Christmas," he answered promptly. "A month come Thursday."

CHAPTER THIRTEEN

Leslie had a nightmare that night for the first time since the year her father died. She dreamed she was walking the upper hall in her nightgown and the distant, dark door in the unlighted corner beckoned. It was cold in the corridor. She could feel icy air around her feet, though she was not conscious of the cold itself. She was not aware of walking, yet the door drew nearer and she was afraid.

At length it was in front of her and her fear became terror. She knew she had to go in. She was being forced by some power she could not control. But she also knew that something lay beyond that door that was too terrible to bear. Even as she stood, the door opened slowly inward, revealing a black interior. The force impelled her forward, though she shrank and tried to withdraw. Ahead there was something in the blackness. Her eyes were just beginning to make it out. It was starting to take shape. She could not discern what the shape was, except that it seemed to be small and not grotesque, and yet it was too horrible to bear and she woke up, uncertain but that she might have screamed.

She lay in the dark in trembling silence for minutes, hearing nothing, and spent more than an hour getting back to sleep.

She thought to ask about the room at breakfast, but Queenie had business with a man in the living room. George did not appear and Leslie had no choice but to eat alone. She was up and leaving by the time Queenie was bidding the man goodbye. Queenie introduced him in the front hall, explaining that the man was Mr. Jasper Lasky, who owned the last house on the road.

Mr. Lasky, who had buck teeth and an obsequious air, allowed as to what an extreme stroke of good fortune it was that he should get to meet the niece of such a fine man as Mr. Walter Barrett. Then he bowed and scraped and assured Queenie that he most certainly had not meant to intrude, but he felt obligated to rectify his bookkeeping error at once. It was only after Mr. Trowbridge had made the monthly collection that he discovered his own mistake, and he couldn't have Mr. Trowbridge or Mr. and Mrs. Barrett discover the mistake and think it intentional.

Queenie yessed him and thanked him and got him out of the house and then stalked off for the breakfast room grumbling about idiot neighbors invading her home with their trifles. She served herself from the varied and plentiful assortment of breakfast fare spread out on the buffet and told Leslie to fill her plate.

"Thank you, but I've eaten."

"You couldn't have. What'd you eat?"

"Sausages, a little scrambled eggs, toast, coffee, and a glass of milk."

"Have some oatmeal or some pancakes. We've got syrup from Vermont, you know. That ought to make you feel at home."

"No, really, I've had plenty."

"Have some more coffee and tell me about last night. You didn't need a chaperone now, did you?"

"No, not really." Leslie poured herself half a cup and sat back down at the table. "I was noticing something, by the way—"

"Where is George?"

"He's not up yet."

"With a beautiful thing like you sitting here having breakfast and he's not up?" She was chuckling when she said it, but then her brows contracted. "The devil you say. What's the matter with him?" She looked at Leslie sharply. "You two have a fight?"

"No, certainly not."

"Well, what kind of a time did you have?"

"It was very nice." Leslie saw that Queenie was dubious. "Really it was."

"You know," Queenie said, pausing in the middle of her trencherman consumption, "you're a very lucky girl."

"Lucky?"

"I mean—George taking an interest in you like that."

"Oh," Leslie said, flushing. "He's only being kind to a stranger in the area."

"Now, don't you try to make light of it," Queenie retorted. "George is taking a shine to you and I can tell." She glared at the doors suddenly. "Except, where the devil is he? You sure everything is all right between you two?"

64

"So far as I know—but perhaps you'd better ask him."

"Like I was saying," Queenie went on, "George is someone to pay attention to. Do you know he's your Uncle Walter's heir? Do you realize that this house and all Walter's mines and oil wells and all the land he owns out in Colorado will ultimately go to George?"

Leslie nodded. "Yes'm. I understand that."

"George, though scarcely older than you, is a man of the world. I suppose you know that."

"I could gather that."

"If he should take a fancy to you, my dear, that would be quite a feather in your cap."

Leslie said politely, "Yes, I'm sure."

"He's a very fine man."

"I'm sure Uncle Walter wouldn't entrust him with so much responsibility if he weren't."

Queenie was obviously looking for more from her. What was she after, Leslie wondered, some kind of commitment? She didn't understand this turn of events at all.

"By the way," she said, as Queenie, somewhat sullenly, devoted herself to several mouthfuls of food, "will you want to be fitted this morning?"

"Good Lord, no," the orange-haired woman said, as if only lunatics would not know better.

"I can't do much more, I'm afraid, without another fitting."

"Well, don't. For heaven's sake, girl, you don't *have* to work, do you?"

"That's what I'm not sure of—what you expect from me."

Queenie gave a full, if slightly sharp laugh. "Lord's sake, you're Walter's niece. Just 'cause you make dresses doesn't change that. The servants work. You don't work. You just sew a little. Get me?"

"Then you don't have any plans for me for this morning?"

"I don't have any plans for you the whole day. George might, but I don't. So do what you like."

CHAPTER FOURTEEN

Leslie was not about to wait for George to plan her day. The morning, at least, was her own, and a whole new country lay at her beck and call. She was determined to see what it contained.

No sooner did she return to her room than she donned her warmest winter clothing—boots, sweaters, scarf, overcoat, hood, woolen hat, and the thick, lamb's-wool mittens that she could double up her fists inside.

Then she set out, going down the front-porch steps, crunching along the path to the heavily packed snow of the plowed drive, and from there to the equally crusted snow of the road. Elsewhere, the level of the soft lying snow was waist-deep with the thick banks the horseplows had raised standing as high as her head.

The sun was well up, tracing its low, southern course across the sky, rising late, setting early, and never reaching a high enough point in the sky to make its warmth felt. It gave light to the countryside and little else.

Leslie did not mind. The pristine fields of snow, the lack of dirt and grime, of slush and mud, the lack of noise and bustle, of the dinginess and despair that hovered over the city of her memory, made this new experience exhilarating, and she forged out into the world with a sense of excitement and adventure that had never before seized her.

A mile to the right would lie Mr. Lasky's house, and she had no interest there. She turned left toward town instead, not intending to go that far, but only to wander along the empty road, explore the route, and enjoy the closeness of nature.

There were snowbirds, tiny, flitting creatures who managed to keep warm and find food in that most inhospitable of climes. Leslie marveled as she walked. The world of Illinois was not devoid of all but human life in winter, after all.

In fact, until she reached the next house, half a mile down the road, she would not have known that human life existed in that area on that cold Saturday morning on the thirteenth of January 1877.

But then the white smoke from a chimney appeared above the snowdrifts, gleaming and curling against the bright-blue sky, and as she drew closer, the house itself came into view. This was the house of the nearest neighbor, inhabited by a family named Cranston, Queenie had said. There would be more than a quarter of a mile more of empty road before another house would appear. Then they would grow in number and the town would begin.

Leslie drew abreast of the house but, except for the smoke, there was no sign of life. The plows that had cleared the road had thrown up barriers against all its exits. There was a barn to the left and behind, but no route had been cleared from there to the road. The house was fifty feet back and the barn still farther, yet the snow between bore not so much as a footmark.

Leslie did not know what to make of it. Were the people inside all right? Shouldn't she make sure? Wouldn't it at least be neighborly to knock on the door and introduce oneself?

She climbed the heaps of snow, sliding and falling, bathing herself in glistening granules. Then, having surmounted the alpine cliffs, she found herself waist-deep in soft, untrammeled white powder.

Through it she struggled to the distant porch, feeling alternately foolish and determined. Perhaps, since they shoveled no paths, they did not want visitors. However, the worst they could do would be to tell her so.

Leslie was panting and exhausted by the time she had reached the porch. The porch was unswept but the snow had drifted against the railings and the route to the front door was no more than ankle-deep. There was a heavy knocker there and Leslie struck with it forcefully.

A long wait followed and Leslie was about to knock again when there was a rasping of bolts, and a crack appeared in which an old man's face was revealed.

"Yes'm," the man said, a startled expression crossing his face. "Do come in." He pulled the door wider—enough to admit the visitor, but not the cold. "Yes, yes." He all but took her arm to get her into the warmth of the home itself, then shut and barred the door again. He was old and bent and gnarled, with the look of something a puff of wind could blow away, but his concern was for her and he was surprisingly spry. "What is your trouble, lass?" he said, his face reflecting his worry. Girls struggling through snow to his door must be in dire straits indeed. "Emily, Emily," he said, his creaky voice calling his wife, "come quick. It's a young girl."

A woman, as bent but as able as the man, appeared through a doorway. She was soft and plump, with a heavily lined face, and her hair, done up in a bun, was as white as the snow outside.

"Oh, you poor thing," the small, round woman said. "What can we get you?" She looked ready to run for the requirement.

"Yes, yes," said the man. "What do you need?"

Leslie felt foolish on the one hand, but relieved and pleased on the other. The couple she had come to was not in trouble. More than that, they were the kind of people she needed. Not since she left Connecticut had she felt so much at home. She owed a great deal to Uncle Walter, Queenie and George, but they did not show the concern for others that Leslie had encountered on that unforgettable Christmas Day when the rich and the poor, when everyone from everywhere, had shown her that they cared.

Quickly Leslie set their minds at ease. She explained who she was and that she was not in trouble. She had merely wanted to introduce herself and let them know she had come to their area. And if, at any time, she could help them in any way, she would be most obliged.

The old man, whose name was Adam Cranston, shifted his cane so that he could shake her hand. His wife, he said, was Emily, and they were delighted to have a visitor. No one came to see them from one summer to the next.

They sat her down to tea and she found them charming. They were not used to visitors and had little contact with the outside world. Two or three times a year they received letters from relatives in far-off places, but, other than that, they lived as shut-ins. They stored firewood in large quantity. Adam was still strong and sawed much cordage through the summer and fall. They raised corn in season on some of their acreage and rented off the rest. This enabled them to stock their larder for the winter months and close themselves in until the late-spring thaws would free them again. For nearly six months of the year they were incommunicado, but they were used to it. This had been, for years on end, their way of life.

Leslie told the Cranstons what she knew of the outside world, but this was little more than what she'd seen of New York and from the window of her train, and the fact that someone named Rutherford B. Hayes would be the next President of the United States. Then, as they refilled her cup and plied her with questions, she told them why she had come to this distant and uninhabited section of the country. It was her Uncle Walter, his wife and stepson who had arranged it.

"Oh, yes," old Adam Cranston said. "He bought the big Morgate house. A year ago. Know the house well. Helped build it. Twenty years ago that was." He stared thoughtfully at the blazing fire. "Strange family, the Morgates. Didn't come from around here. Didn't stay long. House was empty nigh onto ten years before your uncle bought it." He shook his head. "Very strange family."

Leslie said, "Do you know my Uncle Walter?"

Old Adam nodded. "Come here in early spring. Wanted to buy half my land. I didn't want to sell. Seen him in town a couple of times, buying supplies. And he stopped by after the first snow —just before Thanksgiving—to see if we had need. Nice man."

"And the rest of the family?"

Both Adam and his wife shook their heads. "Seen them ride by," he said.

"They should have come to call."

"No, no," the old man said. "More proper this way. They are rich, we are poor."

Emily Cranston said, "Your uncle—he is rich—but one is not aware." She turned to her husband. "How would you say it, Adam?"

"He is of the soil," Adam replied. "He is from the land. Money and riches don't touch men who are from the land."

Mr. Cranston nodded. "Yes, my husband speaks truth. That is your Uncle Walter. He is from the land."

"He is well?" Mr. Cranston asked.

"Very well," Leslie told her. "Right now he's off on a trip."

Old Adam nodded. "He is busy. Supervises many things."

"He'll come see you when he gets back."

"Be nice to see Walter. I like Walter."

"I'll make sure he does." Leslie put down her cup and rose. "But I've taken up too much of your time. You've been most kind."

They saw her to the door, urging that she come again, asking that their kindest regards be relayed to Walter Barrett and the others in his family.

Leslie promised to come back soon, and she meant it.

CHAPTER FIFTEEN

George made an appearance for lunch but he was taciturn and did not meet her eye. Queenie was less talkative than usual and it was left to Leslie to describe her morning. She outlined the difference between the gleaming, clean-white landscape in Fletcher and the dirty slush of a city winter. It elicited no more than polite response. Neither George nor Queenie cared about eastern winters.

She told them next about her visit to the snowbound Cranstons, but that, too, failed to provoke curiosity—until she said they were looking forward to another visit from Uncle Walter.

Then Queenie lifted her head from her plate with her fork half raised. "What's that?"

Leslie repeated herself.

"What do you mean 'another visit'? He's never been to their house in his life!"

"Yes, he has," Leslie said, and explained about the time he

sought to buy some of their land, as well as his stop-in to see how they were. "They said it was just before Thanksgiving."

George's and Queenie's eyes met for a long moment, and it was obvious they were displeased. "He never told me that," Queenie said accusingly. She turned to George. "He should have told me that!"

George nodded grimly and Queenie's eyes narrowed. "I wonder how many other people he's been hobnobbing with in this damned town behind my back."

Leslie was surprised and puzzled by the sudden change in her aunt. Queenie's extreme displeasure indicated that matters in the Barrett family weren't quite as untroubled as she had supposed. "But what is wrong," Leslie could not help asking, "with Uncle Walter calling on his neighbors?"

Queenie was caught at a disadvantage for only a moment. Then she said sharply, "This house is the finest house in Fletcher. It is the biggest and best by far. It is better than any of the houses in Chicago—at least that were available when we got married. Why do you think we're living out in this godforsaken town except that this was the only house we could get that was suitable to our tastes?"

Leslie suspected Queenie really meant "*her* tastes," for she was sure Uncle Walter, from his background and past life, couldn't have cared less for showy houses and an army of servants.

"I can understand that," Leslie answered. "What I can't understand is why Uncle Walter shouldn't call on the neighbors."

"You saw that tiny box of a house they live in. They don't have money and position. Who on earth would even think of calling on people like that?"

"*I* would," Leslie said.

"Oh, yes," Queenie said sourly. "I forgot about you. All right," she went on, stuffing a forkful of food into her mouth, "I'd better explain matters to you. We are worth a great deal of money. Your Uncle Walter must have told you that. When we got married, we wanted to settle down in an area where we could associate with people of class and distinction—people who also had money.

"Like I say," she went on, gesturing with the fork and stabbing

71

more food, "that meant Chicago. Chicago's the only city west of New York that's got any class. But we couldn't get the kind of house we wanted closer to those classy people than this one. Either we bought or we'd have to build, and that would take time. You follow me?"

"A little."

"So we don't do a lot of entertaining, because the people we invite have to come all the way out from Chicago and stay overnight. It's gotta be something special. But that doesn't mean we entertain lower-class people just because we don't see much of the high-society types. Your uncle's got no business going around being friendly with the neighbors. First thing you know, they're going to be trying to get money out of him."

"That's not so. Why, he wanted to buy some of Mr. Cranston's land and he refused to sell."

"He shouldn't've bothered. It doesn't pay to start something up."

"But you see the Laskys. Mr. Lasky was here this morning. You don't mind that."

"I mind his coming to this house," Queenie snapped. "That's just what I'm talking about." She set her teeth grimly. "Well, I'll tell you, your uncle isn't going to be calling on the Cranstons or anybody else when he gets back, and you're not to call on anybody either."

Leslie's mouth came partly open. "I beg your pardon," she said.

Queenie, who had been talking offhandedly while chewing, paid attention for a change. "What?"

"I don't think you quite mean what you said."

"I certainly did," Queenie answered. "I want you to stay away from the Cranstons yourself hereafter."

Leslie noticed that George was paying close attention to the growing confrontation. She could feel the flush growing on her cheeks and the bristling of hairs on her neck. "Queenie," she said carefully, "you can tell me to do anything you want with regard to the clothes I make for you because that is what you are paying me for. But no one, and that includes you and my Uncle Walter, is going to tell me who my friends are going to be and whom I may or may not see."

Queenie's green eyes flashed, narrowed, and grew surprisingly ugly. "My dear," she said, and her tone was harsh, "you forget you are not just an employee. You are a guest in this house."

"That can be quickly remedied," Leslie answered. "I am prepared to leave on the first train."

The women's eyes met unwaveringly for a moment. Then Queenie burst into raucous laughter. "What are we doing?" she boomed, "getting into a fight over nothing? Me and my husband's only relative?" She slapped her thigh. "Dearie, you mustn't take me so seriously. I'd rather you didn't associate with people like the Cranstons, I'll admit, but if it's your honest desire to do so, you won't get no argument from me. You've got the same kind of spunk your uncle's got, and I was forgetting it. Don't you ever think of leaving here, dearie. This is your home. This is where you belong, and don't you ever forget it. You go see anybody you like anytime you like, all right?"

She looked at Leslie, awaiting acceptance. Leslie gave a nod and Queenie, relieved, dug into her food again.

Leslie was on her way back to her room after lunch when George intercepted her. She had thought he'd gone off with Queenie and was taken aback. "Oh," she said. "Where did you come from?"

His brows were dark and his breathing heavy. "What did you tell my mother?" he said by way of answer.

"Tell her? About what?"

"Last night, of course."

Leslie shook her head. "I haven't told her anything."

"Of course you did," he snapped. "You saw how she was at lunch. She's angry."

"But not at you."

"You haven't heard her. What have you been doing to get her upset like that?"

Leslie shook her head in bewilderment. "I don't know what you're talking about."

"Then, why are you running away?"

73

"Running away? From what?"

"From me."

There were sparks in his eyes and Leslie knew better than to laugh. "George, you're crazy. I'm not running away from you."

"Mother says you are, and she's blaming me."

"Your mother is absolutely wrong."

"All right, we'll prove it to her. We'll go dancing again tonight. And in the meantime—"

Leslie hadn't meant to get trapped into that one. "No," she said quickly. "Not tonight."

"What?" he said, stunned in midsentence.

"Thank you very much," Leslie said. "I appreciate your offer more than you can know, but I cannot accept."

She turned for her room, but George's hand clamped fiercely on her arm and jerked her around again. Now his face was dark and frighteningly close. His black eyes smoldered. "What kind of games are you trying to play?" he said in low, taut tones.

For the first time, Leslie was frightened of him. He had shown himself manly, masculine, and moody before, but nothing about him had given hint that he would do harm to a woman. Now she was no longer sure.

"I'm not playing anything," she said, keeping her unease hidden.

His hand was hurting her. His grip was stronger than he knew. "Then, when I tell you I'm taking you out, I don't expect you to play hard-to-get."

"You are hurting me," Leslie said tightly.

He let her go as if not knowing he'd held her. "My apologies," he said, but not as if it meant anything to him.

Leslie, rubbing her bruised arm, swallowed and tried to stand tall. Regardless of how dark, handsome, forceful men might try to dominate her, she was not going to be intimidated. "I am not playing games," she said again. "I choose not to go dancing with you, and while you can break my arm, you cannot change my mind."

"Is it because I fell asleep and you have been insulted? I don't

74

usually fall asleep, but I had been working hard all day and was very tired."

"No, that is not it."

"What, then?"

"Nothing. I just do not care to go dancing with you."

George scowled, more puzzled than angry. "There are girls," he said, "who would get down on their knees to go dancing with me."

"Good, then you should have no trouble at all finding someone else to take out tonight." She turned away, leaving him standing, and went to her room.

CHAPTER SIXTEEN

Leslie, trapped in her room, spent the next hour mulling over her fate. Hiding out from her uncle's stepson was the last thing she had expected on coming to Fletcher. And what was she going to do about it? If he was the hit with women that he said he was— and that she could believe him to be—why did he pester her? Why didn't he go after more willing prey? Did he think she was easy, ripe for the plucking? Plying her with liquor, breathing on her heavily, holding her overclose! No wonder he didn't want chaperones around. And what was she supposed to do in self-defense, lock herself in her room? That would be intolerable. She had better learn how to face him.

There were sounds outside in the drive and Leslie went to the window. It was midafternoon now and she saw that George was in the sleigh swinging into the road and heading for town. That meant she would be spared further confrontations for a while and she could let her tense nerves relax. She would go to the sewing room and work on a dress for herself.

She opened her door and crossed to the one opposite, seeing no sign of Queenie and hearing no sound. That was as she wanted it, and she closed herself in. She needed some time to herself, some freedom from the rest of the family. Give her her sewing box, scissors and materials. Creative design, then cutting and measuring and sewing to make it come true—that was the joy of dressmaking.

Her respite from the family lasted only an hour, however. The sun was still high and she had not yet lighted the lamp when the door swung open and Queenie stood framed in the entrance, arms folded across her stout bosom, her eyes staring accusingly.

"So here you are!"

Queenie's manner had a way of inspiring guilt even among the innocent and Leslie had to remind herself that she had done no wrong. "Yes, of course," she answered. "Where else would I be?"

"I don't know. The last I heard you were off sulking in your room." She came in and closed the door.

So George had talked. George had told his mother that Leslie had refused his invitation and retired to her room. And Queenie was going to—what?

"You must have been misinformed," Leslie said, cutting loose her hemming from the sewing machine. "I haven't been sulking in my room."

Queenie advanced closer, her awesomeness increasing with her approach. "I want to know what's the trouble between you and George."

"Trouble?"

"Trouble!"

Leslie shook her head. "I know of no trouble."

"He's gone to town in a fit of temper because you would not go with him."

"I'm sorry if he's angry—"

"You're sorry, but you made him angry. You refused his invitation."

76

"Which should be my privilege."

"It was totally unjustified. You were being deliberately cruel."

Leslie put down her sewing and turned in her chair. "Just a moment," she said. "Are you telling me that one of the conditions of my employment is that I am to be at the beck and call of your son?"

Queenie's eyes flashed quick fire, which was, with equal speed, banked. "I would think you would be honored—"

"First you try to tell me I am not to see the neighbors, then you try to tell me I *am* to see your son. I thought I was brought out here to be a dressmaker. Now I'm beginning to wonder."

Queenie backed off a little. "I am not trying to tell you whom to see and whom not to see," she insisted, "but I am saying that I cannot understand a girl rejecting the favors of a fine young man like my son, who has money to lavish on those who appeal to him, who is the target of every girl in the area, who is the best catch any woman could hope for for a husband."

Leslie smiled. Queenie must think her exceedingly naïve. "I'm well aware that George has money to lavish upon those whom he chooses. I'm also aware that young men have a habit of expecting something in return for their money. Let him spend his money upon those who wish it. I have no interest in such bargains."

Queenie flushed. Leslie had been quite right. The other woman had not anticipated either such insight or such a refusal. It was a moment before Queenie regained her composure, and then the flush receded. She said, in more than a little surprise, "Are you saying to me that you think George's motives are not honorable?"

"With all due respect to George," Leslie answered, "yes."

"But I thought you understood," Queenie exclaimed.

"Understood what?"

"He's courting you!"

"Courting me?" Leslie erupted in laughter. "I'm sorry," she said when Queenie turned crimson again. "But really—courting me? Surely, you are jesting."

"Why would I jest?" Queenie said, anger in her tone. "Do you think I do not regard such matters seriously?"

"George has known me but a week. Do you think I could believe he would be interested in someone like me in that short a time? Do you really think I could believe a man of his station, with his experience, would even look twice at the likes of me? I'm afraid I am persuaded that George has quite different ideas with regard to me than what you think."

"Rubbish," Queenie answered sharply. "If I thought his intentions weren't honorable, do you think I'd have allowed him to take you out last night unchaperoned? Surely, you must believe I'd take better care of you than that."

"I'm sure that is your own conviction," Leslie said quickly. "But it is not one I share."

Queenie drew herself up. "I know my son, Leslie. And if I tell you that he has been smitten by your charms, I am telling you the truth—as he has told it to me. If he is upset, it is because he has found it no problem to attract young ladies heretofore, and now, when for the first time he meets a young lady who attracts him, he finds his charm has failed him.

"You are from the East," she went on, "and your ways are different there. I do not know what experiences you have had with men back home, but you are using them to wrongly judge my son. What has he done, my child?" Queenie asked, coming closer. "How has he misled you?"

Leslie, chastened, spoke slowly. "I don't know—it's—he rushes everything so fast. Everything he does is too much."

"I don't understand."

Leslie tried to phrase it right. She didn't want to misjudge George. She did not want there to be misunderstanding. "He leans too close. He breathes too near, he hugs too tight, he holds on too much, he's too amorous too soon. He tries to get a girl to drink too much." She looked up at Queenie. "I feel suffocated by him and I want to back away so that I can get to see him better, to know him better. I don't have a chance to get to know him."

"He's a fool," Queenie said, more to herself than Leslie. She turned on her heel and left.

CHAPTER SEVENTEEN

George was dark and moody at dinner and Leslie watched him, nervously aware of his handsome looks and sulky mouth. Oh, but the women would go for George Trowbridge. She could hardly fault him for expecting her to swoon like the rest. And Queenie as well. Queenie was as dour and silent as George and scarcely a word was said through the meal. It was as if Leslie were being punished for being different.

It was so odd, Leslie thought. George was the rich son, the prize catch in town, the object of every girl's desires. Leslie, on the other hand, was the charwoman, the poor girl, the one who scrubbed and cooked and sewed and cleaned. Yet here was the queen, arguing the virtues of Prince Charming to Cinderella. It should be the other way around. The matchmaker should be the poor girl's mother, pushing the daughter's virtues at the prince.

If matchmaking was the purpose! But perhaps it wasn't. Leslie could imagine that George was accustomed to having his way with girls of lower station. Perhaps he was not equipped to handle a balky one, and Mama was pitching in to break down her resistance.

Whatever George's and Queenie's intentions were, Leslie knew only one thing. She would be very careful.

As soon after dinner as she properly could, Leslie retired to her room. It was becoming her refuge and escape. And it was from the corner windows that she saw George, some three quarters of an hour later, again head off toward Fletcher. If she did not go out with him, he certainly did not sit home and pine.

George was not at table for either of the first two meals on Sunday. Queenie took no apparent notice of his absence, and Leslie, trying to hide her turmoil, pretended a similar uninterest. Truth to tell, she had lain awake half the night wondering if she had been needlessly cruel or unfairly stand-offish. Could he be truly smitten with her while she, through false modesty, judged his motives to be base? The possibility that she was doing him a disservice weighed upon her heavily and she blamed herself for his nonappearance.

It was at half-past two, when Leslie was distractedly writing a letter to Mrs. Wiggins, that a chance came to improve matters. Fanny Nils, the other chambermaid, knocked on the door. "Sorry to bother you, miss," she said. "It's Mr. George. He's requesting the pleasure of your company on a ride. I mean, he would like to take you out in the sleigh this afternoon, if you would so oblige him."

Leslie's heart leaped. A ride with George would clear the air. They had parted on a harsh note the previous afternoon and now the fences could be mended. "You may tell Mr. George," she smiled, "that that would be very nice."

"And he says I'm to bring you some extra-warm clothing because it's bitter out. I mean, miss, it gets cold here like I've never seen it before."

"I know. I'm not used to it either. But it's a dry cold, and that makes it bearable."

"That's what I'm finding out, miss."

"You're new here, too?"

"Oh, yes. I've only been here a couple of weeks. I come from Pennsylvania, near Pittsburgh."

"And you came all this way? What brought you here?"

"Oh," Fanny said, "well, cook—you know—Bessie Wood, well, she's a cousin. And she come to work here last month and she said the Barretts were hiring help and needed a chambermaid and would I want the job. They'd even pay my fare." Fanny hitched her shoulders. "And the wages, they was good, and the work no worse than what I'd been doing. So I said, why not? And here I am."

"And Bessie only just came and you only just came? Isn't there anyone in this house who's been here more than a couple of months?"

"I don't know what you mean, ma'am."

"I mean, is there a big turnover in servants? Do you all come and go as fast? Is there something about the work here?"

"Not so far as I know, ma'am. I ain't got any complaints. Leastways, not yet." Fanny was starting to look uncomfortable at the questions and she managed a curtsy. "I'll tell Mr. Trow-bridge you'll be glad to join him for a ride, miss," and she disap-peared.

They rode in the sleigh over back country roads for two hours and Leslie returned home more bewildered than ever. George was a different person from the man she had last seen. This time he did not crowd her too closely nor exhale hot breath in her ear. Queenie had apparently warned him and, instead, he handled her with punctilious remoteness. He assisted her into the sleigh as if she were glass. He tucked her in as if his touch was poison. And when he spoke, it was not to ask where she'd been all his life, or how she had managed to become so beautiful. He was sterilely polite. Did she have a particular place she would like to view? a special road she would like to explore? a length of time she would like to be out?

Leslie had no chance to set things straight between them. He was so stiff and alien she could initiate nothing. What was worse, while his eyes never touched hers, they were not inert. They were dark, angry and bitter, as if his task were unpleasant. Through it all, his forehead was creased, his brows contracted.

Leslie's only recourse was to let him take her where he would, wonder why he did, and enjoy the scenery and fresh air for its own sake. The new George was no more palatable than the old.

The next day was Monday, and whatever it was that George Trowbridge did for Uncle Walter in Chicago, he did not do it that day. He was around the house instead.

His presence, on that occasion, became a convenience. Queenie, going over dress patterns and designs with Leslie, showed pique at discovering she did not have everything she wanted. There was a shop in town that could supply her, but town was a mile away and she did not want Swift to leave his duties, nor would she accept Leslie's offer to walk. George produced the solution. He would take Leslie into Fletcher himself so she could get the items in question without further ado.

Which is what happened. George took Leslie in and brought her back with the same punctilious and distant courtesy, and the ride was as enigmatic as had been the trip through the country-side the afternoon before. George, silent and brooding, carried the errand through with the same apparent lack of interest.

George was still home on Tuesday and it was a time when Leslie really needed help. Tuesday was one of the boring and bad days. Leslie couldn't get Queenie to hold still for another fitting and there was little she could do with the clothes she was preparing. She worked on some of her own designs after lunch, but there came a time when she had had enough of scissors and thread and patterns and material and measuring and the rest. It was then, when Leslie was feeling frustrated, irritated and tired, that Fanny Nils knocked on the sewing-room door and asked once again if Miss Marsh would accept a ride in the sleigh from Mr. Trowbridge.

Despite the dullness of the previous rides, Leslie welcomed the prospect. Anything was better than sewing just then. And this time the ride would be different. This time George would relax and be friendly. This time they would get to know each other. She would see to it.

The ride, however, was as disappointing as the others. Try as she would, she could not break through the stiff, hard shell her companion had developed, and she became increasingly frustrated and depressed. George remained the same silent, moody, morose, untalkative escort. He might as well be one of the cabbies in the hansoms back home. "Why does he invite me out?" Leslie asked herself as she changed for dinner. "He doesn't talk to me enough to notice. He never wonders what my interests are. He never discusses his own."

When Fanny came by the sewing room on Wednesday with another invitation from George, Leslie said, "No, thank you," and closed the door.

CHAPTER EIGHTEEN

Leslie lived in dread of another scene with George and another bruised arm or worse after this new refusal of his attentions. Nevertheless, she had concluded that the relationship was a fruitless one, and the sooner she put an end to whatever intentions he had for her, the better. She was braced, therefore, for the worst and determined that no matter what threats he might make or whatever pleas Queenie might advance, she would not be cowed.

To her surprise, no unpleasantness developed. George, when she saw him, acted in no way disappointed or angry. He behaved, instead, as if nothing had happened, as if the invitation had never been issued. This left Leslie resting easier in her mind, but ever more puzzled. If he could take the rebuke with such equanimity, he must not have been much concerned. Perhaps he didn't really like taking her for sleigh rides. Perhaps he was being made to.

She wished this might be the end of the matter, but she had little hope that it would. Sure enough, George had been undeterred by her refusal of Wednesday afternoon, and Fanny Nils was back Thursday morning with a further invitation to go riding. That George could have asked her himself at breakfast didn't seem to be the point. He preferred to send his invitations through an intermediary.

This time Fanny was being very urgent. "Any kind of a ride," she reported. "Wherever you want to go or do. He says he's your chauffeur." Fanny lifted her eyes. "Some people get all the luck. I can just see some rich man begging for a chance to chauffeur me."

It made Leslie laugh, but Fanny was not amused. Her sympathies were all with George. "How you could turn down the likes of him like you did yesterday—well, that's beyond my ken, that it is."

Leslie was tempted to reply smartly that she could turn down Mr. Trowbridge's invitations twice a day without compunction, but the thought crossed her mind that this might be her future and it would be an extremely trying one. Better that the invitations cease. Better that she discourage rather than refuse them, and an idea occurred. "Did you say, Fanny, that all he wants is to be my chauffeur?"

"That's what he said."

"He'd take me someplace I want to go, then come back for me when I wanted to be picked up?"

"I think so, miss."

"Well, Fanny, you go and find out. If the answer is yes, then I will go for a ride. You may tell him that."

Fanny was back, knocking on Leslie's door, in almost no time. "Mr. Trowbridge says that would be fine. He's having Swift get Brindle out, and the sleigh should be ready in fifteen minutes. He says he'll be awaiting your pleasure anytime after that."

"And he'll drop me off wherever I want to go, and come back for me later?"

"Yes'm. In fact, that's what he was asking me to find out. Where is it you'll be going?"

"You may tell Mr. Trowbridge that I desire to pay a call on Adam and Emily Cranston."

Leslie thought that her announcement would have an effect, and she was right. "You can't really be serious," George grumbled as he helped her into the sleigh a half hour later.

"Serious about what?" Leslie asked innocently, tucking the robes around her while George climbed in beside. She was in control of the situation and she felt chipper and in good spirits.

"About going to see the Cranstons." He clucked to Brindle and started the mare out the drive. "You're doing it to make fun of me."

"Make fun of you, George?"

"Making me pull up at their house like they're important people. They're nobodies. They can't even shovel a path through the snow."

"It's not their fault that they're old, George. There'll come a day when you can't shovel snow either."

"I don't shovel it now," George snapped. "You hire other people to do such things."

"You do if you have the money. Mr. and Mrs. Cranston aren't that fortunate."

"Which is what I'm talking about. What're you bothering with people like them for? You can do better than that."

"It depends upon what you mean by 'better,' George. If you mean money, you must remember I'm poor too."

"No, you aren't. You belong to a rich family."

"*You* belong, George. Not I. Uncle Walter brought me here because your mother asked him to. I can be sent away again anytime he or she decides I'm no longer wanted. All I can count on is the money I can earn, and I don't ever forget it."

"Well," George said, clucking Brindle to a faster pace, "that's going to change, don't worry about that. Pretty soon you won't even have to spit on people like the Cranstons, you'll be so far above them."

And Leslie could only shake her head and say, "George, I don't think you understand. I don't know that you'll ever understand."

It was not long before they were upon the Cranston home and when they reached it, both stared in some surprise. Where, less than a week before, deep snow deterred all visitors, now, through the high drifts, a neatly shoveled path had been cut from the porch steps to the road.

"Well," George had to say when the discovery was made, "they must have inherited some money."

Leslie got out of the sleigh without a word, but inwardly she decided George would not do, even as a chauffeur. "You will come back for me, then?" she said as civilly as she could, walking around Brindle and stroking her nose in passing.

"I said I would."

"One hour, then?"

"One hour." George swung Brindle around in the road and started her off in a trot.

Leslie let him go without a backward glance. He would tire of chauffeuring soon enough and leave her alone. Meanwhile, she could enjoy the shoveled path to the Cranstons' porch and marvel at its accomplishment.

The cause of the feat was discovered as soon as she knocked on the door. It was opened not by old Mr. Cranston but, instead, by

85

a young and personable male with sandy hair, strong, good-looking features, a half-whittled napkin ring in one hand, and a knife in the other.

"Well, what in the world," he said when he beheld her standing there. "What angel of mercy are you?" He was as astonished to find her knocking on the door as she was to find him answering it.

"Who are you?" Leslie gasped in response. "I thought the Cranstons lived here."

"And so they do. Come in at once." The young man hastened her through the door and closed it behind him. Then he drew back to look her over—less, she thought, to appraise her than to discover her purpose. Her garments were Barrett garments and, obviously, quality. Other than that, she left him clueless and he shook his head. "You said 'Cranston,' I believe?"

"They're friends of mine."

"Hah, they do themselves proud. I did not know they had such friends as you." He looked through the window at the now vacant roadway outside. "Where did you come from? Heaven?"

"Heaven?" Leslie found herself put off. "Hardly."

"If not heaven," he laughed, "you must have come from nowhere. But tell me," he continued, his eye once more appraising, "what friend of the Cranstons are you?"

Leslie felt herself flushing under the young man's frank, assessing stare. The men in the West seemed to regard her with a good deal more forthrightness than she had encountered in the East. "I'm Leslie Marsh, their next neighbor," she said, hiding her blush with a toss of the head. "And whom do I have the privilege of addressing?"

"A thousand pardons," the tall young man said, bowing. "I'm Stephen Crawford, at your service—which would be an unmistakable pleasure."

Leslie, noting that the knife he held was pointed in her direction, said, "The pleasure is more yours than mine. Am I being welcomed or turned away?"

Crawford took heed of the knife and promptly turned its point the other way. "My apologies, Miss Marsh. I am a whittler by inclination, not a guard dog. You see?" He held out the piece he had been carving. "I am making a napkin ring, not a dog collar. But let me take you to the Cranstons. They're in the kitchen."

"That sounds like a safer course." She started to follow, then stopped. "It was you who shoveled the path?"

"Yes. Well done, wasn't it?"

"Timely done, at least," Leslie answered. "How long have you been here, Mr. Crawford, if I may ask?"

"Two days. Two whole days. And, of course you may ask."

Mr. Crawford led her to the kitchen then, which was by far the warmest room in the house, for the old wood stove not only cooked the food but heated the room more effectively than any fireplace. Mrs. Cranston was baking and Mr. Cranston was chipping logs with a hatchet for kindling. He'd chipped three loads of logs that morning, he said, and had Miss Marsh met Mr. Crawford?

"At the door," Leslie told him. She refused the offer of hot cookies fresh from the oven, then gave in and tried one.

"Mr. Crawford's renting a room from us," old Adam said. "He's come to Fletcher looking for work."

Fletcher did not strike Leslie as an ideal haven for the unemployed. Though she knew it little, it had not struck her as a rich lode of job opportunities. "I see," she said, not really seeing at all. She turned. "Do you have anything?"

"If anybody needs napkin rings," he said, holding up his half-finished one, "I'm a whiz."

Adam shook his head. "Mr. Crawford thinks Fletcher's a good town, but there just ain't no jobs, especially in winter. You come here in the summer for the farming and the animal husbandry and you might do better."

"What sort of work are you looking for?" Leslie asked.

"Anything a young man can turn his hand to," Mr. Crawford answered. "I'm not fussy."

"Your Uncle Walter wouldn't have anything he'd want done, would he?" Adam asked and said to Stephen, "Miss Marsh here is niece to Walter Barrett, who's got the next place up the road. Walter's got a pack of servants and a big house and stables for I don't know how many horses."

Leslie lowered her eyes but not before she noticed that the news had had an effect upon the stranger. "Walter Barrett?" Stephen said, "yes, I've heard of him. Very rich, if I'm not mistaken." He nodded at Leslie. "Yes, I should have known."

"Should have known?" Leslie asked.

"The elegance of your clothes. So that's where you came from?" He explained to the Cranstons that he thought she'd dropped from the sky. "There she was, out of nowhere. No carriage, no horse, no other house around."

"My uncle's stepson brought me," Leslie explained. "He's to fetch me back again in an hour."

"Well, now," Adam said. "Maybe they could use a groom, relieve the lad of all that work, eh, Steve?"

Emily Cranston said, "Now, Paw, behave yourself. Don't go prying into other people's affairs."

"I ain't prying, Maw. I'm just trying to help out our young boarder here. Don't hurt to ask, does it? Leslie can't do any more'n say no, can she? Steve ain't going to find anything anywhere, lessen he asks."

Leslie said she didn't know what the family situation was, she doubted that Queenie was in need of more servants, but she could inquire.

"Queenie?" Stephen asked.

"My uncle's wife. She runs things because Uncle Walter's away a lot."

Emily Cranston made tea, and Stephen probed Leslie about job prospects at the Barretts'. Since his discovery that she belonged to the family, that Queenie was in charge of the ménage, and that Queenie's son had escorted her on her neighborly calls, he seemed to think she had some influence in the matter. She tried to tell him that she didn't count for anything, that she didn't know of any purpose he could serve, that Queenie would doubtless want references and did he have any.

Stephen, Leslie discovered, was incredibly naïve. Though he

claimed he could turn his hand to any job, he had no letters of recommendation, nor could he produce the names of recent past employers. He couldn't even point to past experience in more than a general way. He had broken horses, he had farmed, he had worked in a store, he was good at mending things. He knew how to wait on table, he said, but couldn't name anyone who had hired him for the purpose. The work in the store was back in the closing months of the Civil War, for heaven's sake, and that was twelve years ago. She doubted he had even reached his teens back then.

"I don't know how you think you can apply for a job without references," she said.

Stephen seemed quite surprised. "Do you think farmhands go around getting letters from the farmers they work for? What about it, Mr. Cranston?"

Mr. Cranston shook his head. "It's not like that out here, Leslie. When I needed a hand, I'd hire any able-bodied young feller who came along. If he was lazy and didn't pull his weight, why, you tell him to get along with him, you didn't want him around any more."

"That's for outside work," Leslie said. "But Mr. Crawford would have to work indoors."

Neither of the men could see what difference that made. Leslie couldn't explain it well, except she knew that Mr. and Mrs. Wiggins wouldn't hire a maid or servant without very good references. If you had a lot of valuable possessions in your home, you had to be careful whom you let loose among them.

Young Mr. Crawford still had hopes. Perhaps if Leslie or the Cranstons put in a good word—?

Leslie nodded politely and refrained from reporting Queenie's view of the Cranstons, or of Leslie, for that matter. She could not think of three people whose opinion would count for less.

Conversation still dwelt upon Mr. Crawford's future when the thumping of the front-door knocker signaled the return of Leslie's "chauffeur."

There was annoyance in the knock, as if Miss Marsh's chauffeur resented having to alight and come to the door.

Leslie wasn't the only one who got that message. "He sounds rather cross," Mr. Crawford laughed and he rose to answer.

Adam Cranston was more affected. "Be nice to the young man," he called. "Make a good impression on him."

"Invite him in," Emily suggested. "Get to know him."

Leslie could imagine George's reaction to such an invitation, but she decided it would do him good. "Yes, by all means," she said. "Tell him I'm not ready yet. I'd like you to meet him."

Thus it was that George, bundled up in his expensive coat and thick muffler, was brought into the kitchen by Stephen, where Leslie made gracious introductions. George nodded curtly at the elderly couple and gazed with a certain annoyance at Leslie, for she was only just beginning to get her things on.

Would he like some tea? No, he would not. As a matter of fact, they were due home for lunch and should hurry.

Leslie said her goodbyes at the door with George, and when they went down the porch steps George strode ahead to the sleigh, waiting there to help her aboard.

"My, what a scowl," Leslie said when she climbed into her seat. "Must you always look so dark and forbidding?"

"The least you could have done was spare me the need to enter that dismal hovel."

"I think their home is very cheery, and I knew they'd want to meet you."

George snorted as he got in beside her. "How can you abide such people?" he growled. "Honestly, Leslie, I don't understand you at all."

"We weren't all born rich, George."

"Nor was I born rich," he answered, gently slapping Brindle into action with the reins. "But when one advances in life, one leaves the laggards behind."

CHAPTER NINETEEN

Neither Mr. Crawford's interest in finding a job, nor George's interest in playing chauffeur, made any serious impression upon Leslie. The rest of her week was spent fitting Queenie for a gown so becoming that, for once, Queenie didn't mind being put through her paces. George did not issue further chauffeuring invitations, and Leslie didn't notice. She was, in fact, so involved with the gown that she had no time for men, so when, late Saturday afternoon, Mabel Tyre knocked on the sewing-room door and said that Mr. Trowbridge wanted to see her in the library, her immediate, startled response was, "Mr. Trowbridge? In the library? Whatever for?"

It was a most inappropriate reply, Leslie decided, for Mabel replied in some alarm, "Miss, forgive me, he didn't say."

Leslie appeased Mabel and told her to report that she would be right along. Then she moved to her own room to inspect her appearance in the large dresser mirror. This was from habit rather than import, for, while she didn't think George was summoning her because he wanted to look at her, the instinct to make herself presentable was too strong to be disobeyed.

The setting was the library, the seldom-used room off the entrance hall, and when Leslie stepped inside, a fire was burning brightly in the grate, the door to the breakfast room was shut, and the trapped smell of George's half-burned cigar filled the room. He held it tight-clenched in his teeth and its size had shrunk to a near stub.

George, pacing to and fro on the oriental rug, motioned for her to close the doors. Leslie did as she was bid, placing themselves in total solitude. The smell of the smoke was distasteful. It was an element of maleness that did not appeal, but Leslie ignored it in favor of the man. Forces were driving him. His brow was dark, his movements awkward, frustrated and erratic. George Trowbridge was under stress and he had called her to him for some kind of succor. Let him smoke, let him be rude and callous. These were the manifestations of his distress. "Yes, George," she said.

"Sit down." He gestured to the couch at the end of the room, opposite.

Leslie went without a murmur, taking the center of the horsehair sofa that would cramp a threesome. The pacing man now strode between her and the door, and Leslie was suddenly reminded of his grip upon her arm. She cleared her throat. "What's the matter, George?"

She was down and positioned and it seemed to calm him. His pace slowed and he took stock of the situation. "Leslie," he said, coming, finally, to a halt in front of her, "look around. What do you see?" He gestured at the room and the windows.

Leslie, not knowing what he was after, shook her head. "What am I supposed to see?"

"Look, look, dammit!" He waved at the surroundings.

"I see a room."

"What kind of a room?" He looked himself and scowled. It wasn't the room he wanted for the purpose. He pointed down at the rich carpet. "See this rug. What do you think of it?"

"It's very beautiful."

"Is that all?"

"What else?"

"It cost a great deal of money, dammit."

Leslie nodded. "I'm sure it did, else you would not have something so beautiful here."

"That's what I'm talking about."

"What *are* you talking about?"

"You, me, this damned rug."

Leslie stared at him. "I don't think I understand what you're saying."

"Well, it ought to be obvious enough."

"It isn't obvious at all. You, me, and this rug? I don't have any idea what you're talking about."

"You like this rug, don't you? You like beauty, don't you?"

"Yes, I like beauty."

"You like beautiful things. Things like this rug, which cost three thousand dollars. This one rug cost three thousand dollars. Did you know that?"

"No," Leslie said. "I had no idea what it cost. I don't know why the price should matter."

"If you had to pay for it, the price would matter."

"But I couldn't possibly pay for such a thing. I wouldn't even think of it."

George gestured at the carpet irritably. "What I'm saying is, you like the rug, don't you?"

"Yes," Leslie answered. "Of course I do. I think it's beautiful."

"What I'm saying is, I can buy things like that."

"I know you can."

George shook his head. He was having a great deal of trouble communicating. "Well, don't you know what it is I'm saying?"

Leslie tried to be co-operative but she had no clue as to what her answer was supposed to be, and all she could do was answer helplessly, "No, I don't have any idea what you're saying."

George took a turn around the floor as if no female could be that demented. He came back and stood before her. "Dammit, I'm asking you to marry me. What the hell do you think I brought you down here for?"

Leslie blinked. Her eyes opened wide and her mouth opened wider. "You what?"

"I brought you down here to ask you to marry me. What are you acting so surprised for?"

The tensions and uncertainties in Leslie had built to the breaking point, and the incredibility of the whole situation suddenly struck her with such force that she burst out laughing. She didn't mean to, for the chagrin that crossed George's face distressed her, but she simply could not help it. She laughed and laughed, rocking helplessly, until she thought she would weep. And through it all, George stood nonplussed in front of her, puffing on his cigar as if it would give him breath, and staring at her as if she'd gone mad.

"Forgive me, forgive me," Leslie cried out, clasping her aching sides, trying to swallow her mirth, trying to make herself realize that this moody and helpless young man in front of her was serious in what he said. It ill-behooved a girl to laugh at a proposal of marriage, yet it was completely beyond her power to stop.

"George, George," she said breathlessly at last, "I apologize. I do not know what possessed me."

"I don't know either," George said sourly. "I think you are quite mad."

"I feel rather mad at this moment," Leslie admitted. "Your proposal has quite loosened the hinges of my mind."

"I utterly fail to see how you could be surprised," George said, eyeing her as if he thought she were putting him on.

"Maybe it's the difference between East and West," Leslie said, managing to become sober once more. "I must confess, George, that a proposal of marriage from you this afternoon was the last thing that would have entered my mind."

"But how could you have doubted my intentions? Did I not court you? Did I not take you riding? Did I not, even more, fetch and carry you according to your desires, even to the Cranstons' farm? Do you believe I did this for no reason whatsoever?"

Leslie's manner took on bite. "I assumed it was for gentlemanly purposes. I did not imagine you had ulterior motives."

"What is ulterior about marriage?" George said, his face reddening. "I have treated you honorably. My intentions towards you are honorable. Why else would I be offering you marriage?"

Leslie flushed and bowed her head. "I'm sorry," she whispered. "I'm deeply sorry. Yes, your proposal is honorable and I did not mean to question your intentions. In my own defense I can only say that I never dreamed you had such feelings towards me."

"Well," George said, turning for an ashtray, "now you know it. So let's have done with all this foolishness." He turned back. "What date would please you? I have no preferences myself, as long as it's soon."

"Date?" Leslie was getting lost again. "Date for what?"

"Our wedding, of course. What else would we be setting a date for?"

Leslie tried to be gentle, but the sharpness of disillusion came into her voice. "George, you have simply got to slow down. You are telling me you're asking me to marry you, but you haven't asked me. And you're assuming I've said yes, and I haven't."

George cast his eyes at the ceiling as if begging forgiveness for

94

not appreciating the Woman that God had created. "Do you need it spelled out to you?" he finally said, looking down at Leslie again. "Do you want it in writing? Is that what you want, a contract?"

"Oh, George, please," Leslie said. "I'm not interested in contracts or how you propose or anything else. I just don't want things to get confused, that's all."

"My point exactly. Let's make it very clear. I've proposed marriage. Can there be any doubt in your mind about that?"

"No, I quite understand you."

"That's fine. The next question is the date. I don't care when, so long as it's soon. Is that clear?"

"You're going too fast again, George. You're forgetting something."

"What?"

"My answer."

"Your answer to what?"

"To your proposal."

"To my proposal? You mean the date? I just told you it's up to you."

"To your proposal of marriage, George. You didn't wait to hear if I would accept or not."

George looked at the ceiling-high heavens once more. "Very well," he said. "I apologize for not having waited for your answer. I ask you, dear Leslie, if you would do me the honor of becoming my bride." He bowed. "I wait upon your answer."

Leslie rose from her seat. "Thank you very much for the honor you do me, sir," she said, extending her hand to him. "It is far beyond anything I ever expected, or could deserve. I regret more deeply than you will ever know that I must refuse. I will, however, always cherish the offer."

She was by him starting for the door when he caught her arm. "What did you say?"

She freed herself gently but firmly. "I said, I thank you very much for your offer of marriage, but I must refuse it."

George shook his head in disbelief. "What are you talking about?"

"Marriage. I do not wish to become married to you."

95

"But," he sputtered. "That's impossible. Why, there are women—"

"Who would fall at your feet," Leslie interjected, "thrilled beyond belief at such a courtesy. Accept them, by all means."

She was almost to the door when George was upon her again. "But I don't want them! I want you!"

"What on earth, George." She put a hand on his arm. "Forgive me, I do not mean to appear dense, but why must you importune a poor seamstress to be your wife? You can have anyone you want. Surely you can do better than me. What would you do with a girl who likes to visit the Cranstons? What would you do with a girl who likes to make clothes and hemstitch and sew in a room you've never set foot inside? What would you do with a girl who doesn't like to go to your dance halls and be coaxed to get drunk? What would you do with a girl who doesn't want to bring you home from your orgies and put you to bed? What would you do with a girl who doesn't fancy the things you fancy or seek the things you seek?"

"What does it matter," George came back, "as long as there's love?"

"Love?" Leslie countered. "*By* whom, *for* whom?"

"By me for you, and you for me!"

"You must have taken leave of your senses!"

George advanced upon her. "You love me and you know it! All that stands between us is that you won't admit it!"

Leslie tried to bring order out of chaos. "George, you're West and I'm East. And as Queenie says, there is a world between us."

"Not when love is involved!"

"But there is no love. I don't *love* you. Can't you understand that? I like you. I feel a kinship to you. But I don't *love* you!"

"Of course you do," George answered. "You just don't understand the meaning of love."

Leslie felt the color come into her cheeks. "Perhaps I don't," she said, "but I do know what's important to me and to my future. And that is that I don't want to marry you."

George shook his head and it was hard to know whether it was from disappointment or disbelief. "If you don't want to marry me," he answered, "then who is it you are seeking to marry?"

96

"I'm not seeking to marry anyone. Can you not understand that, George?"

"You are lying," he said, cutting her off from the door. "You cannot possibly reject me unless you are concealing a better offer."

Leslie, thwarted by George's large bulk against the door, drew herself up very quietly and said, "I am rejecting you, George, on one ground and one ground alone. That ground has nothing to do with your looks or your money. You are handsome, and you are rich, two facts of which you are already more than familiar."

Leslie took a breath before going on. "I am rejecting you because I do not want to spend the rest of my life catering to you because of all the money you've got. I don't want money. I don't want anything except the chance to be myself." She looked George coldly in the eye. "And I don't think," she said, "that this relates to your plans for the future."

George, desperate, snarled, "How do you know what I think?"

"I don't know what you think. This is what worries me. Would you please stand aside now and let me leave?"

"No," he answered frantically. "I'm not through."

"George, there is nothing more to be said."

"Yes, there is," he said desperately. "You've got to marry me. Don't you know I love you?"

"It hasn't been evident, George, but even if it were, the point is, I don't love you."

"But I'll make you happy. I swear it."

Leslie shook her head. "George, you can't possibly make me happy. You're overbearing and arrogant. You think money and good looks are all you need in life. Those are the very last two qualities about a man that interest me."

"Leslie." He got down on a knee before her. "I'll change. I'll be what you want. Anything you want me to be, I'll be. Just say yes. I won't be proud or overbearing or arrogant any more, I promise you. Just do me the honor of becoming my wife."

George looked so crushed, so broken, that Leslie's heart could not help but go out to him. "I'm sorry, George," she said gently, "but I wouldn't marry a man on promises. I would have to see

97

changes in you before I could change my mind. Humility has to be learned, George, and it isn't easily acquired."

He took the hem of her dress. "But I cannot wait. I love you. I want you."

"I'm sorry to be the first thing in your life you've ever wanted and can't have, but I'm afraid that's the way it's got to be. Will you let go of my skirt, please, so that I may leave?"

George rose to his feet, towering grimly over her. "I won't let you go. There's more to be said."

"There's nothing more to be said."

"I can't accept no for an answer."

"If you really mean it about changing your ways to please me, I think you should not try to hold me here against my will. That will only harden my heart."

George weakened and yielded ground. "But what can I do to win you?" he said.

"Start becoming a gentleman."

He looked as if he wanted to ask what a gentleman was, but thought better of it. He turned and pulled open the sliding doors. "You see, I am letting you go," he said quietly. "As you wished."

"Yes," she answered, starting through. "Thank you."

"That ought to prove I love you," he said as she entered the hall.

"Thank you," Leslie said again and went to the stairs.

CHAPTER TWENTY

George was not on hand for dinner that evening, and Queenie learned from Swift that he had gone off in the sleigh. Since she had not been consulted and since she did not like mystery, she was fretful and irritable at the table. Moreover, since George did not customarily act beyond her purview, she sensed something was afoot and eyed Leslie as the cause. For her part, Leslie, though she could guess the reason for George's absence, did not reveal it. As a result, Queenie was impatient and brusque, leaving Leslie to wonder for the hundredth time what forces of fate had acted in the strange conjunction that found her in an alien abode run by a woman who seemed to wish she had never come, and inhabited by a man who proposed marriage as if he were swallowing bitter medicine. And, for the hundredth time, she wished her Uncle Walter would return and take her in his arms and make her feel wanted and at home.

George was gone all evening, and by the time Leslie got ready for bed there had still been no sign of him. Queenie was stalking the house, venting her displeasure on the servants, and Leslie had long since fled to her room for respite.

She turned off her lamp and opened her curtains to look out upon the white, deep-banked landscape. The road lay out there, beyond the edges of darkness, and lights from the windows threw rectangular patches upon the snow.

Even as Leslie watched, the living-room lamps blinked out. Queenie was retiring. The grandfather's clock chimed the half hour, making it eleven-thirty. Queenie was not waiting up for her son.

Leslie groped her way to bed and climbed under the covers. She lay back, but her eyes were open. She should be used to it by now, but she could feel the deep silence of the night press down upon her. In the city it was never this dark and quiet. Street lights, wagon lanterns and the lamps in late-night windows dimmed the blackness so that the soft gray shape of the window could be seen against the darkness of the wall. The clop of hooves on cobblestones, the grinding of steel-rimmed wheels, the squeak of axles and the rowdy voices from late-night saloons kept the city alive. Even at five o'clock, when the city was closest to sleep, there would be the rattle of the milkman's wagon, or the soft thumping of the cop on the beat rapping his billy against the passing trees and posts. To one like Leslie, who

99

was used to light and noise, there was something eerie and disquieting about the unfamiliar black stillness.

She tried to lose herself in sleep, but sleep would not come. George's proposal had had too strong an effect. Over and over she relived it in her mind, feeling not flattered but uneasy. George did not take rejection well and she pondered what she had done that led him to think he would be accepted.

Where was he now, she wondered. What was he doing? Had he gone to some other woman for solace and affection? Or was he licking his wounds in lonely bitterness, planning how to bend her to his will? She sincerely hoped it was the former. That would defang him, and it was his fangs she feared. Let him have his women. Let him have all the women he could want as long as it kept his eyes from her.

Yet what kept her from sleep was the steadfast feeling that her rejection of his proposal was not the end of the affair, but only the beginning.

The clock downstairs chimed twice and Leslie winced. It was two o'clock in the morning and she still had not been to sleep. It was Sunday now, the twenty-first of January, one week before her twenty-first birthday, and she did not have to work. She would sleep late and miss breakfast, and when Mabel or Fanny knocked on the door with the hot water at half-past seven she would say, "Go 'way," turn over and doze off again.

Leslie heard a sound in the soundless night. She stiffened and held still. Was she dreaming? Had she dropped into sleep? No, she heard it again, so faint and soft that only the hours of total quietude enabled her ears to pick up the vibrations. Whatever it was, was a long way away, over on the far side of the house, back where the kitchen was—and the locked room.

Was it George? Had he come back?

Because she was so awake and alert, Leslie was out of bed and pressing an ear to her door before she realized it. There was nothing to hear and she softly opened it a crack. The gaslight in the hall let a dim slit of brightness into the room. Leslie opened the door wider and looked out. The front stairs and the passage beside them were empty. So, too, was the passage that zigzagged to the bathroom.

She heard it again, a soft, shuffling, bumping noise, like someone furtively struggling. It did not sound like George. George would have come in the front door and, even if he came through the kitchen, he would stride. The sounds would be bold and sure.

Carefully Leslie advanced to the railing and looked down into the blackness of the front hall. She had not been mistaken. No one was there.

A faint bumping noise caught her attention once more. Again she didn't know its source, but it sounded from the rear. It didn't have a threatening quality to it and Leslie was moved by curiosity rather than fear. Somebody was up and around. Could one of the servants—?

Leslie crossed to her sewing-room door and looked down that hall. A gas jet was on, but she knew that where the passage bent around the back staircases, there would be a gas jet by a locked door which would not be lighted and the corner there would be very dim.

There was a sound back there, like the creaking of a door, followed by a thump. Could it be from the secret room? Leslie went quickly down the hall and around the back staircases till she could see the dark corner and feel the cold air that crept along the floor.

Silence surrounded her and Leslie looked around. Where had those sounds come from? She tiptoed to the dark corner, up to the door itself. The draft of frigid air from under it was like ice against her bare feet. She tried the knob quietly and put her ear to the panel. Nothing could be alive in there. She was sure of it. The source was somewhere else.

She raised her head. There it was again. She still couldn't ascertain where it was, or what it was. She looked around and, as she did, there was a loud crashing of somebody stumbling and falling, but this was from the kitchen below, as if someone had tripped on the servants' stairs.

Leslie darted down past the bathroom to the head of those

steps. Looking down, she could see two black shapes at the bottom, one huddled on the stairs, the other bending over him. Then the bending figure looked up and, despite the dimness, Leslie saw that it was Stephen Crawford, the Cranstons' new boarder.

She gasped and, as she did, he waved a greeting, then indicated the crumpled figure before him. "It's George," he said in a hoarse whisper. "Give me a hand. I cannot get him up the stairs."

Leslie, forgetting she was barefoot and clad in nothing but a nightgown, grasped the railing and descended quickly. "What's happened to him?" she whispered back. "Is he all right?"

"He will be after he sleeps it off." Mr. Crawford shook his head. "I got him this far, but now he's passed out on me."

Leslie, bending over the fallen man, could hear the bubbling snore of his breathing and smell the harsh, acrid odor of alcohol. "He must have drunk a lot," she said. "What do you want me to do?"

Stephen pulled off his heavy coat, hat and mittens, then climbed past George to the step where Leslie stood. "Grab that arm and I'll take this and we'll drag him up the stairs."

Leslie nodded and together they struggled to get George's hulking, fleshy form to the floor above. The staircase was so cramped that Leslie and Stephen had little room to maneuver and their bodies were in constant contact, rubbing and brushing and bumping. It made Leslie redden with the realization that she had never before been in such close intimacy with a man, let alone with nothing but a flannel nightgown covering her nakedness.

The task of getting George Trowbridge up the stairs, however, was the main concern of Stephen Crawford, and it was a task that required the total efforts of the pair. By the time they had accomplished the feat, Leslie could feel the perspiration running down her body and the dampness of her clinging nightgown. As for Mr. Stephen Crawford, his collar was wilted, the visible part of his shirt was soaked, and his face was dripping. "Mr. Trowbridge weighs much too much," Stephen said when they had him lying on the second-floor carpet. His eyes, while discreet, could not quite keep from glancing at Leslie's thinly clad body.

"How did you come to be bringing him home?" Leslie asked,

ignoring his wayward glance, trying to behave like a properly dressed lady of the house.

"I encountered him in a saloon in town and it was clear that he could not possibly get home alone." Stephen looked down at the snoring man. "Does he always drink like that?"

Leslie, remembering her own experience, could not truthfully call George a moderate drinker. "Not really," was the best she could do. "I've never seen him like this before."

"What he needs is a man about the house."

Leslie looked down at the disheveled, helpless hulk. "What do you want to do with him? Shall I waken the servants?"

"No need. I'll hoist him onto my shoulder with your help and carry him to his room, if you'll show me the way."

Leslie nodded and, after an awkward struggle, she and Stephen got George onto the latter's shoulder and Stephen carried him down the hall, around the front stairs and, with Leslie quietly opening the door for him, into George's room and onto the bed. Stephen sighed with relief when free of his load and shook his head at his charge. "Mr. Trowbridge does tax a man's strength," he said.

Leslie, beside him, whispered, "How are you getting back to the Cranstons'?"

"On foot. It's not far. But first I'll take care of the horse—and Mr. Trowbridge."

"Ssh. George's mother is in the next room."

"And where's your room?"

"On the other side." Leslie hesitated. "Why? What do you want to know for?"

"Don't get startled. No reason. I'm just trying to get the lay of the land, so to speak."

"All right, but you'd better go now. If Queenie wakes up, she won't like finding you here."

"I'm not going to go yet. Is there a candle handy? Do you have matches or a light-maker?"

"Why? What are you going to do?"

"I'm not going to leave poor George like this. I'm going to dress him in his pajamas and tuck him under the covers."

"You can't do that."

"Why? If I don't put him to bed, who will?" He looked at her queryingly.

"Certainly not I," Leslie answered hastily.

"And certainly not Queenie."

"I would assume not."

"Then it's up to me, is it not? But I'll want some kind of light in here. Do you think you could manage that?"

His glance was roaming over her nightgown again and it compelled obedience. "There's a lamp on the table there," she said, "and the equipment to light it should be in the drawer." She turned on her heel and walked out, managing her exit with all the dignity her improper attire could permit. Then, darting quickly back to her own room, she closed the door and, after leaning against it for a moment to regain her composure, turned the key.

Once safe in her own quarters, Leslie stilled her quickened heart, removed her uncomfortably wet nightgown, dried herself with her towel and groped in her drawers for a fresh nightgown. She shivered putting it on and realized how cool the room had become and how much she had been chilled by the cold of the house after her strenuous exertions helping Mr. Crawford.

Once again in bed, getting warm under the covers, she let her thoughts relive the strange events of the night that found her sharing such intimate moments with the Cranstons' new boarder. She would dream of him, she was sure.

CHAPTER TWENTY-ONE

Leslie's dreams that night were not, as she had expected, pleasant reveries about the good-looking newcomer. Instead, they were terrifying nightmares about the locked room. Time and again she heard struggling sounds coming from the back of the house. Time and again, barefoot and in her nightgown, she retraced her steps through the halls, inevitably coming to the locked door and its chilling draft of cold air. Sometimes the sounds were akin to the ones George and Mr. Crawford had made in the kitchen, but other times they became mouthed cries, wordless noises, like someone trying to speak without a tongue. In fear and trembling, she would try the door and it would open. Then she would wake in the inky blackness of her room, perspiring and shaking, taking long moments to gain a sense of her surroundings and realize it was only a dream. She would toss and turn for a bit, drop off again, and the performance would be repeated. It was not until dawn that the nightmares stopped, and not until noon that she allowed Fanny to come in and rebuild the fire.

"You look peaked, miss," Fanny said, peering at her from the stove. "Ain't you slept well?"

"It wasn't one of my better nights," Leslie allowed.

"Miss Queenie's getting techy. She's expecting you for lunch."

"I think I can make it for lunch."

"You should take Lydia E. Pinkham's Vegetable Compound, miss. That'll help what ails you."

"Thank you, Fanny."

"I take it three times a day. Every day. Three tablespoons, I do. And it works wonders, let me tell you."

"Well, then, I'm sure I should try it. By the way, Fanny, do you know why that room at the back of the house over the kitchen is locked?"

Fanny, at the door, looked startled at the question. "Me, miss? No, miss, I don't. It's been locked ever since I've been here."

"And you've never asked why?"

"Miss, if I asked why, they might open it and I'd have to clean it. If they want to forget about it, I don't want to remind them."

Leslie made do with that for the moment, but she was interested in answers and she meant to address Queenie on the subject when she went down for lunch. Why were all the servants newly hired? was one question she wanted answered; and, Why was a large room on the second floor kept locked? was the other.

She was first in the dining room and waited behind her chair.

Then Queenie came sailing in like a steam-powered ocean liner, took her seat at the opposite end of the table and gestured Leslie down with the imperious wave of a Caesar. Her clothes were starched and regal, but her brow was creased and there was an element of wrath in her makeup.

Norma Cash, the scullery girl, was there to serve and seemed uneasy at the prospect. Queenie did nothing to help her. "All right, girl, get to your task, and don't fall all over your feet." She looked briefly at Leslie, then broke a bun and spread butter all over one half. "Damned mistake, I guess I made," she announced in a manner that demanded an inquiring reply.

"Oh?" Leslie obediently responded and sipped water from her goblet.

"Damned stupid mistake," Queenie said when the "oh" became obvious as the only reply. "I should play my hunches."

Leslie sensed she was being set up for something, but she knew she had to play her role. "What do you mean?" she asked dutifully.

Queenie sighed as if it was too painful to bear. She helped herself to the corned beef and cabbage, passed the dish herself and waved Norma back to the scullery. "Leslie," she finally said, "didn't your Uncle Walter explain, when he invited you to come and live with us, that it was because I wanted you?"

Leslie answered carefully, "He said you wanted a dressmaker."

"I wanted *you* for my dressmaker. Did he not make that clear?"

"I'm not sure that I understand, Queenie."

"What I want you to understand, dearie, is that your Uncle Walter invited you here because *I* wanted you, not because *he* wanted you."

Leslie felt her insides shrivel. Queenie could really make you hurt. "Yes, I see."

"I don't mean that your Uncle Walter wasn't delighted to have you move in with us. Your Uncle Walter loves you very much. You understand that, don't you?"

"Yes," Leslie answered because there was nothing else to say.

"I try to do the right thing," Queenie went on. "When I married Walter, I married his family the same way that when he married me, he married my family." Queenie shoveled a new load of corned beef and cabbage into her mouth. "Your Uncle Walter loves George just as much as if he were his own son."

"Yes, I understand."

Queenie, speaking around the food she chewed, went on. "And I love you as if you were my own niece. I love you as much as he does. More, in fact."

"More?" Leslie would have wished it less. She sensed this was going to be a very bad day.

"More." Queenie emphasized the word by leaning closer across the length of the table. "Mind you," she continued, sitting back, "I'm not saying anything against your uncle, but you have to understand that he's very busy carrying on his business. You don't get rich without working very very hard."

"I can understand that."

"He doesn't have time to look after orphaned relatives he's never seen before." Queenie fixed Leslie with a hard eye. "With all due respect to your uncle, I want you to understand that the only reason you're here is because I brought you here." Queenie swallowed one mouthful of food and refilled the void with another. She gulped half a goblet of water. "You sent word that your mother had died. Walter was saddened to learn of the passing of his dearest sister. We all were." Queenie wagged her fork. "But only I devoted attention to the question, What is going to happen to Walter's sister's daughter? Only *I* remembered that your mother had a daughter."

"Yes, I see," Leslie said, fighting back tears.

"I brought you here," Queenie went on, "because I wanted to help you."

"I appreciate that," Leslie said softly. She hadn't asked for help and she hadn't sought it, but Queenie's offer had been providential. It had caught her at low ebb and restored her spirits. Except that she had thought it had come from her uncle.

"So I try to help," Queenie then went on, "and I find I have clasped an adder to my bosom."

Leslie felt a quake go through her. She had been weakened by

107

nightmares, then found the uncle she needed as an anchor had no concern for her. Now the person who professed to be her anchor was turning away. It was more than Leslie, at that moment, could bear. "What do you mean?" she cried out. "I don't understand you! What am I supposed to have done?"

Queenie shook her head sadly. "That's the pity of it," she said. "You haven't *done* anything. It's *my* doing. It's all *my* doing."

"*What* is your doing? Please tell me," Leslie pleaded desperately. "I don't understand."

"When I offered you a home and a position as a member of my family—of your uncle's family," Queenie intoned, "I forgot a terrible fact. I forgot I was bringing a young and beautiful girl into a home with my own young and vulnerable son." Queenie fairly glowered at Leslie. "I did not realize how lovely and charming Walter's niece would be." She shook her head. "And I did not realize what a deadly blow I delivered to my own son." She shook off Leslie's attempted remonstrance. "Had I known what you could do to men," Queenie finished, "I would not have let you within a thousand miles of George."

Leslie finally had her chance. "Queenie," she protested, "I don't know what you're talking about. I'm not beautiful. I don't have any charms. I am scrawny and lanky and ugly. I don't attract men. I never have. I've never even thought about it. The idea that someone like George, who's rich and handsome and experienced, who's had his pick of women, could possibly be interested in me is—like—is—like his being interested in the chambermaids. I mean he might want to—to—avail himself of—" Leslie flushed. "I don't know what I'm trying to say, except that anyone in George's position could not possibly—not in a million years—be interested in someone like me, in any serious, lasting way. You must believe that, Queenie."

Queenie looked haughtily down the table at the young girl. "Are you denying that he's asked you to marry him?"

Leslie swallowed. "You know about that?"

"I found out this morning. Why do you think George isn't at lunch?"

"Well, I—"

"Because he laid his heart before you and you were as uncivil in your response as any human being could be." She leaned forward. "What are you trying to do to my son? All he wants is to marry you. Is that good reason to crucify him?"

"But I didn't crucify him," Leslie protested. "I thanked him for the honor he'd done me—"

"You turned him down."

"But I—I had to."

"You *had* to?" Queenie glowered at her. "What do you mean you had to? Is he not handsome, attractive, rich?"

"Yes, he's very handsome. He's all of those things."

"Would he not be the catch of the season a hundred miles around Chicago?"

"Yes, yes. I was most honored—"

"What on earth more could you want in a man, girl? Do you, a mere seamstress, expect a better offer to come your way?"

"Oh, no," Leslie answered. "Please don't believe that. I never expected *this* offer. I never expected to get any offer."

True bewilderment suddenly took the place of anger in Queenie's face. "Then, what on earth did you say 'no' for?"

Leslie was flustered. It had been clear to her at the time, but Queenie had ways of muddying the water. "I don't love him," she plainted.

Queenie's eyes popped wide open. "You don't what?"

"I don't love him," Leslie repeated. "I hardly know him."

"You don't love him, you don't know him? What on earth has that got to do with it? You'll come to love him later. You'll come to know him later. Leslie, you've been acting like an idiot. You've got to come to your senses." Queenie jabbed a finger at the young girl. "Now I want you to go apologize to George. I want you to tell him you've been an utter fool, that of course you'll marry him and the sooner the better. And I mean that, before he changes his mind. And if I were you, my fine miss, I'd pray to God on my knees that he hasn't changed his mind in the meantime. You have taken a terrible chance, my girl!"

Somehow the things that Queenie was saying brought Leslie's senses back into position. She felt so strange and alien in this far-off land. It was like the world Lewis Carroll described in a book she'd enjoyed, one that Mrs. Wiggins had let her borrow. Everything seemed to be backwards and she got so mixed up she couldn't tell what she was supposed to do. Now, however, she was getting her feet back on the ground. It was that business about praying to God for forgiveness and hoping that George wouldn't withdraw his offer. If she'd wanted his offer she'd have said yes the day before. Nothing had happened in the intervening hours to make her change her mind. Queenie was trying to make her, but Queenie was George's mother and she doted on her son. Whatever it was he wanted, she wished him to have. Her concern was with George, not with Leslie. So were her arguments.

Leslie found herself possessed of a discovered calm. She felt like Lewis Carroll's Alice again, but this time not through the looking glass, but in Wonderland where a little bite of cake made her grow suddenly taller. Leslie felt as if she had shot up five inches and could look down on Queenie from an insurmountable height.

"Thank you for your advice, Queenie," she said with a quiet and telling reserve, "but I don't think I'll pray. If George has changed his mind, I think it's for the best."

Queenie studied her slowly and assessingly, reading her new-found attitude. "You think it's for the best? Why?"

"It would show that his feeling for me was very shallow," Leslie answered. "Which is what I would expect. As I said, we scarcely know each other."

"One doesn't have to know another person to fall in love." Queenie tried to revive her control. "Don't you understand, Leslie? George is in love with you. He's deeply in love."

"But I'm not in love with him."

"What does love matter to a woman? *Men* marry for love. Women marry for advantage."

"I would not take advantage."

"For heaven's sake, Leslie, it's even-Steven. The man gets what he wants and the woman gets what she wants. And both are happy. Don't you understand that you don't have to be in love with George to enjoy the pleasures that George has to offer?

Think of it—all the clothes you could want. A personal maid—like mine. Social position. Important friends. Children—children—you would have those too. You could never have those if you didn't get married, and I know you like children. I can see it in your eyes."

"Yes, I love children," Leslie admitted. "Someday I would like to have some of my own."

"And George can give them to you. Not only that, but they would be well-cared-for children. They would be the children of a rich man, not a poor man. That's important, Leslie. A mother must do right by her children!"

"And what does George get?" Leslie asked. "You've been telling me all the things *I* would get, were I to accept his proposal. Tell me, what would *he* get?"

Queenie compressed her lips. "Of course he would have his husbandly rights," she conceded. "But," she went on, encouragingly, "this is not a great burden upon a woman. When you think of what you get in return, and how little you have to pay, a woman can only give thanks that men were made lustful. It demands but little of us women to sate their lust, but they will pay us greatly for the doing. You have feathered your nest well, my pet. George's love for you assures you a life of ease and comfort, not just for you but for your children."

"You forget," Leslie reminded Queenie, "that I have turned him down."

"I mean," Queenie amended, "once you alter your answer."

"Which I have no intention of doing." Leslie went on. "Queenie, I'm not interested in clothes, personal maids, social position or important friends. If I married a man, it would be because I was interested in *him*, not in the things he could do for me. If I married, it would be because I loved him, not just because he loved me. And if I married a man I was in love with, and if we had children together, I think we could do more for those children, loving each other and loving them, poor as we might be, than people who did not love each other and did not love children could possibly do, no matter how much money they might have."

Queenie started to expostulate, but Leslie was in command.

"You have to understand something, Queenie. I am a *person*, not a thing. There are women who will sacrifice anything to be able to substitute 'Mrs.' for 'Miss.' I am not one of them. You tell me to marry George though I do not love him, assuring me that love comes later. Maybe it does. But what if it doesn't? If it didn't, I would be helpless, frustrated, driven to desperate measures to seek survival. All the money and social position in the world would not compensate for living in a world I hated." Leslie leaned forward. "I have a trade, Queenie. I can make a living. I can support myself. I could not live as well as you do, but I would be my own person and I'd rather make my own future poorly and say what it's going to be than have someone else make it for me richly and have no choice." Leslie rose. "I am extremely sorry if my presence here has disappointed you and distressed your son. If you wish, I would be glad to leave as soon as Uncle Walter returns."

Queenie rose in restraint. "Now wait, now wait, there is no need to be upset. I didn't say I was going to send you home. Sit down and let us be civilized about this."

Both women sat again, Leslie on the edge of her chair, Queenie hitching hers forward. "Let us think carefully about everyone's future," she said. "After all, yours isn't the only one to be considered."

Leslie's eyes narrowed and Queenie became even more conciliatory. "We are at your mercy, George and I," she said. "Are you telling us that George's love for you is hopeless?"

"I could not say that," Leslie answered quickly. "I do not know him. I do not even know myself." She leaned forward. "You must understand, Queenie. Everything's happened so fast. I come here to be a dressmaker and I have scarcely arrived before I'm offered a proposal of marriage. The thought of marrying anybody, let alone marrying George, simply hadn't occurred to me. It's happened so fast I can't think straight. I couldn't possibly say yes on the spur of the moment. Marriage is for life, Queenie. When a woman says yes, she is determining her future for the rest of her life. That's a very serious decision."

"If she says no, she's determining her future too."

"That's true, but when the proposal is unexpected it's a different matter. Saying yes would mean a total break with everything that's gone before. If I say no, at least I'll have an idea what to expect out of life. It's much safer to say no."

Queenie measured her. "You mean, if it hadn't been such a surprise, you would have said yes?"

"I mean that if matters had progressed in a more reasonable manner, I would be able to give more thought to the matter and my decision would have been more wisely reached."

"Are you telling me that if my son courts you proper-like, you could change your mind?"

"Of course I might change my mind. If we get to know each other better, if we find we have things in common, if I find myself falling in love with him, of course the answer could be different."

"How the hell long do you think this courtship business is going to take?" Queenie said sourly.

"I would not have any idea," Leslie answered. "I don't know why it should matter."

It was at that moment that Lambert came in. "Sorry to disturb you, ma'am," he said to Queenie, "but there's a man at the back door wanting to see Mr. George."

"What's he want?" Queenie asked abruptly.

"He says he's Mr. George's valet."

CHAPTER TWENTY-TWO

Queenie's fork fell from her fingers and clattered on her plate. She picked it up again. "He said what?"

Lambert repeated the statement. "He says he's Mr. George's valet, ma'am."

"Impossible!" Queenie got up. "Let me speak to him." She was off, following Lambert to the kitchen, and Leslie, having an idea as to the identity of the visitor, trailed after.

Her hunch was right. It was Mr. Stephen Crawford, standing just inside the door, warmly bundled in a plaid jacket, his cap in mittened hands, a suitcase beside him. Lambert introduced the newcomer in a haughty manner, but the women servants were all but chirping in excitement.

As for Queenie, her manner was imperious and annoyed. "Now what is this you say, Crawford? What is this claim you make about my son?"

"Ah," the young man said with a bow. "Mrs. Barrett. I'm so glad to make your acquaintance. Your son speaks so highly of you. I am looking forward to serving you as well as him."

"You know my son?"

"He could not have hired me if he did not know me. Yes, I have had the pleasure of making his acquaintance, and we have had conversation together."

"How has this been?"

"We first met at the Cranstons' where I have, until now, been boarding. Thereafter, we have encountered each other in town at the—at one of the saloons. In fact, we rode home together last night. He was not feeling well and I gave him assistance." Mr. Crawford's eye caught Leslie's. Hers was uncertain, but his was merry. "It was then that he made the offer. Have you spoken to him this morning?"

"Yes," Queenie said.

"Then he told you about hiring me?"

"He's told me nothing of the kind."

"That's strange," the young man said. "He was most appreciative of the help I gave him and vowed he wanted me around on a permanent basis. He knew, of course, that I have been seeking employment, so he was not being presumptuous. And I," Stephen added, bowing slightly, "was more than pleased to accept." His brow puckered. "But I am surprised he has not told you. Perhaps he was not expecting me until later in the day."

Queenie's mouth was tight with displeasure. Quite obviously

she had not planned her ménage to include a valet for George. She studied the stranger a moment longer. "You are in town looking for employment? Surely you didn't come to Fletcher hoping for a job as a valet."

Mr. Crawford laughed. "No, ma'am, certainly not. That was about the last job I thought would come my way in Fletcher."

"Yes, I daresay. Have you ever been a valet before?"

"Oh, yes. Why the last family—"

"What about references?"

"I don't have any with me, but I'd be glad to write and have—"

"And you say he hired you last night? Are you sure he knew what he was about?"

Stephen arched an eyebrow. "Well, now, Mrs. Barrett, at the time I thought he was his own man. I thought that if he told me I was hired, why I was hired. Otherwise, I would hardly have packed my things and given up my lodgings at the Cranstons'."

Leslie sensed that Queenie was torn, that she wanted to turn the young man out and then go after George; but that would not promote George in Leslie's eyes. She took the other route. "Very well," she snapped. "We'll try you for a week and see. You will bunk in the servants' quarters. Lambert will show you where."

CHAPTER TWENTY-THREE

Leslie could not help but wonder if Stephen—as the new valet would be called—had not taken advantage of George's drunken condition in plying him for a job. If George had hired the newcomer unwittingly, however, he gave no sign. In fact, he went out of his way to take credit for the move.

George was in ebullient spirits when he finally came downstairs in midafternoon. Stephen had already been summoned to his room and had undergone the duty of assisting his master to dress. The George who resulted was a far cry from the one Leslie had expected. He was cheerful, at ease, expansive, betraying no trace of disappointment over her rejection, no aftereffects of the night before. Stephen had decked him out in his Sunday best and he gave every appearance of a country gentleman who had never sipped anything stronger than sherry.

He greeted Leslie pleasurably, as if the previous twenty-four hours had never happened, and so cheerfully sought her company for a ride in the sleigh that she found her acceptance was willingly, rather than dutifully, given. In fact, noting the polish of George's boots, the well-brushed quality of his clothes, the elegance of his appearance that seemed to spark the change in his demeanor, Leslie thought that the addition of a valet might fulfill whatever it was that George had been lacking.

"Here, let me help you," George volunteered when Leslie went to get into her things. He leaped to hold doors, to assist her down the porch steps, and would not let Swift tuck her into the sleigh. That pleasure he reserved for himself.

Leslie was amazed at the difference. George was treating her like a lady instead of a woman of the streets. Had Queenie counseled him? Had Leslie's rejection scared him? Or was it the presence of a valet in the house?

George, usually taciturn, was talkative on the ride. He was trying to be the man Leslie had claimed she wanted—someone she could feel at home with, someone she could get to know.

As for the valet, it was a subject he brought up himself. "I guess you saw Steve," he said, as Brindle clip-clopped along the snowy road. "You were there when he came, Mother says."

"Yes," Leslie answered.

"What do you think about me giving him a job as a valet?"

"Frankly, I'm astonished."

"Astonished?" George turned to her. "Why?"

"Well, partly because of you, and partly because of him."

"What do you mean by that?"

"Because of you, I'd have to say it's because I didn't think you cared much for him when you met. I wouldn't have thought him a man you'd hire for anything, let alone such a personal position as your own valet."

"I know," George agreed. "I wasn't much taken with him at first. I couldn't see a man who spends his time whittling on a stick of wood as amounting to much. But we all make mistakes. That's one thing I've learned. And in certain things Stephen is very good."

"Apparently he is," Leslie agreed, but there was more suspicion in her voice than in George's.

"And what do you mean, 'partly because of him'?"

"He did not strike me as a valet type. I never would have expected him to have any talents at that type of job."

"I wouldn't have either," George agreed. "But he's been looking for work and I thought I'd give him a chance."

"That's generous of you, George."

He sensed the incompleteness of the statement and turned again. "But you don't approve?"

"I do not know," Leslie said, shrugging. "All I mean is, I would not have guessed he'd have experience valeting."

"One wouldn't. But I ran into him in town last night and we talked about his need for a job. That's how it happened. He said he knew how to valet and I decided to try him out. In fact, I brought him home with me last night to put him to the test."

"Oh?" Leslie said. "You put him to the test?" She smiled faintly. "Pray, how did Stephen make out in the test?"

"Very well," George answered without hesitation. "He laid out my pajamas and prepared the bed. He knew what he was doing. I could tell that right away. So I told him he could start work immediately."

"I see," Leslie said, wondering if George were being manipulated. "Are you doing this out of generosity or—I mean, you haven't had a valet before."

"I've been wanting to hire one," George answered offhand-

117

edly. "I've been wanting one for some time, but there haven't been any. There isn't much call for servants out here in Fletcher. You don't have an easy time rounding them up."

"I guess that's right," Leslie agreed. "In fact, I understand all the servants are newly hired. Is that right?"

George looked at her quickly. "Where did you hear that?"

"From the servants themselves. Everyone I've talked to says your mother only hired them last month. That's right, isn't it? I mean most of the servants are new—most, if not all?"

For a brief period, Leslie was afraid George was going to lapse back into the uncommunicative, taciturn escort she'd been accustomed to riding with. His brows had clamped tight and he was pondering long. Then his forehead cleared and he turned, his face steadfast, his voice firm. "That's right," he said. "They're all new. Every one of them."

He said no more and Leslie was left to ask the obvious question. "But why? A whole new household staff?"

George's face tightened. "It's an unpleasant subject," he said gruffly. "Certain valuables disappeared. There was a thief in the house—someone on the staff. Someone very clever. There was no way to catch him—or her. It was critical. There were certain items we had to protect at all costs. We had no choice. We fired the whole lot."

"Oh," Leslie said. "How terrible."

"Terrible?"

"I mean, for the innocent."

"Yes, it was. But we had to. There was nothing else to do."

"I know," Leslie said. "I can understand that. I'm just very sorry."

The ride, for Leslie, was a most pleasant one. George was communicative for a change and, though he steered away from talk about his and Uncle Walter's business affairs, he told Leslie quite a little about his family background. Queenie, he said, had been a buxom belle who had married a well-to-do "old" man of thirty-one when she was a tender seventeen. George junior was the product of that union, having been born in 1854 when Queenie was just turned twenty.

118

George Trowbridge, Sr., was a good provider and the family lived well, but he worked himself into an early grave, dropping dead in late 1867 at the age of forty-six. His estate was sufficient to keep Queenie and young George in reasonable comfort, and this was the situation when her path first crossed that of Walter Barrett in late 1872. Walter was traveling a great deal so the romance bloomed only slowly, and it wasn't until three years later that he finally popped the question and marriage resulted.

Because he could afford it, Queenie wanted a big house. Unfortunately, nothing in the Chicago area, which was where they had courted and wed, was suitable or available. The Morgate house in Fletcher was the nearest thing to Queenie's taste, and she persuaded Walter to buy it.

"I'm surprised," Leslie said, "that she'd pick a place so isolated."

"She doesn't like the country, but she likes the comfort," George replied.

"But there's nowhere to go and nothing to do, except go sleighing like us—and that doesn't seem like Queenie's style."

"Oh," George said, "Mother is very clever at entertaining herself. Sometimes she's almost too clever."

Leslie thought she detected a sour note in that remark and she looked at George quickly. His eyes were straight front, however, his face reflective. It was a mood Leslie sensed she should not disturb and she did not ask him what he meant. Instead, she said, "And the house itself. It must be the biggest one in town."

"It is," George said after a moment. "By far."

"All by itself out in nowhere."

"Built by a strange family," George said. "I don't know whether they thought their friends would build around them or what. They didn't stay long and it sat empty for a long spell before Walter bought it. He got a good bargain."

Leslie nodded. She could imagine he did.

George ordered hot tea for them upon their return and helped her out of her things in true gentlemanly manner. "Yes," Leslie thought to herself, "he definitely is wooing me." In fact, she even sensed that the change in his behavior was genuine, not the result of a crash training course by Queenie. Leslie found herself more favorably disposed toward George than she had ever thought she could be.

It was late after the tea and Leslie wanted to wash and change before the evening meal. Though she would not be taking a bath, she decided to do her ablutions in the bathroom where there was hot water from the tap rather than cold water from her pitcher.

With her dress off and a robe around her, she took her towel and soap dish down the crooked corridor to the door at the end. Her slippered feet were silent on the carpeting, and thus it was that when she reached the bathroom door she did so without disturbing the man at the corner of the opposite hall in front of the locked door.

Leslie, espying him almost by accident, stopped short with her hand on the knob. It was Stephen Crawford, and he was so intent upon the locked door that he had no sense of being witnessed. He twisted the knob, felt the panels, and tried the knob again. Then he knelt and placed his hand by the bottom of the door to feel the cold draft. It was when he then turned to put his ear against the door that he saw her watching him.

He came to his feet quickly. "Oh," he said, approaching her with a ready smile. "I didn't know you were in this part of the house."

"So I observe," Leslie said. "Nor did I know that you were—since George's room is at the front."

"Just learning my way around," Stephen said without the slightest flush of embarrassment. He gestured at the door he had left. "Whose room is that?"

"I don't know."

"It's locked."

"I know."

"Do you know why?"

Leslie shook her head. "Do you think that should be of any concern to you?"

Stephen smiled brightly again. "Now, how could I answer that if I don't know why it's locked?"

Stephen had been open and frank at the Cranstons'. Now there was something devious about him that made him border on the ominous. More than a little lay behind his smile.

"May I congratulate you on your new position," Leslie said. "You didn't have much trouble finding a job."

"Thanks to George—I mean, Mr. Trowbridge."

"He's generous."

"To a fault."

"When did he hire you? I know it was last night, but how did it come about?"

"Hasn't he told you?"

"No."

"On all that long ride this afternoon?"

"We weren't talking about you."

"I'm sure you weren't."

"So I don't really know how or when he hired you."

"You must ask him sometime."

CHAPTER TWENTY-FOUR

George's changed behavior continued throughout the week. Not only that, he spent most of his time in Leslie's company. Business would be at a standstill, he explained, until Walter returned. Meanwhile, Queenie couldn't seem to care less about dressmaking. Leslie was available to be entertained as George was free to provide it. Life for Leslie had become quite delightful. She was sampling it from the Doris Wiggins view—the young mistress of a household without work to do, her time being taken by the courtship of ardent swains. It was a heady feeling.

All was not heaven, however. There was one slight blot on the scene. Stephen was daily becoming more withdrawn around her and almost hostile. She wasn't sure when it had started, but she linked it to the time she had caught him at the locked door trying to learn what lay beyond.

Surely that had nothing to do with it, she thought. Yet from that point on, his manner had become increasingly formal. He addressed her as "Miss Marsh," though he called George "Mr. George," and his manner, when she appeared in his presence, underwent a cooling change. Nor, she noted, was she often in his presence. Though she couldn't be sure, he gave the appearance of avoiding her. Meanwhile, he had become very popular with Mr. George, even with Queenie herself. And the girls in the servants' quarters—they seemed to fall into pieces every time he spoke to them, noticed them, or even walked into a room. But he avoided Leslie so studiously that she thought the others must wonder. Certainly she wondered.

It was on Saturday, the twenty-seventh, that Uncle Walter returned. "Just in time for your twenty-first birthday, my dear," he told Leslie when the carriage he had hired from Chicago returned him to the waiting arms of his family. "I wouldn't forget your birthday," he said with a cupid's-bow smile and a pinch of her cheek. And Leslie, really glad to see her own kin again, hugged him warmly and then flushed at her eagerness.

They gathered around the fire in the living room before dinner, sipping sherry and getting caught up on things. When George and Queenie told Uncle Walter about the valet, Leslie wondered what his response would be. There had been thefts by servants of so serious a nature that the whole household staff had been summarily fired and a new coterie of domestics brought in. Despite this, George and Queenie had engaged a new servant without even a cursory look into his background. Leslie wondered if Uncle Walter would explode in anger at the idea of an additional servant being hired in his absence. Leslie would have expected Uncle Walter to query the newcomer most piercingly.

Instead, Uncle Walter accepted the presence of the new recruit without even raising his eyebrows. That George had equipped himself with a valet caused no comment, and when

Stephen was brought in and introduced, Uncle Walter greeted him in friendly fashion and asked not a single question as to his experience and past employment. Leslie was mystified, but decided it was the difference between East and West. In the more primitive and less staid sections of the country where people did not have long lineages to refer to, they were doubtless accustomed to sizing each other up at a glance, and a person's face was more his recommendation than his list of references. On such evaluation, Stephen obviously passed muster.

"So you've taken on a valet, George," was Uncle Walter's comment when Stephen had been met and dismissed. "I must say it becomes you. You look exceptionally tidy. Is that because of the valet?" he went, casting a glance at Leslie, "or is it because of the dressmaker?" And then he chortled. ·

CHAPTER TWENTY-FIVE

It was Sunday morning, January 28, 1877, and when Fanny Nils brought in the hot water and refueled the fire, she said brightly, "Happy twenty-first birthday, miss."

And all the servants Leslie encountered when she came down the stairs for breakfast also wished her a happy twenty-first birthday. It was no secret that this was a red-letter day for the young niece of Walter Barrett. Bessie Wood served strawberries and cream for breakfast. Norma Cash, who did not know how to write, drew a crude picture of a birthday cake on a card; Paul Lambert, the head of the staff, gave her a corsage he had made of ferns and feathers to wear for the big birthday dinner they would serve at two o'clock; and Harry Best, the footman, recited a birthday poem he had composed. Mabel Tyre and Glenda Peterson gave her small gifts to be opened when the cake was served.

Throughout the rest of the morning, the house was abustle with activity. The birthday dinner was the biggest event in the family's life, and the servants meant to make the most of it. Even Leslie was caught up in the excitement of the preparations and she spent no little time planning her garb, sewing, fixing and preparing. The Barretts, it seemed, did not entertain. They lived in splendid isolation, communing only with themselves, and it left the servants with little to look forward to.

Meanwhile, all that morning, George would hardly leave her alone. With a valet to take of his own needs, he was free to amuse himself as he would, and Leslie, as she had been for the full week, was the object of his attentions. Though such devotion was flattering, it was getting overmuch and she had to shoo him from the sewing room so she could finish her dress.

At half-past one, all was ready and the family gathered in the living room to celebrate the occasion with sherry. Uncle Walter poured four glasses of the dark, nutty-smelling liquid from a cut-glass decanter while Leslie stood near him at the sideboard and George hovered close by.

Uncle Walter handed the first glass to Leslie, then carried one to Queenie. Next came George, who was standing so close to Leslie that their arms and even their bodies kept brushing. She was being wooed not just ardently, but to the point of suffocation. When she sat, she chose a single chair instead of the sofa so that she would be free to breathe, but George was undaunted. He sat at her feet, using the front of the chair and her skirt-covered legs as support. Though she ignored his attentions, Leslie secretly enjoyed them. She had never had a man pay court before, and the experience was flattering and intoxicating.

Then came dinner, with Uncle Walter at the head of the table to carve the immense roast which the footman served and Lambert oversaw. At least at the meal George couldn't crowd too close. He was seated opposite.

It was a happy birthday dinner and Uncle Walter was at his entertaining best. Story after droll story came from his lips, which kept the diners in a constant state of merriment and had Best smothering guffaws and Lambert chuckling quietly.

Then the table was cleared and the time had come for dessert. This consisted of a large cake, crusted with vanilla frosting and decorated with the message "Happy Birthday Leslie" in pink letters, and flower designs in different colored icings, all enclosed in a circle of twenty-one candles. Lambert brought in the cake, followed by Best with a trayful of presents, while Bessie, the cook, watched from the doorway.

Then all the servants were invited to gather 'round for the candle blowing and they trooped in—all but Edgar Swift, the groom, and Stephen Crawford, the valet.

Swift was the one who had given Leslie a gift, and when she had drawn a deep breath and, to the cheers of the assemblage, had blown out all the candles at once, she picked his present off the top of the pile. It was roughly wrapped, small enough to fit into the palms of both hands, flat and roundish, but unusually heavy. "What can it be?" she asked, making a ceremony of feeling and hefting it before untying the ribbon.

Inside was a worn, rusted horseshoe, one of Brindle's castoffs, and it was decorated with a bright piece of red yarn and a card which said, "May this horseshoe bring you the best of luck."

"Oh, I wish he were here so I could thank him," Leslie said, and it was at that moment that the groom did appear. He did not, however, seem to share the joy of the other servants. His face was sober and he circled the group to get to Uncle Walter. He whispered something in the older man's ear and Uncle Walter frowned. He looked around the assemblage. "Swift tells me Brindle's been attacked," he said.

"Attacked?" That was George. "By what? Is she all right?" He was on his feet.

"She's bleeding a little," Swift answered, "but I think she's all right."

"But what attacked her?" Uncle Walter wanted to know.

"Some animal, sir. I think it was a wolf."

"How could this happen?" George demanded, and Leslie, for the first time, realized how strong were men's feelings for their horses. Had Brindle been a human being, George could not have shown more concern.

"The door was ajar. The ice. We haven't been able to close it."

"Never mind the door. What happened?"

"I heard Brindle neighing," Swift explained hurriedly. "I ran to see the trouble. As I got there, something ran out of the stable. I could not see it sharp, but it was like a dog or a wolf, and it ran across the fields, limping. I think Brindle injured it. And I found Brindle bleeding. She's been attacked in her stall, sir," Swift went on to Walter, "and I thought you should know."

At the words "dog or wolf," George and Queenie looked at each other, and Uncle Walter looked at them both. Walter said, "We've never had wolves," but George was the one who took command. "Show me Brindle," he said, starting for the kitchen. "I want to see Brindle."

CHAPTER TWENTY-SIX

"A wolf?" Leslie said in dismay as George disappeared. "Oh, poor Brindle." There were three horses in the stable—Brindle, the spritely mare; Amos, the dray; and Dandy, the riding horse— all of whom had become, for Leslie, distinct characters and creatures she had come to care about. Of them all, however, Brindle was her favorite and she hastened to the front hall closet for her things. She felt the same urge to go to her that George did.

Uncle Walter and Queenie were similarly moved and the three of them put on winter clothes. George had run out wearing nothing but his jacket, but the rest of the family was more alert to the weather.

"A wolf," Leslie said again, still disbelieving. "Are there wolves around here?"

"I never heard of any," Uncle Walter answered, uncertainly.

"But for a loner to come to the stable—to come where people are—I thought they hunted in packs." Leslie, though untutored in the ways of the West, had a level, analytical head and had done much reading. The lore she had accumulated made her view the attack on Brindle as most odd.

"There aren't any wolves around here," Queenie answered with finality. "Swift must be seeing things." Her manner was definite, but Leslie saw uncertainty in her eyes.

"It must be a mistake," Uncle Walter said, pulling his overcoat and muffler from the closet. "Don't get upset now, Leslie. There aren't any wolves about. You don't have to think we live out in the wilderness. Long as we've lived here I haven't heard tell of a single wolf being sighted. They're as scarce as Indians, let me tell you."

"Perhaps, then, it was a dog," Leslie answered, pulling on mittens. "Swift said dog or wolf. It must have been a dog."

"There aren't any stray dogs around either," Uncle Walter said, but he sounded uneasy.

"Whatever it is," Queenie announced without equivocation, "we're going to shoot it. We aren't going to let anything happen to our horses, right, Walter?"

"Absolutely right, Queenie. We'll mount a guard."

When the trio was bundled to brave the bitter cold, they went out the back door, past concerned servants, and down from the small back porch. The barn was but a short distance and they stepped carefully over the ice and snow to the small gap that had been standing between the sliding doors.

Brindle was lying in her stall near a small rear door, beneath the overhang of the haymow. A ladder to the loft stood beside her open gate and George was with her, stroking her, examining a bleeding right shoulder. His wool and velvet jacket was draped over a lantern hanging by a small rear door, and he was in shirtsleeves in near-zero weather. Swift, in warmer garb, was with him, wringing out towels from a steaming water bucket, applying them as compresses to the horse's wound.

"It's a gash in her shoulder," George said when Leslie, Queenie and Uncle Walter appeared. "You women had better stay back. She's bleeding a bit."

Leslie ignored the warning and moved into the stall to assess the extent of the injury. George said, "Leslie, you mustn't. She's bleeding."

"I know she is. I want to see how bad."

"You'll faint."

"Don't you believe it."

Queenie said to Swift, "What kind of animal was it? Tell me what you saw."

Swift, giving over the compress to Leslie, turned uncertainly. "Well, ma'am, I don't rightly know. I'd call it a wolf, except we don't have wolves around here. More likely it was a dog, except we don't have stray dogs either."

"You said Brindle kicked it?"

"I don't know, ma'am. It scooted out the barn door the moment I come from the kitchen and it ran with a limp. And it went like the wind, but one leg wasn't right. That's why I guessed Brindle kicked it."

"Attacking our horses in their stables," Uncle Walter said. "We're not going to have that. We'd better mount a watch."

"I'll stand guard," George volunteered. "This isn't going to happen again, that I'll tell you."

"What are the teeth marks like?" Uncle Walter said.

Leslie, stemming the slow flow of blood, said, "There aren't any teeth marks, Uncle Walter. This is more like a tear."

George said, "I don't care what it is, it needs proper treatment." He nudged Swift. "You—saddle Dandy. I want to get the doctor. Where's Steve? I need warm clothes."

Leslie, noting George's apparel, realized he must be close to frozen. He had been so concerned about the mare that he was only now becoming aware of his own condition.

"I'll get him," Leslie said, handing him the towel. Even as she ran for the house, however, she realized she didn't even know where Stephen was. He had not been on hand at her party. He was the servant she almost never saw.

She paused as she entered the kitchen, wondering where to look for him. The servants' quarters was the obvious place and she went through the pantry into a narrow, L-shaped passageway that gave access to the half-dozen rooms that the quarters contained.

She turned the corner as Stephen emerged from the right-hand door at the end. He looked at her with surprise. "What on earth?"

"George wants warm clothes," she told him. "He has to ride for the horse doctor. Brindle's been hurt."

"Oh? Of course." He passed her, moving quickly.

"You didn't know?" Leslie asked, following.

"My room's away from the stables. I couldn't hear a thing. What happened?"

He didn't wait for an answer and Leslie, following, heard him bounding up the stairs when she reached the kitchen. She did not pursue him, but hurried to the front hall closet to get out George's coat and cap, gloves and boots. George burst through the back door as she returned. There was a rejoining clatter of heels on the stairs and Stephen was back with sweaters and woolen trousers.

George, his thin silk shirt unbuttoned to expose his strong hairy chest, was nearly blue, but recklessly unconcerned as he let Stephen help him into warmer wear.

"What happened, sir?" Stephen asked, dexterously assisting his master. "How did Brindle get hurt?"

"Gashed her shoulder somehow," George said angrily. "I don't know what's the matter with Swift, letting something like this happen."

"Accidental?"

"Swift's clumsiness, more likely."

Leslie said, "What about the animal he saw?"

"*Says* he saw," George corrected. "There aren't any wolves around here. Probably he's trying to cover up his own carelessness."

With Stephen's help, George was buttoned and buckled, ready to ride for assistance. Brindle's cut was a flesh wound but deep, and one ignored such injuries to horses at one's peril. One took care of one's horses—better care, often, than of one's people.

He was off, leaving Stephen and Leslie alone in the kitchen. Through the windows, George could be seen striding toward the stable, meeting the horse that Swift brought out, while Queenie, Uncle Walter and the other servants gathered around.

Stephen did not seem interested. He glanced at the scene, did not look at Leslie, and said, "If you'll excuse me, miss," and started toward the servants' quarters again.

"Steph—" Leslie changed it. "Mr. Crawford?"

He stopped, his back toward her. "Yes, Miss Marsh?"

"What is the matter?"

"Matter?" He turned and smiled. "What makes you think anything's the matter?"

"You've been avoiding me."

"Avoiding you?" He smiled again. "I've only been busy learning my job as Mr. Barrett's valet."

"It's more than that, Mr. Crawford. I've done something. I don't know what, but I've offended you—"

He answered quickly. "No, Miss Marsh. Not for a moment. How could you offend anyone?"

"I've done something. You're so distant. It's bold of me to speak like this, I know—very unladylike—but I'm disturbed, Mr. Crawford—"

"Please," he said. "You should call me Stephen."

"Why?"

"Ladies of the house do not call servants 'Mister.'"

"I'm not a lady of the house. I'm a seamstress."

"Oh come now, you are equivalent to the lady of the house. You are niece to the head of the household and betrothed to the scion—"

"Betrothed? To George?"

"In essence, if not in fact."

Leslie flushed. "But that's not true." She almost added that she had turned him down, but that would not have been fair. "There is nothing between us," she concluded.

Stephen laughed mockingly. "Nothing? When every moment he can manage is spent in your presence? When every other moment is spent in extolling your virtues? Miss Marsh, I am many things, but I am not a fool."

"Extols my—how can you say a thing like that?"

Stephen shook his head. "I have to listen to him, Miss Marsh, and while I do not fault what it is he says of you, I do fault that he says it endlessly."

"About *me?*" Leslie had no idea of this.

"He can't think of anyone but you. Do you pretend you do not know?"

"I don't pretend anything," Leslie said in reply. "George was not intended as a subject of this conversation."

"Which subject was?"

"Why do you avoid me? If I am the attraction you claim I am to George, why am I such a leper to you?"

Now it was Stephen's turn to flush. "You, a leper?"

"You have shunned me. Do you not think I am aware that all the household has seen fit to celebrate my twenty-first birthday, but you have chosen to remain in your room?"

Stephen said, soberly, "Aren't you needlessly upset? One servant, more or less, could hardly matter."

"Stop saying that. You are not a servant. You are no more a servant than I am—or if you are, then we both are. You were friendly enough when you lived with the Cranstons. Now you live here and you have turned to ice."

Stephen looked at her somberly. "Do you not understand that that is what makes the difference?"

"I don't have any idea what you're talking about."

Stephen moved closer to her. "You wonder why I stay away," he said, and put his hands upon her shoulders, staring deeply into her eyes. "We are on separate tracks, you and I, on different trains. We verge near and then we part. You belong to George, whether you know it or not, and I belong to forces quite apart."

131

"But what difference—"

Stephen pulled her suddenly to him. For a moment Leslie was looking up into his dark, terrible eyes. She could hardly breathe in his grasp and she trembled at the feel of him. Then his lips closed on hers and his kiss was as if to drain her of her being. She thought to struggle but she was too overcome. Then wild longings filled her and she thought to clutch him tight, to kiss him back with equal passion, to belong to him, but her senses were reeling and she had no strength.

Then he released her and stepped back, as shaken by her as she was by him. "Now," he whispered hoarsely, "you see why I stay away from you. And why you should stay away from me."

CHAPTER TWENTY-SEVEN

He was gone and Leslie was left alone in the kitchen, trembling and undone. Then she fled to the living room and the giant mirror over the fireplace. Standing on tiptoe before it, she regarded her face. It was flushed, as she knew it would be, but she looked for other marks. Did kisses like that show? She could still feel his lips upon her and thought the world need no more than witness her visage to know what she had been up to.

But except for the fading crimson on her cheeks, there were no telltale signs. She did not have to hide from the others. They could not read her actions from her features, though they might read them from her manner. She would have to compose herself before she appeared publicly again.

From the kitchen she heard sounds of the others returning, eager to get in from the cold. It was too soon. Leslie needed

132

more time to get her quickened heart back to normal. "How is Brindle?" she asked, hurrying back to the kitchen.

"Fussing," Uncle Walter said. "George is fetching the doctor."

"I'll go stay with her."

"Swift is there."

"I know, but I'll go still. I think she'd like a woman's touch." She passed the entering servants, lowering her head as she did, and slipped out again into the cold.

Swift was in the stall, having trouble with Brindle. The mare was struggling to get to her feet, and Swift, holding her halter firmly, was pinning her down on the straw. Though he was talking to her gently, she showed signs of alarm.

"Brindle, Brindle," Leslie cried, entering the gate and kneeling beside the horse, "everything is all right. The doctor is coming. Lie still and behave."

Brindle lifted her head enough to espy the newcomer, and some of the alarm went out of her eye. Leslie stroked her and continued her soothing talk and Brindle's agitation subsided.

"You're good for her, miss," Swift acknowledged. "You have a way with you, that's for certain."

A wet towel had been laid over the wound in Brindle's shoulder and a pail of warm water stood nearby. Leslie felt the towel and said, "This towel is turning to ice. No wonder she's upset."

"Better not touch it, miss," Swift said as she started to remove it. "Better leave it for the doctor."

"Nonsense," Leslie said. "What she needs is a dry towel." She pulled Brindle's covering blanket up close to the wound. "Would you get me one?"

"Who'll hold her halter and keep her head down?"

"She's content now. The wound was cold before. There's no need now to hold her down. Please get me a towel."

Swift obeyed slowly, releasing the halter and finding that Leslie was right. While he went for the towel, Leslie gently bathed and tended the wound. When he returned, she said, "Did you actually see the horse attacked?"

"No, ma'am, I just heard."

133

Leslie took the towel from him. "Heard what?"

"I heard some yaps, like a dog or a wolf, and then there was Brindle neighing and rattling the sides of the stall. I come out running and the critter made tail for it."

"Limping?"

"It was limping all right. Brindle must've caught her with a hoof."

Leslie applied the dry, warm towel, and spoke softly to the quiet horse. She looked up. "The barn door was open?"

"Like now," Swift answered, nodding in its direction. "Ain't been able to close it tight since the snow got rutty and froze. But I'll chop it free and keep it shut now that we got visitors, don't worry none about that, miss. Ain't had anything like that before. 'Course I haven't been here long, but I ain't never heard of wolves in this area."

"It was a dog, then?"

Swift shook his head. "I ain't heard of a dog either. I mean, what would a dog be entering a stable and attacking a horse for? Where would it come from?"

Leslie said she could not imagine.

Leslie and Swift both stayed with Brindle for the hour and a half it took for George to return with the horse doctor, a man named Meddin, who came in a carriage. The wait was good for Brindle and it was good for Leslie. By the time she could turn Brindle over to more professional, if not more caring, hands, she had fully recovered from Stephen Crawford and their encounter in the kitchen.

The doctor did not stay long. He examined the wound while George, Leslie and Swift looked on, pronounced it not serious and was pleased that it had bled profusely. Tear wounds that bled bore a markedly lower fatality rate than puncture wounds that bled little, or bled inwardly, he said. He wanted the wound kept covered and showed the threesome how to change the dressing. He said, "What did she come in contact with anyway, a nail?"

"Swift says she was attacked," George told him. "Some animal got into the barn and went for her."

"Ridiculous," the doctor said. "The wound is a cut, not a bite."

"Argue with Swift," George answered. "He says he saw the critter running away."

Dr. Meddin put his things away and stood up. "Well, if that's your story, that's your story. But that wound wasn't caused by teeth. I can tell you that."

George saw the doctor back to his carriage and Swift returned to the house. Leslie knelt beside the horse for a parting word. "Just what did you do, Brindle?" she asked, stroking the long, warm muzzle. "Did you hit a nail somewhere?"

She rose and looked around. If Brindle had reared while giving forth the neighs that had brought Swift to the scene, how high would her shoulder ride against the siding of her stall? And could there be, anywhere along its length, a carelessly driven nail that protruded and could scratch?

Leslie hunted carefully along the only side the mare's shoulder could have hit. It was ridiculously simple. There, near the front of the stall, in the most obvious place, a half inch of large rusty nail did protrude. Leslie rubbed her finger over it and found it still wet with drying blood.

Brindle had ripped her shoulder open on a nail when rearing in excitement. She hadn't been bitten. And since she was at the front of the stall rather than the back, she might not even have been attacked.

There might not have been a strange wolf or stray dog in the barn at all.

George put his head through the door of the barn. Brindle was comfortable? Fine, then let's get back to the party.

Leslie nodded and followed him, frowning.

CHAPTER TWENTY-EIGHT

After the interlude of Brindle's injury, the party was resumed, the cake was cut and the presents opened. The gifts from the staff were small things, inexpensive and simple—soap, needles, handkerchiefs.

The family gifts were, on the other hand, quite overwhelming. Queenie gave her some beautiful material from which she was to make a gown. George gave her perfume. It was a fine perfume, far beyond anything she had known before, but it was such a personal gift it made her feel uneasy. Stephen had said she belonged to George. Was this a sign that she did? She thanked George graciously but not without a qualm. Lastly, from her uncle, Leslie unwrapped a beautiful fur coat that was warm, thick and delightfully soft to the touch.

"It's the most beautiful coat in the world," Leslie breathed, quite overcome. Now she would no longer have to wear Queenie's things or the old spare coats in the front hall closet. She had a luxurious one of her own.

"Put it on," Uncle Walter said.

She did, drawing it close, turning up the collar to feel its softness against her face. "I feel like a queen," she smiled. "Oh, Uncle Walter, I can't thank you enough." And then, because the gift made her feel, for the first time, as if she really did have a family and that her uncle did care, she ran around from her place to give him a big kiss.

It was the most wonderful birthday Leslie had had, she reflected, up in her room as she put her gifts away. The only flaws were the perfume from George and the absence of Stephen.

Because the Sunday dinner had been so late and so rich, the evening meal was a light supper that wasn't served until after nine and did not end until ten. By then it was nearly bedtime and George arose from the table deciding to take a final look at Brindle. Leslie, bundling herself up in her new fur coat, went with him.

The light from the lantern post guided them and George

brought another lantern to take into the darkness of the barn. Swift had chopped away the ice from the entrance and, for the first time, the barn doors were closed and latched.

Inside, by the glow of the lantern, they discovered Brindle up and snorting in her stall. Except for a barely noticeable favoring of her right-front hoof, she behaved as if nothing had happened.

"You know," Leslie said as they stroked Brindle's nose together, "her wound wasn't from a bite. It was from a nail." She pointed. "Right there, beside you."

George turned, scowling, felt the protruding point and scraped it with his fingernail, gaining tiny flakes of dried blood. "So that was it," he said angrily. "By the lord, what was Swift doing, making up a cock-and-bull story about an animal attacking the horses, getting us all upset like that!"

"He insists he saw one."

"He's making it up, most likely. It's his fault the nail is there. He should have seen to such a thing. He's trying to blame wolves and wild dogs, and there aren't any such things!"

"He sounds sincere."

"He's a liar, blaming animals for his own clumsy—" He stroked Brindle, who flinched at his anger. "I've a good mind to fire him on the spot."

"No, please." Leslie hadn't meant to get the groom in trouble. "George, you can't be sure."

"Brindle bumped against the side of the stall and scratched herself. It's obvious."

"No, George, it isn't." She pointed. "Look how high the nail is. She had to rear to catch her shoulder. She had to go up on her hind legs, and she wouldn't do that without a reason. Maybe an animal *was* here. Why would Swift make it up?"

"There are no strange animals around here," George answered. "Come back inside and get such ideas out of your head. Swift is lying. We don't have any wolves or wild dogs anywhere around."

George led the way back to the house brusquely, and Leslie, following, thought he glanced up in the darkness at the open window to the locked room overhead.

137

Leslie glanced up too and meant to ask about it when they got inside. However, Lambert was waiting for her in the kitchen. "Miss Marsh," he said, "your uncle would like to see you in the living room."

She found him at a small rolltop desk that stood beside the dining-room entrance, busily studying and making entries on papers. "Oh," he said, looking up in surprise. "You startled me. How is Brindle?" He gathered his papers quickly, put them together back in the desk and pulled down the top.

Leslie told him that Brindle was recovering nicely. "You wanted to see me, sir?"

"Yes, yes." Uncle Walter stood up, took a key ring on a long gold chain from his pocket, fitted a tiny key into the desktop and locked it. He did not speak again until he had returned the key ring to his pocket. When he did, his face was serious. "I wonder," he said, "if I might have a word with you—after you take off your things?"

Leslie, puzzled by his tone and sober mien, started to undo buttons. "Of course. I'll be right back."

"I think," he said, gesturing toward the hall entrance, "it would be best if we talked in the library."

CHAPTER TWENTY-NINE

Uncle Walter drew the sliding doors together behind them in the kind of important manner that reminded her of the weekend before, when George proposed. Leslie fancied there was something ominous in the action, that the room itself was ominous. It was a forgotten room that no one ever seemed to use except, as the slow sliding together of the doors suggested, for the discussion of serious and unpleasant subjects. Her birthday had been happy up till now, but she had the feeling that the bloom was about to leave the rose, and that when she went to bed it would not be to look back with glowing pleasure upon a happy day, but in distress and unease.

"Come, sit," Uncle Walter said, gesturing her to the couch near the fireplace. Uncle Walter did not, however, choose to sit himself. Instead, he went to a small cabinet in one of the walls and produced a glass and a bottle of port, filling the one from the other. Then he clipped the end from a cigar and lighted it from one of the lamps. His actions were deliberate, all of them giving Leslie time to build an ever-heightening sense of unease. What had she done?

He turned, puffed his cigar, took a sip of port, and approached the fire. "I understand that my stepson, George, is in love with you," he said.

Leslie almost jumped from her seat. "Oh, no, Uncle Walter," she protested. "You have it quite wrong. There is nothing between us." She was thinking of the perfume.

"On the contrary," Uncle Walter said, "I think *you* have it wrong. My stepson *is* in love with you. You just don't believe it."

"I—" Leslie said, quite flustered, trying to pull herself together. She stared at Uncle Walter. "Does *he* believe it?"

"Does *he* believe—"

"Have you talked to him?" Leslie leaned forward desperately. All she was trying to do was be a seamstress and dressmaker, and everyone was complicating her life. Ever since she had come here she had been pressured and driven. It was not part of the bargain. And what was her Uncle Walter going to do now, drive her some more? Or was he, as her uncle, as a loving older brother to her poor mother, going to be the oasis in the desert, the one person she could turn to in times of stress? Could she divulge to him her secret heart? Was he, a rough-and-ready man whose life had been spent making and losing fortunes, capable of understanding the quaverings and uncertainties of a young girl's mind? Queenie was no port in a storm. George was no succor—he was the storm. What was Uncle Walter?

139

Uncle Walter said stiffly, "Have I talked to George? No, I have not. But I have talked to my wife."

"But she does not know. Only George would know."

And then Uncle Walter turned to her and said, "What about yourself, my child? Perhaps this is the trouble. My wife listens to George, I listen to my wife, and nobody listens to you." He sat down beside her on the couch, blew his cigar smoke in another direction, and turned. "What are you thinking? Are you happy here?"

Leslie, never expecting the forbidding walls surrounding her to melt so quickly, found herself ill-prepared. Her first reaction was defensive. Of course she was happy. Why shouldn't she be? Had he not invited her here? It ill-behooved her to complain.

Yet, if truth be told, she was far from happy. Life in Fletcher, though vastly more luxurious than her life before, had become vastly more complex. Before, her problem had been solely the one of survival, and though it was a vital problem, it was one she could solve through her own striving. The problems she faced now were not so crucial, but they were not so easily solved. Moreover, the answers could not be produced through her own efforts. Others were involved and she was finding herself more and more at their mercy.

"Am I happy?" Leslie said at last. "I suppose I am."

"But things disturb you?"

"Lots of things."

"What, for instance?"

He really cares, she thought. Despite what Queenie had said, that it was she and not Uncle Walter who had arranged for Leslie's coming, he did love his younger sister's daughter. The blood relationship did hold. She would not have to wander through life a homeless waif, unattended, uncared for, scrounging like some alley cat for the food and shelter to keep body and soul alive. She did have "family," after all.

And what, her uncle had asked, disturbed her?

Leslie thought, and she wondered what she could tell him. She couldn't say, "George." She couldn't say, "Queenie." It would not do to bite the hand that fed.

"I feel so strange here," Leslie answered haltingly. "I find it so hard to adjust to your ways. We speak the same language, but it's like living in a different country."

"Don't you mean," Uncle Walter said sympathetically, "that the change isn't moving from East to West, but that you've moved from city to country. I daresay the kind of country you find yourself living in right now can be found in every tiny hamlet in the East. I would also wager that our Chicago can meet your New York on close to even terms and will outdo every other metropolis in the East. There is nothing there that we don't have here, but you have to open your eyes wide and look around with that kind of wisdom to see it."

"Yes, I suppose you're right," Leslie admitted dolefully. He was trying to be helpful, but that wasn't where her trouble lay.

Then he said to her, "Is there a boy back home, my dear? Did we pull you away from a love you held dear? Is that why you wish you had never come?"

"Oh, no," Leslie was quick to protest, and thought she detected a note of relief in her uncle's manner. It encouraged her, for it meant that, though he was glad to have her come West, he hadn't wanted it to be against her will. "There's no boy back home, sir. There's no boy anywhere."

"Not anywhere?" Uncle Walter ventured surprise. "What about George?"

"Oh," Leslie said, recovering and flushing. "I wasn't counting George as a swain."

"Why not, pray tell?"

"I—I—" Leslie stammered to a halt and tried to think, Why not? Then she got hold of herself and her mind cleared. "Because I don't know him," she said.

"Don't know him?" Uncle Walter expressed mild surprise. "You've been living under the same roof with him for three weeks. I believe he has been dancing attendance upon you almost constantly. I'm afraid I don't understand you Easterners. How do you people ever manage to communicate your attentions to one another? How do you manage to get married?"

"Sir," Leslie pleaded in reply, "you must understand that there is a difference between communicating attentions and accepting them. Because one does not accept the communication doesn't mean that he—or, in this case, she—hasn't received it."

"Then, you know that George is in love with you?"

"He's professed this."

"And you ignore him?"

Leslie said anxiously, "I don't ignore him. I have the greatest respect for him. But I do not think I am yet ready for marriage, and I know that he can find many other women who are."

"What does that matter to him if he only wants you?"

She protested against that. "But how can he only want me? He hardly knows me, and there are dozens, hundreds, I am sure, thousands—"

"Love doesn't go by numbers, my dear, and it doesn't go by the clock. Have you ever heard of 'love at first sight'? It happens. And it happened to George."

Leslie was about to protest again, but Uncle Walter raised a hand. "Hear me, my dear. George has had to work and slave since he was old enough to hold a job, helping support his mother. Queenie, my wife, is very charming and I love her dearly, but I think you will agree that she does not have those talents that will keep a single woman alive. She was widowed early, nevertheless, and by a husband who left her in only modest circumstances. If it hadn't been for George, I don't think she would have got through those intervening years until she met me."

Uncle Walter smiled and lifted a hand once more. "Understand me, my dear, I am not suggesting that marrying me is what saved her. She and George would have managed very well even if I had never appeared.

"What I am saying is that, after I married Queenie, for the first time since her widowhood, they had enough money. The two of them could stop worrying about the future." Uncle Walter sipped his port and puffed his cigar. "Now I want to tell you something about that," he said confidentially. "It went to George's head a little. Not a lot, but a little. It's like, you got your hand close over the wood stove and the heat of the old iron is searing you something fierce. But you've got to keep your hand close because the pot roast's fallen into the fire and you've got to get it out or nobody's gonna eat. And then you finally get a long fork into the thing and fish it out through the grate and back into the pan where it's supposed to be. You understand? So then you kind of dance around the kitchen shaking your throbbing hand and shouting 'Whoopee,' because the agony is all over."

Uncle Walter leaned closer to Leslie. "I'm not saying that's good, mind you. What I am saying is that it's understandable in a man. George is out from under after all these years and he's floating on air. Ever since I married your aunt, George has been free to relax and get himself put back together again.

"Now he's just about done that, and you know what the real sign of that is?" Uncle Walter smiled. "It's you, Leslie. It's his falling in love with you."

"Me?"

Uncle Walter moved closer. "Look at it this way. You are a nice-looking girl." He eyed her appraisingly. "In fact, compared to the bag of bones you were when you arrived here, I wouldn't believe a young girl could fill out in such a lovely manner in so short a time. In fact, it's not only George you have to worry about. You're going to have trouble with men everywhere you go. So you'd better get used to it, my pet. It's going to be your way of life. Do you understand me?"

Leslie shook her head.

"What I'm saying, Leslie, is that men are going to chase you, they are going to want to marry you. George is not the only one. He is only the first. And if you should not marry him, then others will pester you."

"Oh, I shouldn't want that," Leslie cried.

"You will have it," Uncle Walter assured her, "unless, of course, you are already married."

"You mean, unless I marry George?"

"Surely you want to get married, my child. Isn't that true?"

Leslie nodded. "I suppose so—sometime. I really haven't thought about it yet."

"Well, you should, my child."

"But I'm so young. I'm just twenty-one."

"That's not young. Queenie was seventeen when she married George's father."

Leslie said, "I don't know how she could manage it. I feel so—unready."

"Is that why you turned George down, my dear, because you didn't feel ready?"

"I don't know. I truly don't. It's that I don't feel I love him."

"I'm sure, on the contrary, that you *do* love him, but you don't yet know what love is." Uncle Walter leaned close and patted her knee. "I would hate to see you lose the best man who'll ever come your way because you didn't understand what it was you wanted."

"You think George—?"

"George is handsome, he is wealthy, he is able and capable. Really, my dear, I have known many men in my life, and I have never known another I would be so proud to have my nephew-in-law."

Leslie was impressed. She knew so little about men she had to rely on the wisdom of others, and she knew that no one would be a better judge of men than her uncle.

Then she was assailed by the recollection of George trying to ply her with drinks in the saloon, of George lying dead drunk on the stairs. Maybe that was the way all men were. Maybe what appeared to be coarseness was really maleness. Perhaps it was foolish to expect sensitivity in men. Perhaps only women were sensitive.

Then the other picture of George came to her mind—the tender George kneeling coatless beside Brindle, the concerned George riding off for the doctor. "He is kind," Leslie admitted.

"Very kind. Very considerate."

"I noticed how he ran to Brindle as soon as he heard she was hurt."

"My dear, you will never meet a finer man. Rest assured of that."

Leslie nodded. She didn't know many men, but if Uncle

144

Walter believed that, she could believe it too. "I suppose you're right."

"Capable in business too, Leslie. Soon to be my partner."

"Your partner? So young?"

Uncle Walter nodded. "Marry him, Leslie. I want the best for you. Don't let him get away."

She was tempted. It had probably been foolish fears that had deterred her before. George had been a changed man since her rejection of him. He had lost the arrogance, the self-assured quality that had repelled her. Perhaps, as Uncle Walter said, it was reaction from those years of poverty. Now he was settling down to become sincere and steady. "I know I should," she whispered softly.

He brightened. "You will?"

She might have said yes. She might have shed her last reservations had there not been, lingering in the back of her mind, the memory of Stephen's kiss. Even now the thought of it and what it had done to her left her flustered and uncertain. "I don't know," she answered Uncle Walter a little desperately. "I need time to make up my mind."

"I would not wait long, my dear. George, feeling rejected, may look elsewhere. Needless indecision could be your undoing."

Leslie hesitated. Should she tell Uncle Walter about Stephen's kiss? Would he understand how one kiss could so unsettle a girl's heart? Or would he fire Stephen on the spot for his brazenness?

At that moment, from out in the cold-black distance of the night, there came a prolonged and baleful howl that could only have been from the throat of a dog or a wolf.

It came again with an eeriness that chilled Leslie's spine. What was even more horrifying was the effect it had on her Uncle Walter. At the first sound of it his face turned ashen and his hands began to shake.

"My God," he said, leaping to his feet with terror in his eyes, and before Leslie could move, he stumbled past her, out of the room.

145

For a long moment Leslie stared at the sliding doors her fleeing uncle had flung shut behind him. What had driven him to run like that? Surely he had heard mournful cries in the night before.

The cry came again and it made her shiver. There was something almost more human than animal to it. And it was closer. She was sure it was closer. She counted the seconds and it came again, closer still, and she began to tremble. It was affecting her almost as it had her uncle.

Outside in the hall, there were hurrying footsteps. People were running, and there were voices.

The cry came again, ever nearer, and Leslie could not stay alone any longer. She hurried to throw open the doors and join the others in the foyer.

Queenie was there, and Walter, and George was coming down the stairs. "What do you think?" Uncle Walter said as George swung around the newel post, passed Leslie, and started grabbing winter gear from the coat closet. He got into his jacket and boots hastily, with Uncle Walter and Queenie trying to assist. Through it all, Leslie watched, unseen and ignored.

When George was buttoned up, he plunged back into the closet and came out with a shotgun that had stood hidden in a back corner. He leaned it against the stairs while he pulled down a box of shells from the shelf.

"What are you going to do?" Leslie asked, moving forward at last.

The long, piercing howl came again as she spoke, and it was very close this time. It sounded out near the barn.

"Don't you hear it?" George answered irritably, selecting two shells to insert in the chambers of the shotgun, stuffing more into his pockets. "I'm going to kill the damned monster. What do you think I'm going to do?"

"But why?"

"Why? Why do you think? You think we want creatures like that coming around our house?"

"Think of the horses," Uncle Walter said.

"But what is it?" Leslie asked. "Why is it out there?"

"Who knows what it is or why it's there," George said, turning on his heel. "It's not going to be there long."

He made off for the kitchen, Queenie and Uncle Walter pressing close behind, with Leslie trailing after. It seemed to her that everybody was overreacting greatly. Why should the sound of a howling animal upset them so? The barn doors were closed. What could the creature do?

"How about a lantern?" Uncle Walter asked when George reached the back door.

"I'll never get close to him with a lantern." He pulled open the door, letting in a blast of cold air from the little porch.

"Good luck," Queenie said, and George gave a determined nod as he went out into the night.

Leslie, looking through the window, could see him move toward the barn in the dim light from the lantern post. The cry came again from out of the blackness and George raised the barrels of the shotgun to horizontal, holding the gun at his waist, aimed at the night and ready.

"How the hell could this happen?" Uncle Walter muttered as George was lost to darkness somewhere beyond the barn.

"How would I know?" Queenie snapped. "So don't talk about it."

"What kind of animal is it?" Leslie asked as they moved away from the windows.

"What do you ask *me* for?" Queenie answered irritably. "Do you think I can see in the dark?"

"I mean, What harm can it do? Why is everybody so frightened?"

Queenie looked at her sharply. "What do you mean frightened?" she said harshly. "We're not frightened. We're just careful, that's all."

Lambert appeared from the servants' quarters, with Bessie behind him. "I never heard such an awful howling in my life," Bessie said. "What would it be, Mrs. Barrett?"

"The servants are frightened," Lambert said. "They're wondering if it's wolves."

"We don't have wolves around here," Queenie told him.

"Is it the creature Swift saw?"

"For heaven's sake, Lambert, how would I know what Swift saw? Just tell everybody not to worry. Mister George has gone out after it. Let that critter howl just one more time, and George'll get him."

Lambert and Bessie retreated and the family waited in uneasy silence. Leslie did not ask more questions. Queenie knew—all of them knew—more than they were saying, and more than they intended to say. But the servants knew nothing. Whatever had taken place with animals in the past was before the whole household staff had been replaced.

The minutes went by and Leslie watched her uncle and Queenie. They were waiting tensely for the sound of George's shotgun. They were hoping to hear it. They were wishing to hear it. But there was nothing but silence. The howling had ceased, and all that could be seen from the windows was the yard area that glowed soft yellow in the light of the post lantern.

"Could the animal attack George?" Leslie asked when she could hold her peace no longer.

"Not likely," Uncle Walter said.

"But if you don't know what it is—"

"George has a gun," Queenie said in a way that ended the subject.

Silence resumed, but as more minutes passed, Queenie's assurance began to dissipate and more and more her eyes clouded and her brow furrowed. Finally she stirred from her musings and wrenched open the tight back door. She stepped out onto the porch and cupped her hands. "George," she called into the night. "George, you hear me?"

Leslie, moving close to the door to catch an answering cry, discovered Uncle Walter beside her. He, too, was wondering.

They listened while Queenie called out again, but there was only silence. Queenie retreated from the bitter cold, back to the fast-cooling kitchen. "Where has the fool gone?" she said, slamming the door behind her. She sounded more angry than frightened.

"Maybe he's getting close," Uncle Walter volunteered, "and didn't want to betray his position."

"All he had to do was go out and shoot it. Ready, aim, fire. That doesn't take an awful lot of brains."

Then Leslie, peering through the window, saw a shadow move. "Here he is," she said as George's dark figure emerged into the light, the gun muzzle pointed down, his legs striding firmly.

He came in in a temper and banged the door. "Not a damned thing," he growled and uttered a curse. "Not even a smell of the damned thing."

Uncle Walter said, "He saw you coming and fled."

"He'll be back. He'll haunt us till we kill him."

"We'll set traps," Queenie said.

"Poisoned meat," Uncle Walter said.

"Is Brindle all right?" Leslie asked.

"He's not been near the stables," George said. "But he'll try again." He stalked off to put away his clothes and the gun.

CHAPTER THIRTY-ONE

It was long after the rest of the family had retired that Leslie at last turned out her own light and climbed beneath the covers. The strange events of her birthday had left her so puzzled and wide-awake that sleep was out of the question, and she had written a long letter to Mrs. Wiggins to calm herself and let weariness overtake her.

Now she drew the covers to her chin and tried to make sense out of the day's events. It was the animal that puzzled her most, but the night would not solve the problem. In the morning, however, its tracks should be easy to find, and that should identify the creature and end the mystery.

She closed her eyes and waited for sleep, but though it was past midnight, her day was not yet to end. From out of the darkness, through the icy, still night air, a new howl keened from the unutterable creature that so upset the family.

Leslie felt a chill go through her, for some of the family's fright had rubbed off onto her. The creature was back.

It howled again, out by the barn.

Leslie clutched the covers around her ears. Where had it come from? What did it want?

She wondered if George had risen to take up his shotgun again. She listened, but there was not a sound in the house. There was only that eerie, ghostly, mournful wail.

For minutes she listened to the periodic cry and could almost believe the animal was calling someone or something. Was it another animal? Was the creature baying at the house? or was it trying to raise an answering cry? How many such animals were around?

At last Leslie sat up in bed. Would no one else stir himself to do anything? Some creature was out in the yard, and it sounded so close that she was sure it must be visible in the light from the post lantern. If she went down to the kitchen and peered through the window, perhaps she could see what it was.

Leslie arose, slipped into a robe and slippers and opened the door. Except for the wails of the beast, all was silent. Leslie went into the chill of the hallway with its whitish, ghostly light and made her way to the kitchen stairs by the bath, the faint brush of her slippers on the carpet making the only sound.

At the head of the staircase she looked down the steep, narrow shaft and started in surprise. Though it was deathly quiet below, a dim, flickering light filled the doorway.

Someone had a candle in the kitchen.

Just then there came another howl from the night and it was close indeed. The creature must be at the barn.

Slowly, Leslie groped for the stair railing and felt with her slippered feet for the dark stairs themselves. Carefully she descended, keeping her approach absolutely silent. Whoever had the candle in the kitchen was as still as the night, and Leslie decided if anyone made a point of being that quiet, she should be too.

She reached the bottom and, keeping herself concealed, peeked around the corner of the door. The candle stood in a holder on the table and a man was close beside it with his back to her, getting into a heavy plaid jacket.

Even as she watched, he picked up something wrapped in paper from the table, pulled open the back door, eased himself onto the porch, and drew the door shut behind him.

Who was it and what was he doing, she wondered. More things were going on in this house that she didn't understand, and she was growing increasingly disquieted. The man getting into the jacket wasn't George and it wasn't Uncle Walter. Perhaps it was Swift, going out to drive the animal away and make sure the horses were all right. She couldn't remember what kind of jacket Swift had.

Leslie waited until the man had left the porch, then she ventured forward to look out the window. The man was by the barn now, moving toward the open space beyond the light. There was no sign of the animal and the howling had stopped.

Leslie stayed at the window until the man was lost to sight, then retreated to the stairway again. When the man returned, she did not want him to see her by candlelight through the window. She did not want him to know his actions had been witnessed.

Back in the stairwell she remained, shivering in the chill of a house whose fires had been banked, wondering what she was seeing, and why. She should go back to bed, she thought, but she was curious. She wanted to wait, and watch, and listen.

Leslie did not know how long she stood there in anticipation, but at last the door opened again and the man who had stilled the beast returned. His face was muffled by the heavy collar that had been turned up over his ears and his brow was shielded by the brim of his cap, but his features were unmistakable. It was Stephen Crawford.

He shut the door, taking pains to be quiet, then removed his cap and gloves. He leaned close by the candle to peer through the window as if viewing his handiwork while he unbuttoned the plaid jacket.

Leslie watched him in fascination, leaning forward to better her view. What was he up to? Why had he gone out? Why had the great beast stopped howling?

Stephen, finishing with the unbuttoning, turned abruptly as he shed the coat. Alas, Leslie had no chance to retreat into the shadows. His eye caught her watching figure even as he swung, and he stopped with jacket still undiscarded. "Who's there?"

There was such a glowering note in his voice that, even if Leslie could have fled, she dared not. Instead, she felt a stab of terror that froze her in position. He was likewise frozen, and Leslie, conquering her fear and determining that, since she had been found out, her best course was to be bold, stepped forward into the kitchen and faced him.

"It's you," Stephen said in amazement, and then he smiled. "I should have known it would be."

He could not help eyeing her appreciatively in her dishabille, the tumbled hair around her shoulders, the figure that her robe could not completely conceal. Leslie drew herself tall, feeling that she was the one entitled to question and he to answer. "What are you doing?" she demanded boldly. "Why are you up at this hour?"

Stephen smiled disarmingly as he pulled off his jacket. "Surely now, have you not heard the howling of the hound? Why else do you think I would not be asleep?"

"I mean—what did you go outside for?"

"To quiet the beast—or at least get a look at him."

"What *is* the beast?"

Stephen shook his head. "He did not wait for me to see. A dog, I would guess, by the sound."

"Who has dogs that would come around here?"

"A good question. Who indeed?"

"Are the horses all right?"

"The barn door is closed. Whatever the animal is, it cannot get to them." Stephen looked at her across the candle, and something in his face softened. "Do you know," he said, "that you are very beautiful?"

Leslie flushed and drew back into the doorway. "I think," she whispered, "since the animal is quiet at last, I will go back to my room."

"I think you should. Goodnight, Leslie."

"Goodnight." She turned and went quickly up the stairs, her heart pounding and her pulse racing.

CHAPTER THIRTY-TWO

For the third time Leslie Marsh had a nightmare about the locked room and she woke, wet and cold with perspiration, not sure but that she had shrieked herself out of slumber. She lay for a while, trembling and wide-eyed, too afraid to try again to sleep, left to wonder what about the room should give her such dreams. On each occasion she had been up late and had been involved in an unnatural situation. First it was after she brought a drunken George home from the saloon, having coped with the predicaments he caused. The second time was after she and Stephen had dragged George up the stairs and got him to his bedroom. Now it was after George and Stephen had both gone hunting a howling animal in the night. Why should these things make her dream about the room, she wondered. Why should she have nightmares at all?

Eventually Leslie's tired nerves relaxed and she fell into sleep again, not recalling any further dreams, and she did not awaken until Fanny brought in her kettle of hot water in the morning and started up the fire. The dream still haunted her, however, and she determined to satisfy her curiosity regarding the strange sealed room.

She thought she would raise the question at breakfast, but the morning atmosphere, after the howling of the night before, was grim and forbidding. Talk was about measures to take against the beast, of stakeouts, of poisoned food, of a hunt for the animal. Leslie felt like an outsider, for she could not feel the animosity toward the creature that the family felt. She could not understand the danger they seemed alert to. As long as the horses were safe, what did it matter what the creature was or what it was howling about?

After breakfast, Uncle Walter went to his desk in the living room, sat down before it and, taking the small key from the collection on his gold chain, turned the lock and rolled up the wooden cover. His ledgers and papers were collected neatly. Uncle Walter was a tidy person, and even as he started to lay out his papers for study, he squared them. He looked up as Leslie approached. "Oh," he said, starting to roll down the desktop again, "I'm sorry, my dear. I didn't see you. Did you want to talk to me?"

Leslie had intended to broach the subject of the locked room, but Uncle Walter was getting to work and her request for information seemed a little untimely. Moreover, she had the sudden fear that if she engaged him in conversation, talk would move quickly from the locked room to her feelings about George, and it was too early in the morning to go through a discussion of her future as Mrs. George Trowbridge. She sensed that she would be marrying George in the end, that the pressures would be too great to resist, but she wanted her freedom as long as possible.

"It's nothing," she said quickly. "I was just passing through. I'm going to be fitting Queenie for a new gown this morning. I think you'll like it."

"I'm sure I will, my dear," he answered and, as she left the room, rolled open his desk again.

Leslie climbed the stairs to the sewing room, glad that she had avoided conversation. The fitting with Queenie would produce conversation enough, and Leslie knew what it would be about. Queenie would be pushing George's virtues at her, expounding on the magnificent husband he would make. Leslie could say no to Queenie, however, and she would work the conversation around to her own subject.

Conversation during the fitting was not about George this time, however. Queenie knew when she was pressing too hard, and there was no point in making the young girl stubborn. Instead, the talk was about the fitting, the material, the plans Leslie had. Though Queenie was not ordinarily clothes-conscious, she was learning much about dressing and style and material under Leslie's tutelage and was actually becoming interested.

Leslie, doing the fitting near the window where she had good light, was pinning the back and smoothing the material to make sure it wasn't gathering, when the time seemed appropriate. "You know, Queenie," she said, "I've always wondered what Uncle Walter keeps in that back room of his."

Leslie wasn't sure, but she thought her fingers, playing over the material, detected a tensing of Queenie's muscles along her spine. "What back room?" Queenie asked in so casual a voice that Leslie decided she was mistaken.

"The one at the end of the hall on this side, past the family stairs, over the kitchen."

"Oh, that?" Queenie sniffed and went on offhandedly. "We don't use it, that's why."

"I know, but why is it locked?"

Queenie smiled. "I just told you. Because we don't use it."

"There are two guest rooms on my side of the house that aren't used either, but they aren't locked."

Queenie turned to the mirror and preened herself. "I think you're making a great deal out of nothing, don't you? Yes, this looks very good. Are you through fitting? Are you ready to take it off now?"

"Not quite. Just another minute." She put some pins in her mouth and started slipping them into place along the route of future seams. She said, "It's something secret, is that it? About that particular room, I mean?"

"Secret?"

"There's something in there you don't want me to know about."

155

"Yes," Queenie said firmly, "there is a secret about that room. Most old houses have secrets about them."

"Is it Uncle Walter's secret?"

"Oh, good heavens, child," Queenie said sharply. "Whatever filled your head with such nonsense?"

"It's a locked room and I've been having bad dreams about it, and I'm wondering why."

"Oh, is that it?" Queenie relaxed and shook her head. "Well, I shouldn't wonder that room would give you bad dreams, my child. It gives me bad dreams as well, which is why I keep it tightly locked. I'm superstitious about such things."

Through the window, Leslie saw Steve Crawford, bundled in his heavy plaid jacket, come out of the house and start past the barn. Like the night before, he was carrying something wrapped in paper. "What kind of things?" Leslie said to Queenie.

"Murder." Queenie turned around solemnly. "I'm talking about murder, my girl."

Leslie's eyes grew wide. "Murder? Who?"

"The murder of Rufus Morgate, the man who built this house."

"He was murdered?" Leslie said, slowly starting to help Queenie out of the dress.

"By his wife and a manservant, in that room. That's why the door stays locked. The walls are covered with his blood."

"Good heavens!"

"That's why the house was empty so long. Your Uncle Walter, he saw the room. I would not look. He wanted to have it redone, but I'm superstitious. I wouldn't hear of it. I wouldn't go near that room no matter what was done to it. It's a haunted room, Leslie."

"Yes, I see," Leslie breathed. "The—ah—I notice one of the windows is open."

"To air it, of course. And to let the ghost come and go." Queenie turned and shook her finger. "Now I've told you, and I shouldn't. But don't you ever breathe a word of it to the servants. Whatever you do, don't let them know."

"No, of course not."

"I can't tell you what a problem we had finding servants," Queenie said, slipping out of the dress. "If they knew there was a ghost in that room and blood on the walls, we'd never be able to keep a one. I wouldn't have told you, but you're family, and entitled. You understand?"

"Yes, of course," Leslie said, assisting Queenie. Glancing out the window, she saw that Steve had turned past the barn across the snow-covered fields towards the forest far beyond.

Queenie picked up the dress she'd shed. "It's going to be lovely, dear," she said, stroking the material. Ghosts were the last thing on her mind when she beamed on Leslie. "Wouldn't it be just the thing to wear to a wedding?"

Leslie said yes and that she'd start sewing now and by tomorrow morning should have it ready for the final fitting.

She saw Queenie out and, when she closed the door, was glad for a chance to be alone with her own thoughts. The idea of a murder having happened in the cold, isolated back room chilled her to the depths, especially when Queenie said the room was haunted and she, herself, wasn't sure but that she had heard strange sounds from it.

That, however, was not all that was odd about her Uncle Walter's house and the people who lived in it. New among the oddities was Stephen Crawford. Leslie looked out of the window again, but Stephen's progress across the fields had taken him past the outbuildings and he was no longer in sight.

Leslie was curious, however, and she was content to bide her time. She took her sewing to the window and worked where she could keep an eye out on the snow that gleamed and sparkled under the wan glare of a growing sun.

It was twenty minutes before Steve reappeared. The paper wrapping and its contents were no longer with him. Whatever it was he had carried, he had left somewhere on the wastes or in the woods.

Leslie frowned and redoubled her efforts with her needle.

CHAPTER THIRTY-THREE

For the next two nights the Barrett household was assailed by the nocturnal cries of the strange howling beast. The subject was not mentioned, however. In fact, it seemed to Leslie that it was studiously avoided.

George went out with his gun Tuesday after breakfast and didn't come back until lunch. He said nothing when he left and nothing when he returned, but his face bore lines of grimness.

By Wednesday morning, after another two hours of the awful nightly sounds, Queenie and Uncle Walter were as dourly visaged as George, and all three looked pale and drawn. Leslie, regarding them over the breakfast table, was struck by the effects the cries were having on them.

Queenie was not in any mood for fittings that day and didn't want Leslie around. "Take some time off," she said. "Go into town or something. George, why don't you take Leslie for a ride someplace?"

"I'll walk into town," Leslie said. She was running low on various personal items. "I can do a little shopping."

"I'll take you shopping," George suggested, brightening.

Since what she was after were feminine garments and toilet articles, Leslie was not at all interested in having George accompany her. "Oh, no," she protested. "I just want to get a few things for myself. I'd much prefer to go alone."

"I meant, I'll give you a lift into town and bring you home," George answered. "I have business in town." He laughed and looked at Uncle Walter. "Walter and I do have to work sometimes, you know. The business doesn't just run itself. Right, Walter?"

The older man smiled agreeably as he got up from the table and started for his desk. "Of course it's right. If we want to keep the money coming in, we have to attend to things. George, you know what to do. You don't need me?"

"I can handle it," George said with assurance. "And I'll give Leslie a ride in and a ride back when she's ready."

"But what do you do in Fletcher?" Leslie asked. "You have an office?"

"Oh, no," George laughed. "It's the town hall. The land records. It's very dull work—a lot of figures."

"Land? In Fletcher?"

"We're interested in acquiring land," George told her, then laughed. "But that's dull work and duller talk. You hurry and get ready and I'll not only give you a ride, I'll take you to lunch."

They left at ten with Dandy hitched to the sleigh. Brindle's wound was healing nicely, but George would pamper her until the scab fell off.

Dandy trotted along the snowy road with a stronger gait than the mare, glad to be out and exercising, and they moved at a good clip. They passed the Cranstons' and, not long thereafter, caught up to a walking figure moving along the road. Before they reached him, Leslie recognized the plaid jacket and the way the man moved.

"Oh," she said, "it's Stephen. What's he doing here?"

"On his way to town, I expect," George answered. "It's his day off."

"Oh, I forgot. Of course, he does get a day off, doesn't he?"

She urged George to stop and give the valet a lift, but George shook his head. "He's a servant."

"But he's on foot. It's a long walk."

"It's good for him."

They went past without slowing. George didn't even pivot his head or call a greeting, and Leslie was left to turn in her seat to give Steve a wave and, at the same time, a shrug of helplessness. Steve waved back with a grin and didn't seem bothered at all.

Leslie was upset nevertheless. "I'm a servant," she said. "How come you'll give me rides?"

"That answer ought to be obvious, my dear," George replied. "Nor are you a servant in the usual sense of the word. If that had been Fanny or Bessie or any of the women, I'd let them walk as well."

Leslie made a face, but what was there to say? She supposed he was right. He was accustomed to wealth and knew what to do with money and the power that money gave. Still and all, she didn't think it would have hurt anything for George to give Stephen a ride.

George let Leslie off in front of the emporium and it was left that he would meet her for lunch at Dewar's, the better of the two restaurants Fletcher had to offer. His business should be over by then, he told her.

Leslie carried out her errands, then went to the post office to see if any mail had come. When she entered the small room with its large street windows, postal boxes and mail counter, the first thing she saw was Stephen's plaid-jacketed back as he bent over a writing table scribbling on an envelope.

"I'm sorry," she said, going up to him. "I really did want to give you a ride."

He turned with a start. "Oh," he said and laughed, casually turning the letter face down so that the name of the addressee was hidden. "I did not mind the walk, but I appreciate the thought."

She couldn't help glancing at the letter. It was long and bulky, containing several folded sheets. "This is your day off?" she said.

"Yes, George—Mr. Trowbridge—set Wednesday as the day, after I'd worked out my first week." He saw her attention was on the envelope and added, "So I'm writing home to let my family know of my position."

"Oh, I see." It looked pretty bulky for a letter home, and she couldn't forget the haste with which he had concealed the address. It made her curious as to who the "family" was.

"By the way," he said, changing the subject completely, "I wonder if you could answer a question that has been puzzling the servants enormously and driving them wild with curiosity?"

"I'll try."

"What's in the locked room on the second floor, and why is the window left open?"

Leslie felt warning signals go through her. It wasn't just that Queenie had asked her not to tell. It was the fact he had pried there and asked about it before. It was the added fact that, despite his claim, none of the servants had ever, to her knowledge, expressed the slightest curiosity about the room. She kept her manner cool and controlled. "The servants are curious?"

"They are consumed with a thirst for knowledge."

160

"Then, why on earth don't any of you ask?"

"Ask—Mrs. Barrett? Mr. Barrett? Mr. Trowbridge?" Stephen shook his head. "It's not a servant's place to ask such things. But you must know how something like a lone locked room in a house will excite speculation. Every day there's a new rumor."

Leslie did not believe him, but she indulged him. "Such as?"

He laughed. "The theories are legion. Do you want to hear some? They run like this." Stephen started counting on his fingers. "Mr. Barrett doesn't trust banks and he doesn't trust paper money. Every cent he gets he converts into gold and the gold is stored there."

Leslie had to laugh. "You mean, while he goes off on trips and leaves it behind?"

Stephen grinned. "I didn't say I subscribed to that theory. I only say that's one of the rumors." He turned down another finger. "A second rumor is that there's a golden idol in there, worth a great deal of money, and members of the family go in when everyone else is asleep and perform secret rites."

"I see. What else?"

"Something or someone is kept imprisoned in that room, and the members of the family hide table scraps and sneak to the food larder at night to feed it without anyone knowing."

"It must be a polar bear," Leslie said. "It's pretty cold in that room."

Stephen wasn't impressing her effectively and his smile was losing some of its dazzle. "Of course that's one of the more far-fetched ones, but you know how vivid imaginations can be."

"Yes," Leslie answered, "I'm getting an idea." She was sure Stephen was making all this up.

"So," he continued, "if you would set us straight on the matter, the whole staff would be forever in your debt."

"Let me tell you," Leslie said. "As, in a way, a servant myself, I have my own theory, and I think it's the best one yet. The house is haunted. Ghosts used to roam upstairs and down, but Uncle Walter managed to lure them all into that one room and then locked the door on them. So, as long as the door stays locked, we are all safe."

Stephen said dryly, "So you don't want to help?"

"Help? It would seem to me that the obvious answer is that it's a storeroom—"

"There already is a storeroom."

"Well, for heaven's sake, if you want to know what's in there, ask someone who would know. Ask my uncle. Ask George. You valet for him."

"Yes, of course," Stephen said. "He's the one to ask." He smiled and switched subjects. "So you've come to town too. How are you getting back?"

"George will be driving me, as soon as he's finished his business."

"His business?"

"Yes, business. Did you not know George has business dealings in town?"

"In the Red Star Hotel?"

A sudden tremor went through her. "What are you saying? He's at the town hall."

Stephen smiled wryly. "My mistake," he said with a slight bow. "I was thinking of someone else."

"Or another occasion?"

"Another occasion."

"Like when you brought him home?"

"Like when I brought him home."

"Like a few other things, I daresay. What is your game, Mr. Stephen Crawford? What are you up to?"

"I, fair lady?"

"You, and never mind the 'fair lady' business. How is it that you appear on our doorstep with a successfully inebriated George on your hands and the next day you are his valet? What did you do to him that night, and where? Was the Red Star your home?"

Steve smiled with conceded pain. "I'm afraid I have pulled the tail of the dragon," he said.

"Yes, you have," Leslie said tartly. "And you've done more besides. What do you know about the animal that's been howling around our doors the past nights—the one I watched you go out and quiet the first evening he howled?"

Stephen shook his head. "I only went out to try to find him and he disappeared and didn't come back."

"Except, Monday morning you went off towards the woods with something in your hands, something in a paper. And you left it there. Why?"

"My," Stephen said with a tint of admiration in his tone, "you are observant."

"What was that for?"

"It was food," Stephen answered. "I thought the beast might be hungry."

"What did you want to feed it for?"

Stephen shrugged in a careless way and moved toward the counter to mail his letter. "So I might befriend it and find out what it was."

CHAPTER THIRTY-FOUR

The rest of the week produced the happiest days Leslie had spent in Fletcher. For the first time since she had known him, George was relaxed and at ease. His great concern was Brindle, and she and George spent many hours together, walking the horse, exercising her, discussing her condition and how she was faring. His knowledge of horses was far superior to her own, but she had, he said, a sympathy for animals that gave her right instincts, and he wouldn't do anything with the mare that Leslie did not think was right. George listened intently to her advice, asked her opinion even as he ventured his own. Restoring Brindle to perfect health was their common goal, and they worked together in pleasant harmony.

It was more than that, though. They tended the other horses as well, George explaining their habits, their needs, their strengths and weaknesses. It was a new world to Leslie and she was delighted with it.

George even started to teach her to ride. Springtime would be better, he said, when the roads would be clear and the meadows green. He was afraid of Dandy slipping, of Leslie falling, and he would not let her go on her own. Riding practice for the present had to take place in the area bounded by the barn, outbuildings and house, with George leading Dandy by her halter.

Betweentimes they sleighrode, and even walked. Leslie was used to walking. It was her mode of transport back East and she had missed its exhilaration. But with George relaxed and natural, she was growing freer and easier with him, and it was she who coaxed him into that endeavor. And he enjoyed it too. At first he thought he would tire Leslie out, that she would soon retreat to the comfort of a horse-drawn sleigh. Then he found it was he whose legs needed toughening, that it was he who came home exhausted while Leslie had scarcely got started.

Leslie who, a few days before, would have been afraid to outstrip the proud, masculine George, now found the competition fun. He did not take umbrage at having been bested. Instead, he told her they would walk again and again until he could match her stride for stride and then do more than that.

He could laugh, Leslie discovered. He was a different person under these conditions—a much more enjoyable person. Around the animals, out in the barn, he was fun to be with. He wasn't under pressure there. He was free of whatever haunted him inside the house, making him seem forced and boorish around his mother and Uncle Walter.

There was one experience with him that Leslie did not enjoy, however. It had to do with the howling animal. George took her with him when he went hunting for animal tracks one morning after breakfast. He'd laid out poisoned meat, he explained, and wanted to see the results.

Leslie accompanied him, but not with relish. If some animal lay dead in the snow she did not want to see it, even if it had threatened the horses.

They found nothing. The deep snow of the fields was crusted, and while a human's weight would break through, something lesser would not. There was no way to tell what the creature was, nor was there a sign of the poisoned food George had laid out.

The howling in the night had stopped as well, and George was satisfied. The creature, he was convinced, had eaten of the meat and had returned to the distant woods to die. That had been his goal. Leslie, while recognizing the need to protect the horses, nevertheless was glad not to have been a part of the killing process and glad not to have come upon an animal carcass out on the frozen wastes.

Except for that, Leslie's week had been almost totally happy. She was feeling at home now and at ease. She no longer feared that a wrong word or move would invite banishment, or at least punishment. It was true that there were many mysteries attached to her new life, but they lingered only in the back of her mind. In the forefront was the fact that the people who mattered—Uncle Walter, Queenie and George—no longer filled her with fear.

In the case of Queenie and Uncle Walter, she knew that it was she who had changed. Her approach and outlook towards them had been altered. With George it was different. He was the one who had changed. He had become so much more nearly the kind of man she could admire that she could even begin to visualize herself as Mrs. George Trowbridge with a certain degree of equanimity if not pleasure.

It is true that she had not been deceived by Stephen's retraction of having seen George in the Red Star the day he had supposedly gone to town hall. Leslie felt worldly enough to understand that men frequented houses of ill-repute—even the most upstanding of men—and she did not expect George to be an exception. If George felt the need to go to the Red Star, he was, after all, not yet married. What else was he to do? Leslie was sure, in the light of the new George, that that was a matter of small consequence. If she should become his wife, there would be no further need for him to frequent such places.

If there was any flaw in Leslie's happiness, it was Stephen Crawford. He had kissed her and he had shunned her and she knew not why. He told her she was too alluring, which could not help but make her whole body tingle, but he gained access to the household under strange circumstances, asked questions about locked rooms, and made mysterious trips into the wastelands to quiet the animal that howled. Worse than that, it was Stephen who made her uncertain about George.

To say that Stephen's presence disturbed Leslie would be putting it too strongly, however. She found herself thinking about him in odd moments, and wondering about him, but it wasn't until the following Monday afternoon that something happened which made her view Stephen more seriously.

She had returned to the sewing room after lunch, hoping to finish Queenie's gown before dinner. What with the time she had spent with George, she had all but abandoned her sewing, and though Queenie encouraged such neglect, her own conscience was bothering her. In fact, George had expected her to go to town with him on an errand that afternoon, but she had, for once, insisted that work came first, and he had, reluctantly, gone off alone. It was quite a feat on Leslie's part, but it was only accomplished because Queenie and Uncle Walter had gone to Chicago on some kind of business with banks and weren't around to insist.

Thus Leslie was alone upstairs and the house was quiet. The servants were taking their ease in quarters and only Leslie was busy, her nimble fingers making the needle fly.

There came a time, however, when she felt the need of a respite and she left her sewing to cross to her own room. There she poured a glass of water and sipped it while looking out the window across the snowy wastes to rest her eyes.

The interlude was brief, no more than five minutes, and she opened her bedroom door just as Stephen appeared from the opposite hall, looked in the sewing room and, seeing no one, went on into the alcove that contained the doors to George's and the master bedrooms.

It happened so quickly and quietly that Leslie had no chance to speak and, since his back was to her, Stephen did not know she was nearby.

Leslie returned to the sewing room again, frowning. Had Stephen been looking for her? She glanced into the alcove. The open door to George's room was facing her and she went to it, passing the door to the master bedroom as she did. It was the second time she had entered George's room, but the first time she had noticed her surroundings. Her glance took in the fireplace on the side, the three windows at the front, the large four-poster standing into the room on her left.

But there was no Stephen.

Leslie paused in surprise, an exclamation on her lips. She had seen him enter. He could not simply have disappeared.

She ventured farther into the room, looking around, frowning in disbelief. Normally she would not have crossed the threshold of another's bedroom, but curiosity emboldened her.

She circled the bed to the closet and peered inside. It was a wide closet and contained an extensive wardrobe of fine clothes. George certainly had more than a man could need. But there was no Stephen.

Leslie closed the closet door slowly. Stephen was most certainly not in the room and she was bewildered. Was he, in addition to all else, a magician?

Then, as she stood uncertainly, she heard the click of a latch outside.

Leslie, starting at the sound, darted around the bed and looked out the door just in time to see Stephen walking away down the hall and around a corner. And in the alcove, the door to Queenie and her uncle's bedroom, the door that had been closed before, was now ajar.

So that was it! It was the master bedroom that Stephen had entered! His glance into the sewing room was only to ascertain that the coast was clear.

What had he stolen?

That was Leslie's first thought, but then she realized his hands were empty.

Yet, why else would he have boldly walked into her uncle's bedroom when he thought the family was away?

Leslie remembered that last batch of servants had been fired because of a thief. Would the same thing happen again? She went quickly into the master bedroom and clicked the door behind her. She must find out what Stephen had done.

The bed was oversized, the brushes and combs on the dressers were silver-backed, the vanity loaded with an abnormally large collection of oils, powders, creams and unguents. Other than that, the room's appearance was ordinary, the furniture heavy and nondescript.

Except for a dainty, high-quality, woman's writing desk in a corner, which lay with its folding shelf down, its papers in disarray.

Leslie's eyes darted quickly. Stephen hadn't been in the room long. If jewelry boxes had been ransacked, they would be lying about. Thus jewels were not his aim, or they were not to be had.

She went to the desk and glanced at the assortment of papers. Surely Stephen wouldn't be interested in those. It wouldn't have been his hand that had messed them.

Some, she noted, were legal papers made out to "Walter J. Barrett." There also was a deed to 1152 acres of land in Colorado with her uncle's bold signature across the front. There were letters addressed to him, some legal, some personal. Leslie did not touch anything, but only looked. Going through another's personal effects was not only unethical, it was immoral. She concluded, however, that the papers were not important, else they would not have been left about. Nor was there evidence that a search had been made for anything else.

Leslie left the room quietly and returned to her sewing bewildered. What was Stephen Crawford up to? More and more she believed he had wangled his job as valet for more reasons than a need for employment.

So far, of course, she had no evidence. Stephen was, apparently, a satisfactory valet. No one among the staff or in the family seemed to fault him for anything. Except he should not have entered the family bedroom, though he seemed to have done no harm.

Leslie's mind was flying as fast as her needle now. Unless Queenie found something had been stolen, Leslie would not tattle on Stephen. That would earn him outright dismissal, and he might not deserve it.

Nevertheless, the valet's actions could not possibly redound to Uncle Walter's benefit, and it was her uncle's welfare that came first. Leslie decided she would henceforth keep a relentless eye upon Stephen Crawford.

CHAPTER THIRTY-FIVE

George and Leslie tested Brindle that Tuesday night. The young mare was so strong and eager that they let her take them to town, where the young couple celebrated her fitness with a dinner together in Dewar's. This they embarked upon, however, only after George and Leslie had spent a quarter hour with Brindle in the stables behind the inn, combing her, talking with her, examining her, and reaching mutual agreement that the mare had not overdone in any way. They were feeling as pleased as if they themselves had created Brindle's condition rather than cultivated it.

The meal was *intime*. George and Leslie leaned their heads close together over the small table and laughed and talked about Brindle and her antics, the way she tossed her head at their examination as if she knew better than they there was no cause for worry. They wondered about the strain of the trip home and talked about Brindle's jealousy at Dandy drawing the sleigh during her convalescence.

Dewar's was a proper setting for their mood. With its dark-paneled walls, sparkling white tablecloths and red-jacketed waiters, it had more elegance and atmosphere than any other restaurant west of Chicago.

They celebrated Brindle's recovery with champagne, and if Leslie drank a mite more than she was accustomed to, it only enhanced the charm of the evening. Leslie was beginning to like Fletcher. She had already started liking George. And on the way home in the sleigh, with Brindle prancing so perkily, she did not mind George sitting extra close and crossing her leg with his under the lap robe. She did not even balk when he slipped an arm around her and eased her head comfortably against his shoulder. The full moon was bright, the white fields glistened, and Leslie had a feeling of closeness to the world about her, and especially to the strong, dark man beside her. It was something she had not expected, but he was turning into the man of her dreams.

Brindle swung into the drive and trotted to the rear of the house where Swift came out to take charge. It was late and the others had retired, so that a dim lamp in the kitchen and another in the living room were all that illumined the downstairs.

"Make sure she's watered," George ordered as he helped Leslie from the sleigh.

"How's her shoulder?" the groom asked.

"Excellent. Right, Leslie?"

"She's better than new," Leslie rejoined. "But she ought to be well blanketed, don't you think, George? Despite the cold, she might be perspiring."

"Make sure she's warm," George ordered. "We don't want that shoulder to get stiff."

"No, sir," Swift agreed. "We certainly do not."

George and Leslie moved inside. The kitchen, inevitably the warmest room in the house, was where they shed their outer garments and George took Leslie's. "I'll hang them up."

"It's all right, I'm very strong."

They went together to the hall and George put the coats on

hangers. "You want something to eat?" he asked as he tucked them in the closet.

"After what we've already eaten? George, you're crazy."

"Or some tea or lemonade?"

"I couldn't look at food now if my life depended on it. Besides, what time is it? Fanny will be bringing my water and poking up my fire before I know it."

"It's not late. Come into the living room for a bit." He took her by the arm.

The house was still and their footsteps soundless. George guided her to the large couch in front of the fireplace. The fires had been banked, but it was still more than warm enough when they moved that close.

He seated her gently, and she, wondering at his purpose, regarded him questioningly. Was he going to sit beside her? Was he going to try to kiss her?

He did none of those things. Instead, he slipped to one knee and took her hand in both of his. In the dimness, his face had a pale, strained look; the darkness of his hair and brows was as black as jet. "Leslie," he said huskily, "I hope you will forgive me. I know you have rejected me once and I have no right to ask you to reconsider. However, I am so enamored of you that I can't think of anything else. I dream of you every night. When you first came, I behaved very badly towards you and I deserved your scorn. But I have learned my lesson. Now there is nothing more in life that would please me so much as to be your slave. I have sought to mend my ways, to please you, to be what you want me to be."

He pressed her hand. "You have been kind to me over these past two weeks since I have undergone my reformation. You give me to believe you no longer regard me with total disfavor. May I take your attitude to mean that I am not without hope?" He leaned forward earnestly and eagerly. "Leslie, do I have a chance? Is there any possibility that you might reconsider?"

Leslie's heart was pounding and she was trembling so that she feared he could read her disquiet through the hand he held. "You mean," she whispered, trying to maintain her composure, "reconsider your—proposal—of marriage?"

He nodded. "Do I have a chance, Leslie? Can you give me any hope at all?"

She could have him, she thought. She could say yes and, in the shortest of times, be Mrs. George Trowbridge, a mistress with servants and a house of her own, with a doting uncle and a delighted aunt. If she accepted him, he would grab and kiss her in rapturous wonder and dash up the stairs to wake the others. Queenie and Uncle Walter would come down in their robes and kiss her and hug her and treat her like a prized possession. She could set herself up for life and make them all happy at the same time. But would she make *herself* happy?

Unbidden, there came to her mind the remembrance of Stephen's kiss and the feel of being in his arms, and she trembled with a different emotion. What were her feelings towards the strange man in their midst? She didn't think it was love, but if it wasn't, what was it? She did not lie in bed and pine for him at night any more than she did for George. If she never saw either one again she would not suffer the loss of a single night's sleep. And yet, if both were suddenly removed from her life, would she not feel a little more regret at losing Stephen than at losing George?

"George," she said gently, smiling at the eager way he hung upon her words. "I do not know my feelings yet. I do not know how to answer you."

"But I do have a chance? You are not toying with my affections?"

"Of course you have a chance. A very good chance."

"That's all I need to know," George said worshipfully. "You have made me very happy. Dearest Leslie, you cannot know the torment I have lived in since you first cast me aside. It has been my goal ever since to earn my way back into your favor. I want only the chance to make you happy, my dearest, and my greatest happiness would be if I could spend my life pleasing you."

Leslie nodded and said, "Thank you," softly.

"How long do you think it will take you to make up your mind, my darling? How long before you can give me an answer?"

"I don't know," Leslie answered, "but I'll do it as soon as I can."

She knew as she said it that the answer would be yes, and she sensed that he knew it too. It was not a matter of *what*, but only of *when*. And the when, she felt, would be soon as well. In fact, as he rose from his knees, gazing happily into her eyes, she wondered why she wasn't saying yes right then. What was the point in holding back? She would not be learning anything so new and different about him that she would change her opinion of him in the next few days.

Still, Leslie felt that tonight was not the time. Still, some little uncertainty about her feelings made her reluctant. A few more days of waiting would do no harm, and it would give her a chance to get used to the idea. That was what she thought she needed, the opportunity to condition herself to the idea of being married and to the idea of being married to George.

CHAPTER THIRTY-SIX

Leslie tossed sleeplessly in her bed long after midnight. Fresh in her mind was George's second proposal and his gleaming countenance when she gave him hope. He had seen her up the stairs, holding her elbow, but aquiver to gather her in his arms. Only by the slenderest of margins could he restrain himself. It was flattering to find oneself so irresistible, but it was frightening too. Stephen Crawford had not restrained himself. He had seized and kissed her. George had shown greater control, but, then, George was taking a long-range view. He was looking to the future. Stephen knew he had no future, so what did he have to lose?

Most girls, Leslie thought, would lie awake in the pleasure of a safe, luxurious life ahead. It was so far beyond anything she had contemplated. The only future she'd ever seen was that of seamstress, her greatest ambition being to open her own shop. Now she could look forward to a fine marriage and family. She only wished she would stop having misgivings.

Her thoughts were interrupted by a far-off cry.

She heard it again, close now. It was the howl of the beast.

Leslie shivered. They had had a week's respite from the creature, had thought it dead and gone. Now the animal was back, its cry as piercing and ghostly as ever.

It was as if the creature had returned from the dead. She even began to imagine that the beast had been killed over and over, that George had shot it before she came and the family thought itself free. But its ghost came back and terrorized them until they fed it poisoned meat. Once again the creature had died, and once again the family had gained release. But now it was alive again, returning to drive the owners of the household mad.

Perhaps the creature had been a dog belonging to the murdered Rufus Morgate. Perhaps—

Leslie gritted her teeth and rebuked herself. Where did she get such foolish ideas? "Shame on you," she told herself. "What would Mama think?"

The howl came again and Leslie wondered what Stephen was doing. Was he going out to feed the beast? Could she see it from the sewing-room window?

Leslie rose, slid her feet into the slippers by her bed and groped for her robe on the bedpost. Slipping into it, she opened the door and stepped out.

She crossed quickly by the staircase to the sewing room. In the alcove the doors to George's and the master bedroom were closed with no lights showing. Leslie couldn't believe they were all sleeping, but they were pretending to. In any case, they were ignoring the animal, as she could not.

Inside the sewing room, Leslie felt her way towards the dimly outlined windows opposite. There, she parted the curtains and looked out. To the right, below, the barnyard was bathed in pale light from the post lantern, but the glow was feeble. Above, the moon was high and the nearby coop cast sharp shadows across the gleaming snow. Leslie's eyes roved over the broad landscape while her ears were tuned to home in on the next cry. Yes, it did come from around the barn. She stared fixedly there and the moon was more help than the pale lantern light. She could see the barn well enough to make out that its doors were shut. Elsewhere, the trees across the drive and the sheds and the silo were sharp shapes against the snow and sky.

The cry came again and she redoubled her efforts to make something out. It seemed, from the sound of it, that the creature must be in view. Still she saw nothing.

But wait—there—blending with the snow— She had detected a movement. It wasn't a ghost. The animal was there indeed.

She tried for a better look, but it was fruitless. Perhaps if she went down to the kitchen—

Leslie turned away and came out of the sewing room. Below, the front hall was dark, but there was a tiny glow of light in the living room.

Leslie stopped and stared. She and George had turned off the lamps before climbing the stairs. Someone was down there, someone with a candle.

Leslie paused and swallowed. The howling of the beast was forgotten. Who was downstairs? She listened and there was no sound. Only the periodic mournful cry interrupted the silence. Leslie's heart doubled its beat. One hand grasped the bannister and the other clutched her bathrobe to her throat. She felt a momentary urge to flee back to her room, jump into bed and pull the covers over her head. But she could not do that. She had to see why a candle was burning. She had to see who was there.

Slowly she tiptoed down the stairs, concentrating upon silence, her ears no longer hearing the cries from outside, her eyes fixed on the entrance to the living room and the faint, orange, flickering glow that filled it.

The bottom step stopped by the ornately arched entrance and Leslie paused there for a moment, listening for sounds. There was a faint rustle from the living room, unidentifiable but real. Leslie stepped down to the floor, keeping her heels close to the

175

stair risers, her body against the wall. She took a breath and slowly looked around the corner.

The flickering light came, as she had known it would, from a candle. The candle, in a holder, stood atop the rolltop desk her uncle kept locked. Only now the desk was open, the flexible cover pushed full up, and bending over the opening, going through her uncle's papers with his back to her, was Stephen Crawford.

Leslie was so startled at the valet's boldness that she could not hold back a gasp. Her intake of breath was so loud that she was sure he heard her and she began to tremble violently. Stephen, however, continued his careful ransacking of Walter Barrett's desk without so much as a tremor, and Leslie realized that her ill-concealed surprise had coincided with a howl from the beast outside.

With Stephen between her and the desk, blocking her view, she could not see what he was doing, but it was obvious he was going through her uncle's papers. He had broken into her uncle's preserve and anger rose in Leslie's breast. How dare the man!

She was tempted to storm into the room with threats and calumny, but an instinct warned her it would be at her peril. All at once she knew it was not chance that had brought him as a boarder to the Cranstons'. Stephen had intended to raid her uncle's possessions for a long long time. That was what had brought him to Fletcher, and he would not be stopped. Leslie knew with certainty that it was worth her life not to be discovered, that if he were interrupted or learned he had been found out, she would be in great danger.

Her urge was to flee, yet she did not move. She wanted to watch. She needed to find out what he was up to. The more she could learn, the more she could report to her uncle. So she stayed against the frame of the arch, her face peeking around the corner, her heart pounding, her breath coming in short gasps, her feet planted, ready to run screaming for help should she be caught and pursued.

So she stayed, watching Stephen and listening to the howl of the beast for what seemed an interminable period. She studied the man at the desk, trying to fathom from his behavior what he was after. The only thing she knew for sure was that it must be of vital importance. This was no simple burglary. It was a planned campaign.

For twenty minutes Leslie watched as Stephen carefully and methodically went through the contents of the desk and put things back. His actions were competent and unexcited, free of worry and complications. Stephen knew what he was after and how to get it. He showed none of the furtiveness of the amateur.

Then, finally finished, Stephen carefully and quietly slid down the cover of the rolltop desk. He worked on the lock for a little and then ducked off, taking nothing with him but the candle.

Leslie breathed a sigh of relief. She had escaped detection. And, she thought, Stephen probably believed he had too. The desk, she was sure, had been relocked, the papers inside back where they belonged. If she did not tell him, she was sure Uncle Walter would never know his secret papers were no longer secret.

CHAPTER THIRTY-SEVEN

Leslie determined, before she went to sleep, that she would reveal Stephen's treachery to her uncle first thing in the morning. Then she dreamed of Stephen all night and woke up uncertain.

He was, in her dreams, taking food to a wounded animal out in a strange place. She was with him and she was frightened, but Stephen soothed her and said it was all right. He laid out food for some giant beast she could not see, but whose presence she could feel, and when he had done that, Stephen kissed her.

It was in the middle of that kiss that Mabel knocked and came in with the morning kettle. Leslie wished she could throw Mabel out and resume her dream. Indeed, she tried to go back to sleep while Mabel refueled the fire, but the moment had escaped and she knew that, tired as she was, her sleep was over for the night.

She lay in bed musing after Mabel had gone. Stephen's phantom kiss still tingled her lips and she was re-experiencing that delicious, yielding sensation she had felt in the kitchen the time when Stephen had really kissed her.

She could not believe he was evil. Surely, an evil man could not have had that effect upon her. She would have felt the evil.

She reflected that sometime before she had gone to sleep, the beast had stopped howling. Had Stephen gone out and fed it again? How different that was from George going after it with a gun and laying out poisoned meat.

But if Stephen were not evil, then his activities were not undertaken for the purpose of harming her uncle. Strange as his behavior seemed to be, there could well be a perfectly logical explanation for it. If he were given a chance to explain his actions, Leslie might find them completely innocuous and justifiable.

If she reported him to her uncle, she knew she would never hear Stephen's reasons. He would be dismissed on the instant. She probably wouldn't get to see him go. Perhaps that punishment was too severe for the crime. It was only fair, she felt, that he should have a chance to explain himself. Should not a defendant be given a fair trial? Then, if his tale did not bear scrutiny, if his alibis and excuses were flawed, he could be given the dismissal he deserved. First, though, he should be heard. But who would give him a chance to speak in his own behalf other than Leslie herself? It would have to be she.

Thus, when Leslie arose from bed, it was with the conclusion that, unless her uncle discovered that someone had been through his things, or found something missing, she would hold her peace for the moment. She would give Stephen a chance to justify his actions, and only then would she decide what steps should be taken. She would bide her time that morning, she decided, and call him to her after lunch. That would be the best time—while Queenie, Uncle Walter and George were resting and before

George would want her to go walking with him. Meanwhile, there was much sewing to be done and she needed the time to prepare.

Throughout the morning, from breakfast till lunch, Leslie thought about her plan, and she went about her work with her pulses pounding and her spine tingling. Over and over she visualized the confrontation, she with her knowledge, demanding answers. Should she sit in the large winged chair in the living room while a craven Stephen cowered before her? Perhaps she should be seated at her uncle's desk. She could place her hand imperiously upon the locked, roll-down top and frostily ask if Stephen liked what he had found inside.

On the other hand, maybe she should be standing and make Stephen sit. She could pace back and forth, pointing an accusing finger at the humbled valet, and make clear that she was giving him a chance to save himself before she presented the facts to her uncle.

Over and over she rehearsed her remarks, often muttering them aloud as she bent over her needle. Could she speak in a properly firm voice? Could she eliminate the touch of a quaver? She must be in control. She must not let her fear of the encounter show.

How she got through the family luncheon she did not know. George looked at her with aching eyes while Queenie and Uncle Walter uttered inanities. She found responses without knowing what they were, and she must have looked at George encouragingly, because his eyes grew ever more bovine. Inwardly, however, her only thought was of the importance of protecting them all and the need for her to determine what was the danger that threatened them.

At last they were gone and Leslie was back in her room standing before the dresser mirror, pinching color into her cheeks, adjusting her hair, smoothing all wrinkles from her dress, and wishing she could make her bosom less noticeable. Really, she had gained a remarkable bit of weight since she had come West, and most of it had, discomfitingly, gone to swell that particular area. She had never paid attention before, but more and more male glances were making her aware of the difference. It was distracting. A girl tried to make some sense to a man, to explain something, to take a stand. And in the middle of it the man's eyes would wander to her bust, and a girl got the feeling that his mind was not on what she was saying at all.

Leslie smoothed her blouse over her bosom and fluffed the ruffle. That was the one thing she feared. She felt she could handle Stephen if he showed anger, fear, penitence, cowardice, or even threat. But if, while she addressed him, he started looking at her bosom, she would be destroyed.

Leslie examined the critical area again. If she wore her gold nugget outside her blouse instead of inside, as was her custom, that would only draw his eye to the area she wanted to discourage. It had best stay hidden inside.

What about a shawl? She put a white one about her shoulders. It was loosely woven, long, wool and warm. It made her look like an old grandmother. That was the very thing.

Leslie, draping the shawl properly, her bodice covering the golden nugget, left the room at last, closing the door softly. It was the afternoon rest period, when even the servants had nothing to do.

She went to the kitchen but it was empty. She went through to the servants' wing and looked around. Lambert's room was beside her at the head of the corridor to her left. Leslie hesitated a moment, feeling like an intruder, then she rapped.

In a moment, Lambert opened the door and she had a glimpse of a cluttered desk and a picture in a silver frame.

If Lambert were surprised that it was Leslie standing there, he gave no sign. He inclined his head a little and said, "Ma'am?"

"I want to see Stephen Crawford," Leslie said.

"Oh?" Was there a slight arch to the eyebrows? "Yes, miss. His room is around the corner, last door on the right."

Leslie drew herself up. "I did not say I wanted to go to his room. I said I wanted to see him. Will you send him to me in the living room, please?"

In the dimness, Leslie could not be certain whether Lambert's response was to hide a flush of embarrassment or the hint of a smile. "Yes, miss," he said and started down the hall.

Leslie returned to the living room to await Stephen's appearance and she was seething. What kind of a head butler had her uncle hired? Who were all these people who had been working for him less than two months? She remembered the help she knew at Mrs. Wiggins', so well trained and polished. Surely there were more able servants in Fletcher than those in her uncle's house.

It was Lambert, not Stephen, who came to her. He was sober and careful. He was very sorry, but Stephen was not available. It was his day off and he had gone into town.

CHAPTER THIRTY-EIGHT

Leslie sat in dismay for long minutes after Lambert had gone. Her shoulders were bowed, her hands worked together in her lap, and she stared emptily at the toes of her shoes projecting from under her skirt on the footstool.

What had she done? What a fool she had been. How could she have forgotten this was Stephen's free day? He had walked to town again, as he had the previous week. And, of course, he would visit the post office and mail some kind of letter to whomever it was he sent letters to.

Meanwhile, stupid Leslie had thought she was in control. Stupid Leslie had eschewed going immediately to her uncle with the news of Stephen's perfidy. Instead, she would be magnanimous. She would give him every chance to explain himself when there was nothing to explain. She should have reported him instantly, but she had not. And, deep down, she knew why. It was because he had kissed her and she had been undone.

Now she had given him a respite and, in so doing, had endangered her uncle. Whatever damage Stephen was plotting might now have been carried out. He had gone through her uncle's papers in the desk upstairs and the desk downstairs, and whatever he had meant to do with what he learned, he had probably now done. If harm came to her uncle because of Stephen's prowling, the blame would be hers.

A tear ran down Leslie's cheek as she contemplated the disaster she might have sponsored. Her uncle and Queenie had taken her in. Her step-cousin wanted to marry her and she was on the verge of accepting. She had been given everything. And now, because she had been influenced by Stephen's kisses, she had, perhaps, brought ruin on them all.

So Leslie wept and wondered what, if anything, she might do to make amends. It would be fruitless following Stephen to town. She could not stop his letter from being mailed, nor could she make him reveal what he was after. Telling Uncle Walter would not help matters. He would learn that he might be damaged, but he would not know how. If Stephen did not choose to reveal his purposes, could anyone make him talk? She envisioned Uncle Walter and George tying Stephen up and threatening him with torture, and it made her shiver. She did not think she could stand that.

Then there was always the possibility that Stephen had not yet accomplished his mission. If he posted a letter in Fletcher, it might be only an interim report.

Leslie rose at last and went to the window. The sky was bleak and the first few flakes of new snow were falling. They were the first she had seen in Fletcher.

And where was Stephen out in those first few flakes? Was he homeward bound, gleeful with success?

Yet, if he were returning, would this not mean the job had not yet been completed? What was it he was after? It occurred to her that there might be one way to find out. His room was at the end of the servants' hall, last door on the right. Perhaps the answer lay there.

It was not proper, Leslie knew, to search another person's room, but it was the least she could do for Uncle Walter and she acted without further thought, crossing through the house to the servants' quarters, pausing in the entrance to listen. From around the corner came the giggle of female voices. Leslie ventured to the bend and found the sound came from an open door to one of the rooms. The maids were having a social gathering.

Leslie went ahead carefully. The door, fortunately, was only ajar and she was able to slip by without anyone knowing. Now she was at the end of the hall at Stephen's door. Out of habit she raised her hand to knock, then realized the room was empty and reached for the knob. It turned, but the door did not budge. She tried again and shook her head. Stephen had locked it. Was there any reason why she should have believed he would not?

Darn, darn, darn, Leslie thought. Now what was she to do? The first order of business, of course, was to get out of the servants' quarters again without being seen, and she moved stealthily back the way she had come. As she got to the partially open door and the gabbling voices behind it, it was suddenly jerked open right in her face. Leslie gasped and froze, her brain racing in search of an excuse.

Mabel Tyre was standing there but it was her back that faced the hallway, for she was still in conversation as she took her leave.

Fortunately for Leslie, Mabel's broad figure denied the others a view of the startled young girl in the hall. Leslie darted around the corner and out into the safety of the kitchen before Mabel could turn around.

There, Leslie panted for breath and removed the shawl, for she had quite suddenly become overwarm. That was too close a call for her poor nerves, and it was several minutes before her breathing returned to normal.

Even while she was regaining her composure, Leslie was planning her next move. Unlike the windows she knew back home, these in Uncle Walter's house were newfangled gadgets that had sash weights for counterbalance, and they didn't need catches to hold them up. That meant, if they were unlocked, they could be opened from the outside. It was worth a chance.

Leslie donned coat, boots and mittens, then ducked out the back door and circled around to Stephen's room via the path to the privy. There were three windows on his corner room, and the first she tried opened easily to her touch.

It was but the work of a moment for Leslie to slip in over the sill. Then she was inside Stephen Crawford's room, sliding the window shut behind her, and turning to view her surroundings.

There was a wardrobe next to the door, a bed against the opposite wall, with a washstand, bureau and chair between. Though the room was rudely equipped and Spartan in appearance, it was neatly kept. The washbasin and pitcher were clean, the soap in the soap dish dry, the dish itself shiny. The towels on the side racks were neatly folded, the used clothes were stored in a laundry bag inside the wardrobe door, and the only outward sign that the room was inhabited was a folder on the bureau beside a pen and inkwell.

Leslie opened the folder. Inside there was nothing but writing paper and envelopes and, in a pocket, one sheet of paper upon which was written, "Leonard James, Household Supplies: Utensils for the kitchen. Linen. Drapery. Boudoir accessories."

Leslie pulled that sheet from its pocket, read it and scowled. It made no sense. Surely she must have misunderstood everything she had been seeing.

She tried to slip the sheet back into place, but it jammed against something else inside the pocket. She reached in and drew out a scrap of paper which was the torn-off end of some kind of document, and scribbled boldly across it was the name "Walter Barrett" in the hand she knew so well. Stephen had, then, in his possession, the name and occupation of somebody named Leonard James. In addition, he had a torn-off piece of document bearing her uncle's signature. She studied the piece closely, hunting for clues as to its origin, but no other writing could be found and, though the paper was stiff and like parchment, she had no idea from where it had come.

Leslie explored the pocket to assure herself that nothing further was hidden inside. Then she returned the folder to its exact position so that Stephen, upon his return, would never know that it had been touched.

Leslie went on to the wardrobe. She was finding things, even if she did not know what her findings meant. What else of meaning was there in the room?

In the wardrobe was one of Stephen's suits, two hats on a shelf, a pair of polished black shoes, and a suitcase lying on its side. The catches of the suitcase were unfastened and Leslie knelt on the floor to lift the lid. Inside there seemed to be little, only a scarf and a heavy sweater bundled together against one side. Leslie put her hand on them and discovered there was more. Something hard was wrapped inside. Her heart pounded harder. Without an idea as to what it was, she knew she had stumbled onto an item of importance. Its feel and the secrecy of its location told her.

Carefully Leslie brought the sweater out and opened it on her lap as she knelt on the floor. And when the heavy wool came away and the thing lay exposed to view, she gasped and a quiver of fear went through her. It was a black revolver with the glint of copper bullets in the chambers. It was a six-shooter, meaning it could fire six bullets without reloading. Leslie had heard of such guns, though she had never seen one. In fact, she had never seen any kind of a handgun before.

For a long time she stared at it, afraid to touch it, afraid it might go off. What should she do with it? Should she put it back and tell Uncle Walter? Should she take it with her out the window and back to the house? What would a man have a gun for? What would he want to shoot? Or was it—Who? Would he want to use it against Uncle Walter or Queenie or someone in the family?

Leslie could not believe that, nor did she want to handle the gun. Best to rewrap it in the sweater and restore it to its place in the suitcase. Let Uncle Walter decide what to do about it.

She repacked the sweater, arranging the scarf as she had found it so that Stephen would not know anything had been touched. Then she rose and was about to close the wardrobe door when her eye fell on the good suit hanging on the rack. It was not the one he wore around the house or into town. It was his dress-up suit, the one that went with the shiny black shoes, and it looked very well made and form-fitting. The pants were neatly suspended from the hanger by clips, and the vest, hanging inside the coat, had three buttons done up. Leslie looked at it wondering if she had seen it before, and then, on an impulse, slipped her hands into the pockets.

There was a folded piece of paper in the jacket pocket on the right-hand side, and when Leslie drew it out she saw that it was an order slip. Across the top was printed "The Red Star Hotel," and the lined front of the paper was blank. When Leslie opened it, however, she found a message written on the back. "George T. just came in," it said. "He's in 12 with Lil." There was no signature, but the handwriting looked like a girl's.

Leslie's breath caught and then came very slowly. That was the night she had rejected George's suit. Fletcher's house of ill-repute was where he had gone, and Stephen had been waiting for him. Stephen had the barmaids and waitresses briefed to let him know when George showed up. Stephen had not run into a drunken George by accident; he had laid for him and got him drunk, and brought him home and put him to bed and said that George had hired him as a valet. And George didn't know that he hadn't.

It was all a scheme so Stephen could infiltrate the household and do what it was against Uncle Walter he had set out to do. And the kisses and his claims that Leslie was too irresistible for him to be around—that was more of his scheming. That had been to lull her suspicions. Where had he been during her birthday party? Everyone else in the house had gathered. Stephen alone had been absent. Never mind his false excuse. What had he been up to? What was he up to now?

Whatever it was, Leslie knew it boded ill for her uncle. She tucked the note into her coat pocket and then, without any reluctance whatever, she reopened the suitcase, took the revolver from its hiding place, gave a hasty readjustment to things and closed the wardrobe door. She had to get out the window again and to her uncle as fast as possible.

CHAPTER THIRTY-NINE

Hiding the revolver under her coat, Leslie slipped back to her own room without encountering a soul. She did not, however, breathe in relief until she had the gun buried at the bottom of her laundry bag and her coat, boots and mittens put away. Only when she had viewed herself in the mirror, tucked back the loose strands of hair, straightened her bodice and could get her face to look relaxed, did she feel safe. Now no one would have known she had left her room at all.

Getting to her uncle was the next thing. He would be readily available, of course, but so was Queenie, and Leslie wanted to keep her case for his ears alone, nor did she want to appear either secretive or alarmist. The best approach would be to go back to work, acting as if nothing had happened, and bide her time.

This, she accordingly did, busying herself in the sewing room, from which vantage point she could look out upon the rutted driveway, keeping watch for Stephen's return. It was snowing harder, but the flakes still fell gently, though far more thickly. The gray mass of woods in the distance was only a blur now.

Across the room the door was open, so Leslie could monitor the family comings and goings. Queenie and Uncle Walter went downstairs, looking in with a greeting as they passed. George went by, but she looked out at the drive so that he would not stop for comment. She was not up to talking to George just then.

At four o'clock Queenie reappeared, entering the room to comment upon Leslie's diligence and to note her progress. At this moment she did not want to be fitted, but she did want to match the dress against her figure in front of the mirror.

"Where's Uncle Walter?"

"At his desk," Queenie told her. "Yes, I do like this color with my hair. I used to be all for red, but I don't like red any more."

"I still want to see you in a pearl gray—"

"Nonsense. Grays are too flat and unflattering. I like color, color, color." She gave the half-completed gown back to Leslie.

"Where are you going now?" Leslie asked.

"To change."

Queenie left for her room and Leslie, taking one last look out the window for the absent Stephen, put her things quickly away and darted back to her own room. There, she retrieved the revolver, wrapping it in a flannel nightgown, and started on her mission.

Uncle Walter was doing figures at his desk by the light of the oil lamp on top, going over his papers soberly. Leslie, coming down the back family stairs to keep from being seen, startled him as she came in through the dining-room entrance almost beside him.

"Oh," he said, gathering his papers quickly, "George is out in the barn exercising Brindle."

Leslie said that it was he she wanted to see, and Uncle Walter said, "Oh, indeed?" and pushed his papers together, sliding down the desktop and turning around in his chair. "Now, then," he smiled. "What can I do for you, my child?"

Leslie moved right to the point. She placed the nightgown-wrapped object in his lap and said, "First, sir, would you look at this?"

Uncle Walter opened the flannel garment slowly and stared down at the revolver. "Where did you get this?" he said, looking at her in puzzlement.

Leslie told him and he stared at her. "But what on earth—how on earth—were you—"

"And that's not all. Look at this!" She showed him the message she had removed from Stephen's jacket pocket. He read that wonderingly while she explained its purport. "You see," she said, "it's all a scheme. He got George drunk, don't you see?"

Uncle Walter nodded, but his eyes narrowed warily as if he was not convinced. Leslie knew the reason. "Don't pay any attention to the 'He's in 12 with Lil' part," she said. "I know what that means. I'd turned him down that day and I understand about men. If a woman rejects them, they go find a woman who'll be nice to them. It's all right. I don't hold that against George. That's the way men are. What I'm talking about is that Stephen waylaid George afterward. He waited for George and plied him with drink. It's the only answer, Uncle Walter, especially after the rest."

"Rest?" Uncle Walter shook his head. "You mean there's more?"

Leslie nodded vigorously. "Much more. Did you know that he's got a piece of paper in his room that's got your signature on it?"

That news opened Uncle Walter's eyes more than the gun and the note had. "My signature? How can you tell?"

"I know how you write your name, silly. Didn't you used to write Mama and send her money?"

"Of course, but I didn't realize— So it is *my* signature? What's it on?"

"It's torn from the bottom of a sheet of paper of some kind, like a letter or a contract or something. There's no way of telling."

"And what else?"

"There's another name, and I don't know what that means. It's written on a small piece of paper and it said, 'Leonard James—'"

Uncle Walter came half out of his chair, his jaw sagging, his face blanched white. "Wha—wha—?" he said as if he'd heard his death knell sound.

Leslie reached to support him. "Uncle, uncle—are you all right?"

The gun and nightgown fell from Walter Barrett's lap as he rose, and now he sagged back weakly, sweat starting to break out on his ashen face.

"I'll get you some water," Leslie said, turning to run to the kitchen, but her uncle, seeming to have aged ten years in ten seconds, cried hoarsely to her to desist. "No, no," he said. "Tell me —what else was there?"

"Just that," Leslie answered, returning. "It said 'Leonard James,' and after that it said 'Household supplies, utensils for the kitchen. Linen. Drapery. Boudoir accessories.'"

She watched her uncle lest he have another attack, but he only nodded weakly, the sweat beaded on his face. She could not imagine the cause for such a reaction and she was seriously concerned. "Uncle," she said, "what does it mean? Are you in danger?"

189

He nodded, unable to talk, his eyes almost lolling in his head.

"Uncle Walter!" She knelt beside the stricken man. "Tell me what the trouble is. Tell me what I can do."

He turned his ghastly face to look down at her upturned visage close by the chair arm. "What else—" he gasped. "What else have you found?"

She told him all of it then, how Stephen went out at night and the howling animal became quiet, how she had caught him sneaking out of the master bedroom, how she had caught him at the rolltop desk, studying all the papers inside. Through it all, Uncle Walter listened, absorbing and unmoving.

"I should have told you sooner," Leslie said at the end, and her voice choked on a sob. "I should have told you right away— before he went into town today."

He patted her hand absently, his eyes looking beyond her. "Oh, Uncle," she cried, "is it very bad?"

He nodded and a corner of his mouth twitched. "Very bad. Very, very bad."

"Are we in danger?"

Now he looked at her. "Grave danger," he said soberly. "He is a very evil man. He may destroy us all."

"Destroy us?"

"All of us. You, me, Queenie, George." He shuddered.

"If I had told you sooner—before he went to town—would this have made a difference?"

Walter struggled to his feet. "I don't know," he said, shaking his head. "I do not know whether it's too late or not."

Leslie started to weep, burying her face in her hands.

Walter touched her hair with an awkward, gentle hand. "Thank God you've told us now," he said. "All may not be lost. Give me the gun."

She picked up the black revolver, rewrapped it in the flannel nightgown and handed it to him. "Dry your eyes," he said. "And whatever you do, do not let him know what you've done and what you've seen."

"No, never!"

"Because if he suspects, you'll be in the greatest of danger.

What he wants to do to us is more horrible than you could imagine."

He left her, going to the front stairs like an old man. The vigor was gone from his step, his back seemed more bent, his graying hair grayer.

Leslie watched him and, when he had disappeared, she burst into fresh tears of remorse, feeling as if the responsibility for the change in her uncle was her doing. If only she had let him know before Stephen got away! Now they all were in danger, and though she did not know what the danger was, she was aware that it was very real and very present.

It was as she was drying her eyes, still seated on the rug beside her uncle's chair, that George returned from caring for their beautiful mare. He saw her in her distress and cried, "Leslie," coming instantly to his knee beside her. "My dearest one, whatever can be the matter?"

"I'm all right, really," she answered, trying to force a smile.

"You're far from all right," George said, his face clouded with concern. He took her by the shoulders and held her firmly. "Something is troubling you and I won't have it, not when I'm around. Tell it to me so I may remedy the matter."

Leslie had botched things enough already and she wasn't going to make things worse. If Uncle Walter wanted to tell George what had transpired, that was up to him. She only knew she must not tell anyone. "It's only girlish things," she said. "Don't you know girls often cry for no reason at all?" She smiled beamingly. "See, it's all over. The sun's out."

"Oh, no," George said. "You don't cry without a reason. Not you. You're unhappy, and I want to know why."

"All right," Leslie said, "I'm really crying for a very silly reason. It's because I'm happy and excited and nervous and all kinds of things."

"You are?"

"Well, wouldn't you be, if you were a girl and had just decided to accept a proposal of marriage?"

George rose up on both knees. "You—mean—?"

"I'll marry you," Leslie said simply. "If you still want me."

"If—I—want you?" He gazed at her. "Oh, man, do I!"

He grabbed her, kissed her hard, and leaped to his feet. The last she saw of him he was rounding the corner to the hall stairs whooping like an Indian.

CHAPTER FORTY

Despite the joy her acceptance brought to George's heart and the pleasure it gave to Queenie and her uncle, it was an unhappy and miserable Leslie Marsh who climbed into bed late that Wednesday night. Hanging over the family, smothering the happiness that should have been theirs, was a heavy pall of gloom, and this was also Leslie's doing. Stephen's treachery, which Leslie had been so delinquent in reporting, was in the forefront of everyone's mind, banishing conversation and involving the soberest of faces. Even George, who had rushed upstairs in the height of ecstasy to relate her acceptance, returned at dinner defeated and withdrawn. Queenie and Uncle Walter had kissed her and wished her happiness, but their faces were troubled.

Though not a word of chastisement or rebuke was uttered, Leslie knew it was all her fault. She toyed miserably with her food and wished she were dead. Perhaps George no longer wanted to marry her. Perhaps the family no longer desired her presence. If only they would say something, cry out at her, call her names, berate or scream at her.

Instead, there was that distracted silence, the three people around her eating without conversation, each lost in his own thoughts. What was the danger, she wondered. What was Stephen going to do to them? What could he do? What could be done against him?

Leslie did not even know if Stephen had come back, or if he would ever come back. She did not know what would be done to him if he should return. She wished she could bring up the subject, make inquiries, ask what Stephen's power was, explore the possibilities of blunting it. But the others said nothing, so she did not dare.

In bed at last, she tossed sleeplessly. It was going to be one of those bad nights. The rest of the house was bedded down, but she was going to lie awake crying over spilt milk, castigating herself for the damage she had done to those she loved, wishing a great hole in the ground would open up and swallow her. Outside, the snow was swirling, whitening the blackness of the sky, building ever deeper, closing them in. Outside the night was quiet, the snow thickening its soft, peaceful blanket. And inside there was terror.

Leslie turned over again. Her jaw was tight and her fists clenched in self-condemnation. It was a useless exercise, but she could not control it.

Then, out of the silence of the night it came: the eerie howl of the beast.

"Oh, God," Leslie thought. "Not again. Not tonight."

It was repeated, a wailing, painful cry, as if the animal was calling someone—a dead mate, or a lost child.

Leslie shivered and pulled the covers around her ears. Was Stephen back? Would he go out and soothe the beast or do whatever it was that made it go away? The beast and Stephen. He had some power over it, as he had some power over the family. The terror that had seized her uncle seemed to go deeper than threats to his fortune. Stephen exercised a strange power that smacked of the unwholesome, the supernatural, the threat of death, or something worse than death.

The howls continued, reaching Leslie's ears despite the covers she clutched. They were periodic and drew nearer. Leslie squeezed her eyes shut. "Make it go away," she thought, distraught and miserable in a far-off house in a far-off town. "Won't somebody make it go away?"

The howls continued, beyond the barn, and she thought she

would have to bear them through the night. But suddenly they were interrupted by the explosion of a gun going off. It rattled the windows and reverberated in the distance. Then all was still.

Leslie sat upright in bed. It was the second time a gun had been taken out against the animal, and a strange, uneasy feeling went through her.

Without knowing why she was doing it, Leslie slipped out of bed, undid the pink ribbon at her throat, dropped her nightgown to the floor and started to get into her clothes. She was sure the man with the gun was George, and for some reason she felt she had to see him. For some reason she wanted to be dressed when she did and she worked rapidly to clothe herself in the dark.

When she was done, she opened her door and slipped into the hall. Around were only the quiet night lights, but even as she paused, a sound came up from the hall closet below, followed immediately by footsteps on the stairs.

Leslie advanced to the rail as George's head and shoulders came into view. He was dressed in the clothes he had worn at dinner, except that his jacket had been replaced by a heavy sweater. His back was to her and there was a ponderousness in his tread, but also the sense of a duty done.

"George!"

He turned at her soft call and grinned. "Oh, hello."

"What happened?"

"I shot the brute."

"Did you kill him?"

"I don't know. I hope so."

"What was it?"

"I don't know. I didn't go close enough to see."

"You didn't find out?"

George shook his head with a disconcertingly malignant gleam in his eyes. "It's pitch-black out there. If I went close and it wasn't dead, I could be in great danger. Time enough to find out tomorrow."

"But what if it's only wounded?"

"Then it will go away. Either way, I hope it's never going to bother us again."

"I think you should go put it out of its misery."

"It might be out already."

"But you aren't sure."

"No, and I'm not going to find out tonight. I'll go out in the morning, but not before."

"Even if the creature—"

A stern, cold look came into George's eyes. "That's the last of it, Leslie. Go back to bed." He went up the rest of the stairs and disappeared around the corner to his room without giving her another look.

CHAPTER FORTY-ONE

Leslie returned to her room, scowling darkly. George, who had, in proposing, professed himself Leslie's slave, willing to do anything to please her, had just ordered her around as if she were one of the servants. Could it be that, having won her consent, he no longer need treat her with courtesy and concern? Did he think he now owned her? Was he reverting to the old George she had turned down?

She leaned against the door of her room, fuming at the offhanded treatment, but also reckoning her future. If he could dismiss her in such a manner before he had even put a diamond upon her finger, what would he do when the knot was finally tied and she was unable to escape? Leslie well knew that once a woman accepted a man as her husband, he became her guardian, mentor, lover, determiner. Every request she wished to make, every need she wanted fulfilled, every hope she wanted sparked, had to go through her husband. If he were of a like mind, a woman might find marriage a blessing. If he were not, it would be a prison.

Suddenly, Leslie was torn by doubts. For most women marriage was their only hope of achievement. Without it, life was disaster. Spinsters were doomed to live in the households of married relatives, the maiden aunts of another's children, the in-home teachers and disciplinarians, the household help. These were women whose identity was the effect they could have upon another woman's child. They were displaced persons, harbored, sheltered, even loved, but dependent. Always dependent.

The rest became teachers or worked in factories sewing clothes or, like her mother, cleaned houses and took in laundry. No wonder women would rather live in prison, with her husband the jailer. No wonder men thought they could deal with women however they chose.

But Leslie was not thus beholden to men. She could make a living with her needle, and a good living at that. She did not have to get married to survive. She did not have to learn to cope with an unmanageable man, to coax and sweet-talk him if she wanted something, seduce him with her body to get special favors. She would not have to feign ignorance of the drunken brawls George might enter into when he went salooning, of the girls in room 12 or 14, or however many rooms they had on the second floor of the Red Star that men went to visit.

"Well," Leslie thought, coming away from the door at last, "I haven't promised to love, honor and obey him yet. And maybe I just never will."

And damned if she was going back to bed because George told her to. She took a turn around the room and frowned anew. She was worried about the animal. No matter how hideous the beast might be, it did not deserve to be wounded and unable to get itself to safety. By morning, if the snow was still falling, it might be buried under several inches, and might have slowly frozen to death in the process. A proper hunter should track down wounded prey to put them out of their misery.

The more she thought about the animal, the more she knew she could not sleep until she had learned its fate. George was afraid to go near it, but somebody ought to.

There was but one thing to do and she knew she was going to do it before she even considered the consequences. She was going out into the snowstorm herself and find the answer. What George might think of such an action did not bother her, for George was not going to know about it, ever. Nobody was going to know about it.

She put on her boots and heavy sweater. It was much colder than when she had climbed through Stephen's window, and she needed to dress still more warmly. Coat, scarf, thick fur hat, and wool-lined mittens. She was perspiring before she had everything on. Then she removed the milk-glass shade from over the chimney of the oil lamp, lighted it, turned the flame down low and went with it into the hall to the back servants' stairs. Except for the night lights, all was dark.

Quietly she went down to the dim, empty kitchen. Outside, dense, falling flakes were caught in the glow of the post lantern, but the snowfall was so thick the lantern was helpless against it. One could see scarcely ten feet beyond the post.

Leslie's heart was filled with sudden misgivings. Where should she look for the animal? The area out there was vast, and she doubted that a trace of George's tracks remained. With the feeble lantern she carried, she could pass within three yards of the creature and not see it.

Leslie hesitated uncertainly. It would be foolhardy to venture forth. George had been right to tell her to go to bed.

Just then, from out of the darkness, there came a cry from the beast. It was a wailing, plaintive sound, a new kind of call. The beast was in trouble. There was a pleading note in its cry, a call for help which Leslie could not ignore.

She went out onto the back porch. It was drifted with snow, though sheltered on three sides. Gingerly she groped for a footing on hidden steps and started forward. She crossed the rutted drive, nearly falling because of the icy depression that underlay the thick, covering snow and paused by the lantern post to adjust her lamp wick for a brighter flame. She looked around for tracks, but the footsteps George had left had already been obliterated. "Curse the snow," Leslie thought. It was nearly to her knees and the falling flakes were heavy and determined.

Out in the darkness the creature moaned again and Leslie

started in its direction, feeling the large melting snowflakes chill her cheeks, ducking her head to keep them out of her eyes.

The great red hulk of the barn was visible on her right, but it dimmed as she went past. By the time she had reached its far corner, the glow from the post lantern was behind her and all she could see was the small yellow circle of snow that was created by her own lamp.

The cries were more frequent now, hopeful, encouraging cries. The creature had seen her light, knew someone was coming.

Leslie held the lamp higher and there, ahead of her, was the red glow of eyes. She advanced a step and a little of the creature itself became visible. It yipped and she took another step. It looked like a large dog with light-colored hair, but she could not be sure.

She ducked her head against the snow and waded forward. As she looked up, the animal leaped away, advanced, and then barked. It was a dog. But it did not seem to be hurt.

Leslie plowed through the snow a little farther and the dog, as she drew near, leaped away again. She stopped.

The dog barked. It came forward and leaped away again, came forward and barked. Leslie advanced again. The dog was leading her on, but for what purpose?

The dog bounded away in the deep snow and floundered. There was something wrong with it and Leslie remembered Swift saying the animal that ran from the barn had gone off limping.

The dog barked again as Leslie took another step, and then she saw something else. It was a great black form twice the size of the dog, and it was lying half buried in the snow.

Leslie advanced cautiously and, as she approached, the dog withdrew. The snowy black shape before her did not stir. She took another step and then gasped. It wasn't an animal, it was a man.

Leslie leaped forward and dropped to her knees beside the still figure. He was clad in coat and cap, and a coating of snow already covered his back.

She put the lamp beside him in the snow, brushed some of the coating from him, and moaning in dismay, tried to roll him over. The feeble glow from the lamp showed that the jacket was plaid and Leslie gasped in horror. She had seen but one plaid jacket in Fletcher.

Her efforts to move the still form were futile. She raised him only a matter of inches, then had to let him slump again, but the doing shifted him enough so she could see the white, still face. It belonged to Stephen Crawford.

CHAPTER FORTY-TWO

A sob broke from Leslie's lips at sight of Stephen's face. No matter what he had done, she did not want him shot. "Oh, Stephen," she cried, heartsick at the thought that he might be dead and George had killed him. Oh, please God, not that.

She seized him frantically and, with strength she did not know she had, turned him onto his back. "Oh Stephen, oh Stephen," she cried, pulling off her mittens to feel his cold face with her hands. If she could unfasten his jacket—

His eyelids trembled and she leaned closer. "Oh, Stephen, say something. Please don't die."

His eyes opened and he looked up at her, his gaze, in the lamplight, more alert than she could have hoped. "Stephen," she said, leaning close. "It's me, Leslie." She touched his face with both hands. "Do you know me?"

"Leslie," he said with difficulty. "I—I've been—shot."

"I heard. I heard. I came looking. Oh, Stephen!" She fought back tears. "Thank God I found you. Is it very bad?"

"It's—my leg," he groaned. "I—can't walk."

She saw then that he had been dragging himself through the

snow, but that his progress had been painful and slow. He could never have got back to the house before he froze to death.

Leslie pulled on her mittens again. "I'll get help," she told him. "You'll be all right." She started to climb to her feet, but he grunted a hoarse, "No."

"What?"

"Don't. No help."

"I'll get George. You can't do anything yourself and I'm—"

"No. Not George." Stephen gasped for breath. "He—tried to —kill me."

"It was an accident. He thought you were the beast."

"No—no accident—"

She went to her knees. "What are you saying? Of course it was an accident. He—"

"No accident," Stephen repeated. "He—saw me. I—spoke— and he—fired."

"No, Stephen. You must be mistaken." And as she said that, Leslie remembered Uncle Walter's fear of Stephen, the sober faces at the dinner table, the family dread of what Stephen might do. And she knew that the shooting hadn't been a mistake.

"Don't tell George," Stephen said with all the strength he could muster. "He will—kill—me."

Leslie knew he spoke the truth, but would not let herself believe it. It was too monstrous. "Swift," she said. "I'll get Swift."

"No—please."

Leslie leaned close. "You're getting weaker, Stephen. You can't stay out here much longer. I've got to get somebody. Tell me whom to get."

"No one," he pleaded. "George will—find out—and—kill me. That's why I played dead just now." He lifted a weakening arm. "Help—please."

He wanted her to help him. He trusted her not to betray the fact that he still lived. He believed she had the strength to get him to safety.

And help she would—at least she would try. Nor did the thought that he might be conning her again, the way he had when he kissed her and called her irresistible, come into her mind. He had tricked his way into the Barrett household, he had opened her uncle's locked desk and read his secret papers. He sent reports to someone outside, he endangered her uncle and his family, and he had used her as well. He was an enemy spy, and if he died her uncle might be safe. But she would not let him die. Later he would pay for his sins, but first he must be saved.

Leslie put her arms around him. "Can you sit up?" she asked. "Can you get up and lean on me?"

Stephen struggled and did sit up, but Leslie sensed his weakness was due more to cold than injury. If only his leg had been hurt, then his arms and upper torso should have been more limber.

But Leslie was feeling the weakening effects of the cold as well. Kneeling and talking had drained much of the warmth from her own body. If she didn't make her muscles work, she, too, would become sluggish and unable to function.

"On your feet," Leslie said and struggled with the fallen man. He strived and, together, they made it slowly. She supported him and his weight was heavy upon her shoulders. She looked around and could not see the light of the distant post lamp through the blinding snowstorm. She felt a moment of panic, then remembered the tracks she had made. At her feet, the kerosene lamp stood half sunken in a crater of melted snow. She could not follow the trail without it, but she could not stoop for it without letting Stephen go.

"Steady yourself," she told him. "Can you keep your balance? I have to pick up the lamp."

Stephen nodded and said, "Go bend," but he kept a steadying hand on her shoulder when she let him go to retrieve it.

Then she was back, beside him. His weight came against her again and very nearly brought her down into the snow. "Easy," she said.

"Hold me," he said. "I can't stand."

"Can you take the lamp? Then I can put both arms around you."

He did so, and so did she. He said, "What do we need the lamp for?" and his speech was sluggish. He was starting to fade.

"To find our way back. We have to follow my tracks."

"Oh."

"Can you hold it?"

Stephen indicated that he could and she put it in his free hand. She got his other arm over her shoulder and put both hers around his waist. Then, very slowly and carefully, they started through the deep snow and heavily falling snowflakes back along the rapidly fading path Leslie had made.

The lamp wavered in Stephen's grasp, but it did not fall. Though the snowstorm was thick, there was no wind, and drafts did not sweep across the top of the glass chimney and suck out the flame.

They inched their way along, following Leslie's fast-filling tracks until they could make out the faint glow of the post lantern ahead. After that, it was easier and they came in past the nearly invisible barn to the safety of the porch.

Leslie opened the door and helped Stephen into the kitchen, closing out the cold again. Stephen was holding onto Leslie with one arm, the lamp with the other. His teeth chattered violently and his right leg was dragging and almost frozen.

But now they were in the kitchen, and while the temperature was far from warm, it was half as high above freezing as the outside temperature was below.

Leslie helped him to the staircase and he stumbled on the steps, almost dropping the lamp. He was living on nerve now, dragging the crippled leg, leaning ever more heavily upon her, blotting pain and progress from his mind. He did not ask where they were going, but only struggled to keep erect.

Leslie got him up the stairs as quietly as she could, took him to her own room, helped him onto the bed and locked the door. Stephen lay there with a sigh that was half a moan, and gave himself up to her efforts to unbutton and remove his heavy outer garments.

She felt his hands and face and they were like ice. His lips were blue. The room was cold now, but he was colder. Leslie did not know what to do, yet she responded, acting automatically, tending to his needs without thinking.

His coat, hat and mittens and boots were heaped by the door.

The snow on his trousers was melting, and in the lamplight she could see the dark-red stain against dark trousers, more because it was frozen than because it was evident. She undid his belt and unbuttoned his trousers, then worked them down over his hips. There was full-length woolen underwear beneath, and when she got his trousers down to his knees she saw that the underwear was stained deep red around a bullet hole that went through it and through his thigh. Stephen had lost a lot of blood. He was wounded and nearly frozen. What should she do about the wound? The bleeding seemed to have nearly stopped. Only a little blood was oozing.

Leslie got his trousers off entirely, then undid his shirt. Stephen was all but unconscious, yet able in some small way to assist her, as if he knew she was trying to help. If he did not have the strength to raise himself, he could help her raise him, and together they got him out of his shirt.

Now he lay atop the bed, clad only in his longjohns, the right leg bloody from short of the hip to below the knee. He was starting to shiver now, given to violent spasms, and Leslie was frightened. She was tempted to strip off the underwear, but something about rendering him naked stopped her. No matter what the need, she could not bring herself to do that.

But she had to get him warm. She had to do something for him. She knew that getting him under the covers would help, but the bed had lain open since she had left it and, even if she could stretch him out in it and pull the sheets, blankets and comforter over him, his own body temperature was so low that it would do him little good.

Yet she could not leave him exposed. She felt his cold feet and rubbed them, then his hands, but it was of little avail. His shiverings and spasms continued.

Leslie tucked his feet under the sheets and pulled the covers up to his chin, pushing them in tight around his face. Still, he lay there as if dead, except that he shivered and shook.

Leslie wished she could call for help, call for hot water, for hot irons wrapped in towels to put around his feet, for a fire he could be moved close to. Yet she dared not. She had to help him herself, but what could she do? He had to be made warm and there was no heat.

Again it was mechanical. Leslie didn't think it out, she just started undressing. And when she was stripped as far as she could without being totally bare, she got under the covers with Stephen, put her arms around him and tried to warm him with her own body.

How cold he was. She thought about his wound, but attention to that would come later. The first thing was to overcome his violent chills.

For a long time he kept trembling and shaking, lying still, with his eyes closed. And for a long time, Leslie, absorbing the cold of his body, wondered whether she would ever succeed or whether he would ultimately drain the heat out of both of them.

Slowly, however, her hugging and squeezing, her lying on top of him, pressing her legs against him, her arms around his, her head against his chin, began to take effect. Slowly the shuddering and shaking lessened and grew still. Slowly his body began to warm hers back. Slowly he was coming to life. She could feel the blood coursing through his veins once more, she could feel his strength reviving, the vibrance starting to return.

And the more like Stephen Crawford he became, the more his maleness came through to her and the more her femaleness responded. She began to tremble. Never before had she been so close to a man. Never had she been in so tight an embrace. Never had she and a man been so near nakedness together, lying snuggled under the covers. Never had she felt the stirrings of emotion that were gripping her now, strong, frightening emotions that made her want to stay with him and find ways of getting still closer, emotions she knew a girl shouldn't feel, that she didn't know she had.

His hand moved, the first response he had given. It started to inch around her waist and Leslie was seized with a sudden terror. She jumped from Stephen and the bed itself as if catapulted. Then she was standing beside it, trembling as violently as he had been. "No, please," she said desperately. "You mustn't."

He was regarding her weakly from the bed, her flushed face

and tumbled hair, her figure, covered by only the thinnest of undergarments. "I know," he whispered. "I didn't mean to. You shouldn't come so close."

"I wasn't—it wasn't— I was only trying to get you warm."

He nodded feebly. "Thank you. You saved me."

"You're better? You're warmer?"

"I'm getting too much better."

"Your wound—" She gestured at his blanket-covered leg. "We should look at it?"

"In a little while. It's still numb."

"You should have a doctor."

"Later." He looked at her. "Leslie, would you put something on? You're driving me crazy."

CHAPTER FORTY-THREE

Though better, Stephen was far from well and he had slipped into slumber by the time Leslie, quivering with strange desires, had donned a robe, tied the sash, and, out of his sight, put hands to her hot, flushed cheeks. She awakened his animal instincts, she decided, and knew she should feel horror, but instead she felt excitement. Whatever she was doing to him, he was doing to her, and she found she liked it. She shouldn't, she knew, and wondered guiltily about George. What kind of a wife would she be if a strange man should arouse her in such a way? But perhaps, she told herself, she would feel the same sensations when she was with George. After all, she and he had not been in such an intimate situation. That was probably the reason, she decided, why girls were supposed to wear so much clothing and stay so far away from men. Because if they didn't, their animal passions would get the best of them. Now she was finding out what those animal passions were like, and she could well see the danger. Stephen was right. She must keep herself well covered and at a considerable distance.

Now, when she went back to him, she found his eyes were closed and his breathing even. She could not address herself to his wound then, but if it wasn't paining him, she was glad to leave it alone. Rest was the thing he needed most.

Rest was something she needed as well, and how was she going to get it with Stephen occupying the bed? She solved that problem by laying a blanket on the floor and taking a spare comforter from the closet shelf. Using the extra pillow, she tried to make herself comfortable on the floor.

The cause was hopeless. It wasn't the hardness of her bed that kept her awake, it was the turmoil of her situation. How long could she keep Stephen secreted in her room without its being known? How could she forestall Fanny Nils when she came to make the beds? What would happen to her reputation—to her engagement—if Stephen were discovered?

Then, there were her ambivalent feelings about Stephen himself. She knew he was some kind of villain, that she should hate and fear him, yet she was attracted. To a villain she felt attraction, while to George, her betrothed, a man who found favor in her uncle's eyes, she could only feel a sense of duty.

And George had deliberately tried to kill Stephen. Stephen seemed to be in no doubt of that, and much as she wanted to deny it, she believed him.

So Leslie tossed, turned and stared into the darkness. Once or twice she heard Stephen groan and wondered if the injured leg were waking him with pain and he was as sleepless as she. When she heard his restless stirrings, she was tempted to relight the lamp and see to his wound, but a strange fear kept her from it. Some instinct told her that if they were both awake together in the dead of night in her bedroom, wound or no, pain or no, no good would come of it.

Thus, it was a wretched and haggard Leslie who heard Fanny's morning rap. "It's seven-thirty, Miss Marsh," Fanny said in that slightly cracked, high-pitched, early-morning voice of hers. She twisted the knob but the door was locked. "It's locked, miss."

"Just leave the kettle by the door, please, Fanny, I'll get it later."

"But the fire. You'll be wanting me to build up the fire."

"I'll take care of it this morning, Fanny. I'm not quite ready for it yet."

"I see. Yes, miss," Fanny said disapprovingly. She wasn't accustomed to breaks in the routine. There was the sound of the kettle being placed on the floor. "You'll be wanting new towels and washcloth."

"Leave them with the kettle, Fanny. Thank you."

"Yes, miss." The voice held even more disapproval. There was the sound of them dropping, and footsteps retreated. Leslie, on her feet by now, advanced to the door and listened until there was silence. Then she turned the key, peeked out, made sure both corridors were empty, and brought in the appointments of the bath. She relocked the door, deposited the kettle and accessories on the washstand and, when she turned, found Stephen regarding her soberly from the bed.

He looked pale and his eyes stared at her from darkened hollows. He said hoarsely, "I've got to get out of here."

"Out of here?" She shook her head. "You are not well."

"If I stay, you'll be compromised. Already Fanny is suspicious. She knows something's not right in this room."

"She doesn't know what it is that isn't right."

"No, but she's going to be watching to find out. If anybody gets the idea that I've been in here, you're ruined."

"Nothing happened."

"You know that doesn't matter."

"But your leg. You can't just go. You're injured." She moved toward the bed. "Does it pain you much?"

"It throbs like a freight engine. It woke me scarce after I had gone to sleep, and has tortured me since."

"May I see?"

Stephen turned back the covers, exposing his leg and the blood-soaked woolen underwear he wore. "Scissors," he said, and when she brought them to him, he cut the leg of the underwear above the wound. The injury was high, near the hip, and Leslie gently pulled the severed legging down over his knee.

There was a small but ugly-looking hole in the front of his leg, and a jagged, larger hole in the back. Leslie discovered the second hole when she had him turn on his side.

"Oh no," she moaned. "It's worse than I thought. It's two wounds."

Stephen twisted to see and gently felt the large wound. "That's good," he said. "The bullet came out. It isn't festering inside."

"Good?" Leslie didn't fancy the looks of the large hole.

"And it missed the bone. I knew that last night because I could stand. I'm lucky."

Leslie knew nothing about bullets, but she sensed that Stephen did, and if things weren't as bad as he had feared, then her own mind was eased. Nevertheless, it wasn't as if nothing had happened. "But you should see a doctor," she said.

"All in good time. The main thing is to get me out of here."

That wasn't the main thing with her. "I think you should rest and regain some strength."

"Leslie," Stephen told her, "you have to wash and dress and go downstairs to breakfast, and while you are there, Mabel will come in to tidy your room. Already you've got Fanny worried because you wouldn't let her fix the fire. You can't go to breakfast and lock me in here, because then all kinds of rumors will break out in the servants' quarters. Do you know what servants talk about? The family. Do you know why? There is nothing else in this desolate place to talk about, except what happens to them on their days off. So the slightest deviation from the routine is the instant cause of intense speculation." Stephen looked hard at her. "Do you understand me, Leslie?"

Leslie nodded and conceded he couldn't stay. But what was she going to do with him?

Stephen had the logical answer. He would move to one of the two unoccupied guest rooms down the hall.

He acted upon the suggestion without giving Leslie a chance

to object. He pulled himself up and got into his trousers—at least got his left leg into his trousers. Try as he might, he could not manage his stiff, throbbing, wounded leg and Leslie had to assist him.

"I've got to get you to a doctor," she said in alarm as she helped him complete his excruciating task.

"All in good time," Stephen said, breathing heavily and resting from his exertions. He struggled to a sitting posture on the side of the bed. "But please. Don't tell anyone I'm in the house. Not anyone, do you understand?"

Leslie nodded and gave her assurance.

When Stephen was dressed, with his boots and outer garments in hand, she checked that the halls were empty and sent him quickly on his way. He was limping badly but, for all of that, he was far spryer than the man she had half dragged into her room those short hours before.

She locked her door behind him and felt relief in the act. Hiding him had put her under more tension than she had realized. It wasn't just that she was risking her reputation by keeping a man in her room, she was protecting an enemy of her uncle and her fiancé. She would not have liked trying to explain herself to them.

CHAPTER FORTY-FOUR

"Where the devil is my valet?" George said, entering the breakfast room while tying his tie. He was late and Leslie, Queenie and Uncle Walter were already on their eggs and sausage. Lambert entered from the kitchen with a pot of scalding coffee as the dark-haired young man helped himself to food at the buffet. "What about it, Lambert?" he said. "Where's Stephen this morning?"

Lambert said he hadn't seen him but he'd go rouse him. Perhaps he'd overslept.

"He'd better not have," George said tartly. "That's not what he's being paid for." He sat down, facing both Leslie and the kitchen door and looked around conspiratorially. "I don't know what he's up to, my dear," he said, talking to Leslie, yet addressing them all, "but while he's employed in this house he's going to earn his wages and do his job."

"Maybe he knows he's not going to be employed long," Walter said.

There were long looks and George put his finger to his lips. Very little of what went on in this house could escape the servants' attention.

George tucked his napkin in his neck and started on his eggs, and Leslie, watching him, realized that he had hardly noticed her this morning. He had not sought to kiss her cheek, he had not given her an especial greeting. Now he was bent over his plate, chewing noisily, and his thoughts seemed to be anywhere except on his surroundings.

"Everybody sleep well?" he said, chuckling with his mouth full and looking around.

Queenie and Walter grinned. It seemed like a private joke.

"How about you, dear?" George asked, looking now at Leslie. "I mean, after I shot the wretched beast?"

Leslie had trouble breathing. What was going on? How much did George know? "I slept all right," she said at last.

George was beaming. "I guess I got that critter. I guess we won't be bothered by any more wailing half the night long."

"Good shooting, George," Uncle Walter said. "You drop him dead?"

"Couldn't tell," George answered. "It was snowing too hard. But I know I hit him. I heard the critter yelp."

Leslie felt an icy twinge in her stomach. George sounded as if he really believed he had hit the dog, that he hadn't been gunning for a human target. Had Stephen lied to her? Was he using her against her own kin while he worked behind their backs? "You don't know what kind of animal you hit?" she said slowly.

George shook his head and stuffed more sausage in his mouth. "Naw. Like I told you last night, that beast was something I wasn't going near in the dark, even if I did have a gun." George gestured with his knife. "Not that I'm a coward, mind you, but if I'm going to take chances, I'm going to make sure I can see what I'm doing. Time enough to go see what I hit when I finish eating."

There was speculation then as to the nature of the beast and its purpose in coming around. The curiosity was so normal and the attitudes so natural, that Leslie began to think she was imagining things when she thought her uncle had blanched at its mournful howl.

Lambert came in through the kitchen door. "I'm sorry, sir," he said. "Stephen isn't in his room."

George, about to sip coffee, paused, then sneezed. Hot coffee slopped onto his hand and he yelped and put the cup down. "Close the damned door," he snapped. "Can't you feel the draft?"

"I'm sorry, sir." Lambert came quickly into the room and made sure the swinging door was shut. "I didn't realize—"

George was wiping his scalded hand with a white napkin and Lambert hurried around the table. "Some butter, sir."

"Get away," George snapped, working the thumb and fingers. "Damn it, it may blister." He put some butter on the injured tissue with his knife. "Now, then, what were you telling me?"

Lambert, flustered and uncertain, said, "Stephen isn't in his room, sir. He must be in another part of the house."

"Well, he's in the wrong part, wherever he is. He should have dressed me this morning. Go find him and tell him I want him."

"Yes, sir." Lambert withdrew quickly.

"Hey," George called, and the man came back. "Are you sure he's not in his room? You sure he's not snoring his head off in there?"

"Oh, yes, sir. I looked inside. I have a duplicate key to all the servants' rooms."

"All right, then go find him. I want him found immediately."

"Yes," Uncle Walter put in. "Today isn't his day off, yesterday was."

Lambert disappeared and George looked at all the others. "What do you think?" he asked uneasily. "You think he got what he came for and has run for it?"

Uncle Walter was scowling and making marks in the tablecloth with his fork. "I don't know," he said. "I don't know what he was after."

Queenie said, "Do you think he's stolen anything? What do you think he might have taken?"

Leslie shifted nervously in her seat. Stephen was in a guest room and even the most cursory search would uncover him. Then it would be learned that he had been shot by mistake and Leslie had been hiding him. All eyes would fix on her. Why hadn't she roused the household? Why didn't she seek help for the injured man? Where had she kept him and why? Leslie knew it was going to be very very bad.

All she could think of to say was, "If he's gone, don't you think Lambert would have told us his bags are missing?"

That impressed the others. They had to agree that Stephen must still be around the house, but where he might have gone remained a mystery.

When Lambert returned, the mystery grew even greater, at least for Leslie. Lambert reported that he and the upstairs maids had gone through all rooms (except the locked room, of course), had checked downstairs, and even in the cellar. They had looked under beds, in closets, and in the attic, and Stephen was not in the house.

CHAPTER FORTY-FIVE

Leslie all but gasped at Lambert's news. The idea that Stephen could have escaped detection had not occurred to her. What she also did not expect, and hardly noticed, were the meetings of eyes that went on among the other three finishing coffee at the table. The looks were accompanied by that slight nodding of heads and knowing glance that said, "We knew he wasn't here. We knew he had gone." It made Leslie dimly aware that, though she had expected Stephen to be found, they had not, and theirs was the expectation that had come to pass.

They arose from the breakfast table, leaving a mystified Lambert to ponder Stephen's doings, and George went directly to the clothes closet under the front-hall stairs to get into his boots and jacket. "Well, now," he said, "it's time I went out and saw what kind of a beast I hit last night. What do you think it'll be, Walt? A coyote, a wolf, a dog?"

"Maybe you only nicked it," Uncle Walter said. "Maybe it got away."

"Then I'll track it." George reached into the deep pocket of the jacket ad pulled out the revolver Leslie had taken from Stephen's trunk. "And with this gadget in my hand, I'll see to it he never bothers us again. You know, this is quite a thing to shoot. It's got a helluva kick to it."

The day outside was bright and cloudless, and eighteen inches of new-fallen snow had blanketed the landscape. It caused Walter to look out the window and remark, "Maybe it won't have left any tracks. It snowed most of the night."

"We'll see," George said confidently, starting for the kitchen. "We'll see."

Leslie followed with the others and they watched him embark. Fortunately for Leslie, the tracks that she and Stephen had made were totally covered and George could be seen struggling through a deep, pristine blanket.

After a moment, Uncle Walter went to his desk and Queenie went upstairs with Glenda. Leslie, however, remained at the window, ignoring the servants and wondering at Stephen. What magic had he worked so that, wounded and hardly able to get around, he had avoided discovery?

Out in the yard, George's dark figure slogged through the snow, his boots plowing a path into the distance. He moved confidently, enjoying the presence of the revolver in his pocket. It was a strange weapon to someone who had fired only muskets or shotguns theretofore, but he had mastered the art quickly and appreciated the value of a gun that could shoot six bullets without reloading.

And what would George think when he discovered nothing was out there lying half buried under the mantle of white? All that joy and confidence would be replaced by a slowly growing wrath that would turn into a towering anger that would make her afraid.

Leslie turned from the window with a shiver. Norma was washing the breakfast plates in the scullery, and Bessie was making early preparations for lunch. The other servants were elsewhere about their duties.

Leslie went upstairs and searched the guest rooms herself. Stephen had to be in one of them. She was sure he had bribed the maids—perhaps with nothing but a kiss—and she meant to find him. However, her search was fruitless. Gone not only was Stephen, but his jacket, hat, boots, mittens, everything. It was as if he had never been.

Leslie hurried to her own room. Perhaps he had returned to that. It, however, was equally empty. The bed had been made, there were new towels and a full pitcher on the washstand, but there was no sign of life.

Leslie, her hunt at an end, sat down on the bed. Stephen was most definitely not in the house. But where had he gone? and how?

Horses. Dandy! It came to her. Stephen would be struggling to get to a doctor. He had used her to keep his presence secret. Now, while she was eating, he had stolen off to make good his escape. But he could not escape without a horse. And the riding horse was Dandy. Stephen must be in the barn saddling Dandy! But there were no footprints in the snow. How did he get to the barn without leaving a trail? How did he get out of the house without being seen?

Then, suddenly, she knew. That draft that had made George sneeze and scald his hand, that hadn't been caused by Lambert coming in from the kitchen. It had come in through the front

214

door that Stephen was quietly opening and closing. Right now he was in the barn. She knew it.

Quickly she donned her winter things from her wardrobe, then slipped from her room and down the front stairs, making sure her progress went unwitnessed. She went out onto the porch, opening and closing the door so softly that only the chill air that drifted into the house betrayed the fact. The porch, the steps, and a path to the driveway had been shoveled, but this did not hide the evidence of Stephen's passage. At the bottom of the steps his tracks were evident, moving away from the path, circling the house to the east. The deep snow not only revealed his route, but that he was limping badly and dragging one leg.

Leslie went quickly down the steps after him. The air was crackly cold, the landscape a solid, unspoiled white, save only for the gray of far-off woods. The tracks Leslie followed stayed close to the house. His path took him under the windows so that no one inside could see.

Leslie, keeping herself as invisible as he, worked her way around the back of the dining room, past the scullery, to the windows of Lambert's room. Here she had to stoop, for the ground rose and the sills were no longer over her head.

She turned ninety degrees, ducking under Lambert's second window, under Harry Best's, and lastly, Stephen's. Then she was around the corner to the back of the quarters.

Stephen's path led to the window of his room that Leslie had entered. The sill was clean of snow, which told her he too had climbed inside. He was not still there, however, for the tracks continued on, out behind the plantings and fences that screened the path to the privy and, from there, across open snow to the back door of the barn. Leslie nodded in satisfaction. It was as she had expected.

She plowed after him, knowing he had a long headstart, yet confident he was still in the barn. No horse had tramped through the snow before George left the house, and she was sure no horse had tried to leave since. There would have been sounds and shouts. Stephen could hardly make an escape unnoticed.

215

Leslie crossed the open snow to the back entrance, where the tracks stopped. The door was small and slid on wheels along a steel track overhead, and it stood half ajar. She stepped onto the sill and looked inside.

Dandy, fully saddled, stood before the front doors opposite, while a sweating, struggling Stephen Crawford tried futilely to mount him.

CHAPTER FORTY-SIX

As Leslie watched, Stephen tried first to lift his crippled right leg into the stirrup, but he was unable to raise his foot high enough. He shook his head and hung onto the pommel and rear of the saddle to take as much of his weight as he could. Next he tried to lift his good leg. The injured leg, however, buckled instantly, and he nearly fell. He had obviously tried that before and it worked no better this time. Finally, he tried to spring aboard the horse, but he could only leap with one leg and he fell heavily against Dandy, who was forced to give way a step and, regaining balance, stand patiently.

It was then that Stephen, mumbling curses, leaning his weight against the horse, resting his leg and massaging it, saw Leslie in the doorway. He started, gave the quick look of a trapped animal, and said, "Are you alone?"

Leslie nodded and stepped inside. "What are you trying to do?"

"It's pretty evident, isn't it?" he said, panting. "I'm trying to get astride Dandy. Maybe you can give me a hand."

"Where do you want to go with Dandy?" Leslie asked. She stood where she was and her voice was cool. He had used her to hide; now he wanted to use her to escape.

216

"To a doctor," he said. "I've got to get to a doctor." He was flushed and perspiring. "Help me."

She might have believed him, and certainly he was in need of medical attention, but she had noted his snowless windowsill and she knew that, in the midst of his flight, he had taken time out to climb into his room. It was obviously to get something, and Leslie knew he was after his gun.

"You don't want to go anywhere," she said.

"Oh, but I do. But I can't mount the horse."

"You should have hitched Brindle to the carriage."

"I think maybe I should."

"Except you were afraid someone on Dandy could catch you?"

"Yes."

"Why?"

Stephen, still resting against Dandy, stroked her rump briefly. "I told you last night. Because George tried to kill me."

"Or so you say."

"It's true, even if he is your fiancé."

"You know about that?"

Stephen smiled, albeit dryly. "Servants know more of what goes on than you think." He sighed. "We're talking and time is passing. Would you help me, Leslie?"

"I don't think you want to leave right now," she answered. "George is outside with a gun."

She detected a quiver in Stephen. He said, "Looking for me?"

"Looking for what he hit last night. He thinks it's a dog."

"It *is* a dog. A lame dog."

"What do you know about that dog?"

"I don't know anything."

"You do. It called me to you last night and then disappeared. Why?"

"I don't know the animal, Leslie. I've set out food for it and tried to befriend it because I want to know. I want to find out whose it is and why it comes around." He shook his head. "It's let me come near, but not too near. Not yet, at least."

"Well, that's what George thinks he hit."

"You don't think he aimed at me?"

"Deliberately try to shoot an unarmed man? Never. It was an accident. He and Queenie and Uncle Walter were talking about it at breakfast. He thinks he hit an animal. He isn't aware he hit anything else."

"You know better. At least you did last night."

Leslie felt color come into her face. "Just because I helped you—"

"You know things," Stephen said, testing his weak leg and wincing. "You know a lot of things, Leslie. You know, for example, *why* George wants to kill me."

"I do not. He doesn't want to kill you." She defended him hotly. "He's no killer."

Stephen shook his head. "You didn't talk that way last night, my girl. When I told you he shot me, though I had called his name, you did not challenge the claim. You did not say, in righteous wrath, that your fiancé could never in his life do such a thing. You knew he could. You knew he had reason to. You know why he wants me dead." Stephen pointed a finger at her. "*I* don't, but *you* do!"

Leslie stood straighter. She was not going to give ground. "Are you sure you don't?" she said haughtily. "Do you really believe he has no reason to fear you?"

"Fear *me?*"

"You've been found out," Leslie said. "You've been seen spying, snooping, prying into places you should not be. You are very clever, Mr. Crawford. You have fooled a lot of us for a very long time, but in the end you have been found out."

The flush of effort that had been on Stephen's face was gone now and his skin was pale. Leslie, aware of his pallor, eyed him ever more critically. He was facing a reality he hadn't expected. For a moment, he looked tempted to ask in innocent tones what it was that had been discovered. He could read knowledge in her eyes, however, and a certain gleam came into his own. "This was *your* doing, wasn't it?" he asked.

"I passed along certain information, yes."

"Like what?" Stephen's face had grown dark, making Leslie

suddenly aware that they were alone together and no one else in the world knew where she was. She did not feel more than a passing moment of concern, however, for Stephen's injury rendered him incapable of catching her, and his strength had been so sapped by his wound that, even if he could, she would be able to hold her own.

Therefore, instead of cringing or drawing back at Stephen's anger, Leslie stepped forward. "Like prying through my uncle's desk," she said. "Like sneaking into his bedroom when he and Queenie weren't around. Like the way you got your job here. You came here to hurt my uncle and you aren't going to succeed." Leslie's eyes flashed fire. She was protective toward her family and she would cast off those who would do it harm.

Stephen, resting lightly against Dandy, pursed his lips. "That explains it, then," he said. "These are things you found out, didn't you?"

"I'm not saying."

Stephen even laughed. "You don't have to. I already know. None of the others are as bright as you. None of the others know as much as you. You found me out and you told them, isn't that right?"

Leslie lifted her chin. "Yes."

Stephen laughed without mirth. "And what is it that you conclude I am after? Do you think it's the combination to a safe full of stocks and bonds? Do you think I'm after the family jewels? Does your uncle have a million dollars lying loose that I'm planning to steal? What is it that I'm supposed to be after?"

"I don't know."

"But George tried to kill me, and you believe that—or you did last night. What can I do to him that would make him act in so desperate a fashion?"

"I don't know, but I'm sure *you* do."

Stephen shook his head. "I don't know either. Not if what you're telling me is true. I can't imagine why your uncle would want to do more than throw me out of the house for looking through his papers. Believe me, there's nothing in them that makes any sense."

"Nothing you're saying makes any sense either."

Stephen laughed with a sudden sadness. "You have no idea how fetching you are, standing there in righteous indignation. You are too good for the likes of George. Much too good."

Leslie said dryly, "I'm more for the likes of you, I suppose."

"I'd give the earth if that were so," Stephen replied. "But that seems not to be my fate. I would like, however, since you have caught me in shameful deeds, to tell you what motivated me, why it is that I came to Fletcher, why I tried to work my way into the household, and why I wanted to see your uncle's papers. It was not to rob him, as you presume. It was not to do him any harm at all. It was, rather, to keep him from doing harm to others."

"That's ridiculous," Leslie answered tartly. "My uncle is an honorable man. He wouldn't harm anyone."

"This is what we've always believed," Stephen responded. "That is, my family—my father."

"*Your* father?" Leslie did not understand any of this.

"My father and your uncle," Stephen said, "have had large business dealings together over the past few years. With them, a handshake has been enough. But something happened. Over the past couple of months your uncle has behaved very strangely. A meeting just before Christmas that he was supposed to attend he did not come to, nor did he send word. He had committed himself to a certain course of action. He had given my father assurances, and my father entered into certain transactions accordingly. My father did certain things—made certain deals and commitments on the basis of agreements previously made with your uncle.

"But then, when he was supposed to carry out his agreements, your uncle didn't show up. He did not send word, he did nothing. When my father wrote him, seeking reassurance, your uncle wrote back in such vague, general terms, that my father had the very great fear that he was being betrayed."

Leslie said staunchly, "I'm sure my uncle wouldn't betray anybody."

Stephen nodded quickly. "This is what we hoped. Because, if it was your uncle's purpose to betray my father and throw in with another group, a group that my father has been fighting, this could very well ruin my father. Surely you can see what kind of position this put my father in."

Leslie nodded with a quick movement, but remained silent.

"My father tended to believe this could not happen. He's known your uncle for more than twenty years and trusts him. Now, then, I did not know your uncle and, with all due respect to your feelings about him and my father's feelings about him, I was not nearly as sure of his honesty as you and my father were. The fact that his betrayal could ruin my father gave him enormous power. If he threw in with this other group, that should not bring him as much financial gain as teaming up with my father, but there are games within games here and, because of your uncle's behavior, I was very suspicious as to his motives.

"There wasn't much my father could do except, perhaps, to hedge his bets, pull back and set up defenses. He couldn't, of course, say to your uncle, 'What are your intentions towards me?' My father could do nothing but retreat.

"I didn't want to see that happen unless it was necessary. I proposed to my father that, since your uncle did not know me, I come out here to Fletcher and try, by whatever means I could, to find out what your uncle was up to. If your uncle meant to continue the relationship, we would both do very well. If your uncle merely wanted to remain neutral, my father would do quite well. If, however, your uncle was going to throw in with the other side, then we would have to take fast steps to avoid disaster."

Stephen shrugged. "I came as a spy. It was my choice and my responsibility. I frankly did not expect to gain access to the house. I fully expected to spend my time renting a room from the Cranstons and trying to pick up what I could around town—from the servants I could befriend, from the girls, from the family members I could befriend. My father knows I am doing this, though he did not approve. He can't, however, stop me, and I know he reads the weekly reports I send him." Stephen gave his bitter laugh again. "The trouble is, I'm doing all this and nothing I discover does me any good. Worst of all, I meet the girl of my dreams, and she's on the other side."

CHAPTER FORTY-SEVEN

Leslie held very still through all of this. She tried not to believe it when he called her the girl of his dreams, but it was hard, just as it was hard not to believe the story he told. It sounded so sensible, it answered so many questions.

Stephen, turning in the ensuing silence, started to unsaddle Dandy. Leslie watched for a bit and said, "Did you find what you wanted?"

"I found *whom* I wanted," Steve answered, unfastening the cinches. "I didn't find *what* I wanted."

She felt her heart stop again. What was the matter with her? She had to keep her mind on the things at hand. "You saw the papers in my uncle's desk," she said. "Didn't they tell you whether he was honest or not?"

"You know about that?"

"I watched you that night. I told my uncle what you had done."

Stephen looked at her quickly. "Is that why George tried to kill me?"

Leslie shook her head. "He didn't try to kill you. You're mistaken. What would he do that for?"

"I don't know. There was nothing in the papers that made any sense." He lifted the saddle from Dandy's back and hobbled awkwardly to hang it on its peg. Leslie moved quickly. "Let me." He would not let her take it, but he let her help. Stephen returned and backed the horse into his stall before slipping off his halter. He turned to Leslie. "Where did your uncle go on his trip?"

"To Colorado to look over his properties."

"Then, why did he go east to Chicago when the train has to go through Fletcher anyway? And why did he come back from Chicago when the return train stops at Fletcher—on a different day?"

Leslie hadn't thought of that. "He has business offices in Chicago," she said defensively. "He undoubtedly had matters to take care of before he came home from the trip."

"Granted that's possible," Stephen allowed. Then he said, "What do you know about a man named Leonard James?"

Leslie blinked. "I?" She shook her head. "You're the one who knows. You and Uncle Walter."

"Your Uncle Walter does, but I don't. That's the name I kept finding in your uncle's desk. Papers that were signed by him. Statements in his handwriting, all having to do with household goods—supplies that salesmen in wagons sell from house to house."

"You mean you think my uncle's getting into the housewares business?"

"He's not getting into it, he's in it. And my father's never heard him mention it. It's a totally new thing."

"I've never heard him mention it either."

"No, and he keeps the papers locked up tight in his desk. It's a big secret, but I don't know why. The papers aren't anything but sales reports—Leonard James's sales reports. Why doesn't he want anyone to know how many pots and pans Leonard James sells door to door?"

"I'm sure he doesn't care who knows," Leslie said. But then she remembered how carefully he locked his desk and the dismay and pallor that had come into her uncle's face when he learned that Stephen knew about Leonard James. No question about it. The matter was meant to be secret.

Stephen was alert to her uncertainty. "You hesitate," he said. "You don't really believe that."

And Leslie, in all honesty, had to say, "No. He's my uncle and I believe him, but there's something there, and I don't know what."

"Would it have to do with that locked room up on the second floor that everybody tiptoes around? What's he got in there?"

"Nothing," Leslie answered quickly. "He doesn't have anything in there."

"You're sure it's not full of household wares? You're sure he's not opening a store?"

"You're being silly."

"Of course I'm being silly, but I don't know what's silly and what isn't silly around here. Your uncle locks papers in a desk that don't need to be hidden. They deal with businesses he's never shown an interest in before, businesses that, on the surface at least, there's no reason to keep quiet about. The place where his own papers are kept is in the desk in his bedroom—yes, I've been through those, and you know it—but there's nothing among those papers that shows he's trying to cheat my father, or anybody else. Everything is straightforward, yet the whole family goes into a panic when they learn I've been looking at their records. They don't fire me, accost me, accuse me. Instead, they sneak out at night and try to shoot me. And don't tell me it was an accident, my dear Leslie. I know your feelings towards George, but please allow me the conclusions of my own experiences."

"I don't believe you," Leslie said. "George went out to shoot that beast and the beast stopped howling, and George thought he'd hit him."

"All very easy to explain, right? Except, why does a lame dog come around and howl at night? And why is it that all the servants are new? What happened to the old ones?"

"Some were thieves. They were stealing."

Stephen frowned. "There's something in that locked room on the second floor. I know it."

"There isn't," Leslie answered tartly. "Queenie keeps it locked because it's full of bloodstains."

Stephen looked at her. "It's full of what?"

"Bloodstains."

"Whose bloodstains?"

"Rufus Morgate's, the man who built this house. He was murdered in that room. That's why Queenie keeps it locked up."

"Did she tell you that?"

The conversation got no further. There was a sound against the barn and it moved to the door. Stephen put an instant finger to his lips and looked around. Then he more leaped than hobbled, grabbing Leslie by the hand, dragging her to the great pile of hay that filled the half of the barn opposite the stalls. He pulled

her with him into the hay, burying them both, as the barn door
slid open. "Ssh," he whispered and held her still as there came the
sound of people entering.

Leslie held her breath and trembled. She didn't have to be
warned to silence. Every instinct in her body told her she must
not be found.

CHAPTER FORTY-EIGHT

The first voice was George's and he said, "No, the horses are all
here." There was bitterness and frustration in the tone.

Leslie heard Uncle Walter respond. "Then, where the hell did
he go?"

"I don't know," George snapped. "If I knew, do you think I'd
be looking for him?"

Uncle Walter wasn't happy about things either. "I don't think
you even hit him. You probably never even saw him."

"Of course I hit him! I dropped him, God damn it."

"Like hell. He was playing possum on you. You thinking he
was going to freeze to death in the snow. He fooled you. Now
there's no telling where he's gone. He could be fifty miles away
by now."

"I hit him," George answered irritably. "I ought to know
when I hit something."

"Well, if you hit him, where is he? If he was so crippled by
your fine marksmanship, what happened to him?"

"Listen," George snarled, "I didn't bring you out here to
bellyache. I got you out here to help me find the dastard. I hit
him, I tell you. Even if he's not hurt bad, the only way he can
get out of here is with a horse."

225

"Why did you leave him? Why didn't you go see? What were you scared of? Now he's got away."

The pair moved around the barn, leaving the stalls and roaming, looking for clues. "I wasn't scared, you God-damned fool," George snapped. "What do you think I'm going to do, put a second bullet into him?"

"It would have been a damned sight smarter than coming back to the house crowing about solving all our problems."

"Maybe you didn't stop to think that one bullet is an accident, but two bullets makes it deliberate. And it's me, not you, pulling the trigger. Maybe you didn't stop to think about that—or maybe you did. Maybe that's just what you *did* think about."

They were standing beside the giant pile of hay, not more than five feet from where Leslie was buried. The covering over her was thin and she was sure that patches of her jacket must be visible. At that close range, Uncle Walter's voice boomed stridently: "I'm not thinking anything of the kind. What I'm thinking is that you shot that revolver at the sky and then came back and reported that we would have no more trouble. Only now you go out and can't find what it was you were supposed to have hit, and you come back to Queenie and me and want us to help you hunt for your supposed victim." Uncle Walter's voice became even more harsh. "You failed, George. You promised us a victim and you have no victim."

"I didn't shoot at the sky," George shrieked. "I hit him. I know I did."

"Tell it to your mother."

"I'm not going to tell it to my mother. Give me some help, damn it. What are you alive for?"

"I'm alive," Uncle Walter answered, acidly, "for the sole purpose of keeping *you* alive." He went on: "If you are smart, George, you will go back to the house with me and confer with your mother. I think she knows better than you."

The pair moved away and when heard next, George was saying, by Dandy's stall, "Damn it, there's no way the man could have walked away."

Then the voices faded, followed by the sound of the barn door shutting.

Leslie, more in relief than of need, sneezed, and Stephen, casting off their covering, smiled. "Thank you for not doing that earlier."

Leslie came up out of the straw beside him. Her eyes were round. "They were looking for you!"

"Yes," he nodded. "They were."

"They really meant to kill you."

Stephen's face was solemn and his eyes had a faraway look. "I think you have your tense wrong, Leslie. They mean, and will mean, to kill me."

"But you haven't done anything."

"I haven't done anything worthy of being killed for, that I'll agree. But that's not *their* view. And I don't know why."

"And if you're smart," Leslie said, seizing his arm, "you won't stay around to find out. Let me hitch up the wagon and—"

Stephen put a hand on her hand. "Now, Leslie," he said, "let's not be too hasty. Let us keep our wits about us."

"But you're in danger."

"So are you, if you insist on staying here."

"I'm not going to stay here, but you mustn't either. If I hitch Brindle—"

"If you hitch Brindle and I ride out on her, you're going to be in trouble. Do you realize that, young miss?"

"I don't care. I'm not going to have you harmed."

"And, my dear, sweet child, I'm not going to have you harmed. So what—" He put a finger to her mouth to silence her. "Hush, my sweet. What you are to do is go back to the house— and do it as stealthily as you can. And whatever you do, don't let anyone know where I am."

"Never. Not ever," she breathed.

"Then I, when the coast is clear, will get away. But only after you have gone back to the house and are not in any danger."

"Yes, but where will you go?"

"I should go to a doctor, don't you think?"

"In Fletcher."

"Of course, in Fletcher. Doctor Payne."

"I won't tell anyone. And I'll come see you."

"If you do, I'll kiss you."

Leslie stopped and blushed, moving flustered hands. "Stop it, will you?"

"You like being kissed."

"Please," she said desperately. "Will you be serious?"

"I will be serious—so long as you come and see me. But please don't bring your family."

"You aren't being serious at all. Stephen, you have got to be careful."

"That," he answered, being very serious, "is true. Now go, will you? And would you hand me that scrap of wood over there?"

"Listen, if you think you're going to whittle napkin rings—"

"Fetch, Fido. Please?"

Leslie climbed over the low rail of the hay crib to get it for him. "What do you want a piece of wood for?" she asked, bringing it back.

"Never you mind," he said. "Tell me, are you still in love with George?"

"In love with him?"

"You're supposed to marry him."

"Yes, but I—don't—"

"But you don't love him."

"I didn't say that."

"You don't have to."

"I don't think I know what love is."

She was standing before him, the piece of wood in her hand, her eyes questioning. Stephen said, very seriously, "I think you do," and then he folded her in his arms.

His kiss was deep and savoring and Leslie, enveloped and defenseless, felt the strength go out of her so that she could not have stood had not Stephen been holding her so tightly. Then, brazenly, helplessly, she was kissing him back and her arms grew taut around him, trying to embrace him as closely as he was holding her. She felt wanton, and she knew she shouldn't. For the moment, though, she didn't care. She didn't want to think about George or her uncle or what might happen next. For just this one moment she would let herself go completely and accept the kisses and caresses of this man who held such a power over her as she had not suspected one person could have over another.

She pulled herself together at last and pushed him away, for it was clear he would not be the one to stop. "You must behave," she said, catching her breath.

"You're not going to marry George, you're going to marry me."

"Stop it. I'm not going to marry anybody right now. I've got to go back to the house and see what's happening."

"Tell me you're not going to marry George."

"Please, please. I have to go."

He held her hand. "Tell me."

"All right, I'm not going to marry George." Then, because she had a sudden craving, she kissed him quickly and broke away.

"What's that for?" he asked.

"Because I felt like it." Then she darted back to the rear barn door, looked out quickly, and then hurried into the brisk, frigid air, back across the snow, around the screening, to the path that led to the privy and, via that, to the back door of the house.

She found Queenie, George and Uncle Walter by the hall closet. The men were taking off their things and all were in a conspiratorial conversation that ceased upon Leslie's appearance. "Oh," she said. "You're back. What did you find?"

"Damned dog got away," George said.

"You're sure it's a dog?"

"I ought to know. I got a shot at it last night."

"I thought you hit it."

"I thought I did too. Damned if I know what happened out there."

Uncle Walter said, "Well, at least you drove it away."

"I don't know where I drove it," George said, hanging up his heavy coat and shaking his head, mystified.

CHAPTER FORTY-NINE

Leslie spent the rest of an anxious morning working with needle and thread close to the window from which she could see the yard, the barn, and the projection of the servants' quarters. From that vantage point she could monitor who came and went from the back porch and whether their route was to the barn or the privy. She had to hope that the latter path was sufficiently well screened to bar notice of her crisscross trail.

The morning passed without event, but at lunch she sensed from the others that Stephen's whereabouts was a matter of undiminished concern. George had ordered the sleigh made ready and talked of business in town that afternoon. Nor did he suggest that his newly won fiancée accompany him. Leslie asked no questions, but many were on her mind. Was George tracking Stephen? Was he, perhaps, going to visit the Cranstons to see if their old boarder had returned? Was he going to check the inns for late arrivals the night before? Would he ask Dr. Payne about a patient with a bullet hole?

There was an air of mystification at the table as well, a kind of unease. George, Queenie and her uncle were not the vibrant, cocksure trio she had seen at breakfast. The bold George who had gone confidently forth with a revolver to look for the "animal" he had shot, had been replaced by a puzzled George who did not quite know how to explain matters. Equally at a loss were Queenie and Uncle Walter. If Stephen had fled in the night, why had he not taken one of the horses? If he were in hiding, where were his tracks? He had vanished into the air, and since they did not know how he had accomplished the feat, they did not know when or where he might reappear.

It was well after George's departure, when the servants had cleaned away the luncheon things and were taking their respite, that Leslie made her next attempt to see Stephen. Putting on a wrap, she grabbed half a loaf of bread from the pantry and went outside, following the path toward the privy till she reached her detour to the back door of the barn.

She slipped through, closing it behind her, and looked around.

The big doors opposite were shut and the vast interior was dim and quiet. Swift, having prepared the sleigh for George, had long since gone.

Leslie moved to the stored hay where she and Stephen had hidden and called his name softly. There was no response. She frowned and circled around to the stalls. Amos and Dandy snorted and stamped, but otherwise it was silent.

"Stephen," Leslie called again, a little louder. He had to be somewhere.

A soft answer made her turn but she saw no one. "Where are you?"

"Up here."

She was standing by the ladder beside Brindle's stall, and when she looked up she saw his face peering down at her from the hay loft above. "How did you get up there?"

He grinned. "By the ladder, but it wasn't easy."

"Are you all right?"

"Of course. Anyone know you're here?"

"No." She held up the bread. "I brought you some food." She tested the first rung of the ladder and mounted it carefully. He held it in place while she climbed up to him, and when her head came above the loft level he extended a hand. "Here, I'll help you."

"No, I'm not coming any higher. I can't stay."

"But you came."

"I thought you must be hungry." She gave him the bread. "I couldn't bring water. Would you like some snow?"

"No, but thanks for the bread. It's the finest feast I've ever had." He laughed and leaned forward to kiss her on the mouth. "But if you're going to run all this risk, you might as well come up here and keep me company for a bit to make it worthwhile."

"No. If I come up there, you're just going to kiss me."

"Of course." He kissed her again as she stood on the ladder. "After all, if you're going to marry me—"

"I'm not going to marry you. Where did you get that idea?"

"When you told me you weren't going to marry George." He kissed her again.

231

"Stop it. If you keep kissing me, I'm going to fall off this ladder. Besides, I've got things to tell you. George has gone into town. I think he's looking for you."

"What makes him think I'm in town?"

"Because he doesn't know what happened to you and he wants to find out. At least that's what I think he wants."

"But you don't have any idea what he's got against me?"

"No, but it's something. I can tell. Which is why you've got to get away. But you can't go now, because he's gone and you'll meet him. And I think he's got your gun."

"Because you gave it to him."

Leslie nodded. "I'm sorry. I didn't know."

"You're forgiven." He kissed her again. "I can't stand having you look so forlorn."

"But if he really wants to kill you—"

"He does. Believe me."

"All right, when he comes back, then you can saddle Dandy again—"

"Can you do something for me?"

"What?"

"Can you get me a key to that locked room?"

Leslie gasped. "What?"

"A key to the locked room. I want to see what's inside the locked room."

"But I told you what's inside."

"No you didn't. You told me what Queenie *said* was inside. But she's lying. There wasn't any murder in that room."

"How do you know?"

"Because Rufus Morgate and his family were very much alive when they sold the house to your uncle."

"You must be mistaken."

"The Cranstons knew them, Leslie. The Cranstons were friends of theirs and they told me about them. The murder tale is a lie, Leslie, to keep you from going near the place. There's something in that room they don't want anybody to see, and I want to get in there and take a look."

"You can't," Leslie whispered. "They'll find you. You've got to get away, to a doctor, to safety. They're trying to kill you."

232

"And that room must be the reason why. There isn't any other reason."

"But you can't get in. That's all there is to it. The door's locked. I don't know where the key is. I don't know if there even is a key."

"Queenie has the key, you can bet on it."

"It wouldn't be where anybody can find it, though. Not if she really doesn't want anybody going in there."

"Maybe your uncle—maybe if you sweet-talked him—"

Leslie shook her head vehemently. "I can't. I wouldn't. I wouldn't dare. If you're right and it has something to do with why they want to kill you, then they won't like me even asking about a key, let alone letting me have one. They'd want to know why, and if I got persistent—honest Injun, Steve, I'd be scared."

Stephen patted her hand. "You're right. I've no business asking you to do anything like that. You wouldn't know where Queenie or your uncle might hide such a key, would you?"

"No, and I don't want you looking. You've got to get out of here. Besides, you've been through their things. If there are any keys, you're the one who'd know where they are."

"Yes, you're right. And I never saw any."

"Forget about the room. Forget about business deals. You get away from here and get your father to come see Uncle Walter. That would be the best way to do it. Uncle Walter wouldn't cheat anybody. I'll bet if your father were to just ask him plain outright, he'd explain the whole thing."

"Yes, I'll just bet. Especially if George has my gun."

"My uncle is a fine man. I know he is. If he knew you're not really a spy—"

"Don't you dare tell him about me," Stephen said. "Not a word."

"All right, but you've got to escape. You've got to go. You can't stay here."

"Yes, you're right."

"As soon as you get the chance."

Stephen laughed and kissed her as she started down the ladder, but he didn't look convinced.

233

George didn't return until just before dinner, and he'd been doing more than "conduct business" or search for Stephen. He'd been drinking. Leslie, on hand with Queenie and Uncle Walter to welcome him, could detect the slight weave in his step, the slight blowsiness in his manner. But if he'd been drinking, it hadn't been in celebration. His face was grim and sullen, his brow furrowed in still deeper puzzlement. And, though Leslie was his fiancée and the professed love of his life, his eyes were on Queenie and Uncle Walter and he treated her almost as an underfoot encumbrance he couldn't wait to slough off so that he could get into conference with the others.

All through the dinner that followed, Leslie had trouble sitting still. Conversation was tense and she knew that much was on everyone's mind. George, Queenie and Uncle Walter were disturbed by Stephen, though they never mentioned his name, whereas in the servants' hall curiosity ran rife and his was the only name spoken.

As for Leslie, she hardly touched her plate. What was Stephen doing at that moment? Was he saddling Dandy? Had he already made his escape? It was dark and George was back, so the coast was clear. Was he taking the sleigh? How much headstart could he get before Swift would find one of the horses missing? Though Leslie tried to concentrate on the meaningless conversation, her thoughts and attention were directed at what went on among the servants and what they would discover.

No messages were delivered, however. Swift did not report that a horse was stolen. No one brought word that the missing valet had been found. The ritual of the meal was fulfilled as if nothing out-of-the-way had been transpiring.

It was more than Leslie could bear and, at its conclusion, she pleaded a headache and retired to her room. The only way she could hide her increasing nervousness was to flee the scene, nor did her equally nervous family seek to delay her. They were as eager to stop dissembling before her as she was before them.

Though her room was a refuge, it was for Leslie, equally a

prison. It was not her room she wanted to be in, but the barn. Had Stephen gone yet? She was dying to know, but she was powerless to find out. The family was up and the servants were only just finishing their chores and preparing for social activity. Leslie thought she would go crazy if she had to wait for the house to quiet down, for the household members to go to bed. Yet there was no alternative and she paced the floor and washed and bathed and read and did everything she could think of to make the time pass.

When the hall clock struck ten, Leslie was sure she could slip out to the barn unnoticed. But no. A glance from her windows told her that lights were still on all over the house. It didn't matter where George or Queenie or Uncle Walter were—the servants were still up.

Leslie waited another half hour until the living-room lights went out, then opened her door and listened. The house had still not settled down for the night. Damn it, what were people doing up and around?

Leslie made herself stay still until midnight, though it all but cost her her sanity. When she finally opened her door to the dim glow of the gaslights and realized that slumber, or at least retirement, had at last overcome the household, she was still fully dressed. Nor was she wearing the gown she had been seen in at dinner. She was in coarser garb, outdoor garments and warm woolens that would protect her against the bitter cold of a northern February.

Now, sensing the way was clear, she tiptoed quickly to the head of the stairs and down to the front hall. Fearing being seen should she go through the kitchen, she slipped out through the front door and took the dark east route around the house through the deep snow. All the servants' rooms were dark now and no one but she was stirring. With her clothes only whispering through the snow, she made her way to the rear barn door and slid it open. The interior was blacker than the night, but directly across from her gleamed a tall, narrow slot of light. The front barn door was ajar, and it was the glow from the post lantern that filled the gap.

Stephen was gone, she thought. He had made away on Dandy and she had missed him. She could breathe relief, but even as she did, she felt a sense of loss. She had wanted to *help* him escape.

Or could Swift have left the door ajar? She had to be sure that Stephen was indeed gone. Leslie removed a glove and groped carefully beside the door for the lantern that hung there and the box of matches on the beam beside. Ah, there was the metal base of the lantern, there was its glass chimney. And there were the matches. Leslie lighted a match, a large wooden splinter that threw an orange glow all over the barn. She lifted the lantern's chimney and realized, as she did, that it was warm. The lantern had not long ago been lit.

She touched the burning splinter to the wick, watched it leap with flame and settle to a steady, comforting glow. She slid the chimney back in place and looked around.

Stephen, she discovered, had not fled, after all. From their near stalls, Brindle and Dandy stared at her curiously while Amos, the dray horse, snorted from the one beyond. The sleigh and carriage were in place. She began to worry again. What was keeping him? Why had he not left?

Leslie looked to the hayloft, thinking to see his face at the edge, but there was nothing. She thought to climb up for a look and discovered the ladder was missing. Stephen was gone and the ladder was gone.

She turned to the gap in the barn doors, wonderingly, and as she did, Stephen hobbled through it. "The light," he whispered hoarsely. "Put out the light!"

She quickly did as she was bid and Stephen, close to her, said, "Anybody looking out the windows might see it."

"I didn't realize," she answered. "I wasn't thinking."

He left her, limping back through the doors, and she followed. "What are you doing?" she whispered. "Why aren't you gone?"

Then she saw what he was up to. The ladder was propped against the house where the top just reached the sill of the open window to the locked room. "Stephen," she whispered. "You're crazy."

"I'm curious."

"But you can't get up there. You could hardly get to the loft. Stephen, you've got to get to a doctor."

"If I'm ever going to get into that room it's got to be now."

She trailed him to the ladder, still carrying the lantern and matches, and she walked slowly, staying behind him. Stephen was so weak, she thought, so crippled. He tried not to show it, but he was in pain. He wanted to limp more than he let himself, wanted to go more slowly than he dared let her see.

They were at the foot of the ladder now, close enough to the house to avoid accidental discovery, and she felt relief. The trip from the barn door across the lighted yard was the danger.

Leslie peered up at the dim dark open window above. Why that one lone window was open had always puzzled her. Now it provided their entry, which might provide a reason.

"Let me have your lantern," Stephen whispered.

"Stephen, you can't climb that ladder."

"Yes, I can." He held out his hand. "I need the lantern."

She gave it to him, and the box of matches. He stuffed the matches in his pocket, put the handle of the lantern between his teeth, gripped the ladder hard with both hands to ease the weight on his wounded leg, and gained the first rung with the other. When he tried to shift weight to the weak leg again, however, he gasped in pain and couldn't do it. He tried to adjust his foot more securely.

Leslie, beside him, holding the ladder, said, "Stephen, you can't do it. Will you please, for heaven's sake, get out of here and go to a doctor?"

"I don't need a doctor," he answered, taking the lantern out of his mouth, but without ungritting his teeth. "My leg is fine. Just give me a minute."

"I'll give you a minute. Get down and rest."

Stephen did and, under his breath, cursed his weakness.

"Forget the room," Leslie said, kneeling beside him in the snow. "It's your leg that matters, your leg and getting away before they find you."

"Spoken just like a woman," Stephen said. "Always caring."

"Somebody has to care about you. *You* won't."

"Have I ever told you I love you?"

"Stop it. Be serious."

"I am serious," Stephen said. "It's not just the room that keeps me here, it's you. I can't go off and leave you trapped."

"Trapped? But I'm not trapped."

"You are and you don't know it. If I left you you'd marry George. You don't want him. You want to be rid of him, but you don't know how to escape. George, his mother and your uncle—they'll make you marry him. You're trapped here, Leslie, unless I take you away."

"I am not. I am the master of my own fate—"

Stephen shook his head. "You are trapped. You are the damsel in distress, the princess in the castle, forced to marry the ogre for the sake of—God only knows; perhaps your sense of obligation. And I am here to rescue you."

Leslie lifted her chin. "There are times, Stephen, when I don't know if you know yourself. I am not a damsel, let alone a damsel in distress. And I am not in need of rescuing, whether you think so or not. I can take care of myself and my own fortunes very well, thank you. In fact, my late concerns have been and are with you and your ability to manage your own fortunes. If you had any sense of your own peril, you would have been gone from here five hours ago."

Stephen pulled himself to his feet. "Very well, I thank you for your concern." He slipped the lantern handle over his arm and clasped the sides of the ladder with his mittened hands. He gripped hard and lifted his strong foot.

"Stephen, you don't listen to me."

"Yes, I do, but I'm going to find out about that room."

"You can't climb that ladder."

"Yes, I can. I climbed it to the loft this morning."

"That wasn't anywhere near as high, and you were stronger then. This would take you half the night."

"I will still climb it."

Leslie put her mittened hand on his, looked up at the high window overhead and back to Stephen. "Please," she said, "give me the lantern. Let me go in your place."

Stephen shook his head, smiling. "Leslie, you're crazy. You can't climb ladders. You'll get dizzy and fall."

"No, I won't. I'll hang on very tight."

"It's too high. You'll be scared to death."

"I'll close my eyes. I won't look down."

"Leslie, you can't be serious."

Leslie nodded and the tears came. "Yes, I am," she said. "Because you're sick and I love you."

CHAPTER FIFTY-ONE

Stephen touched her cheek with his mittened hand. "Oh, my darling," he said, and pulled her to him for a kiss. It was a gentle, sealing kiss, one that promised himself, and it was more affecting to Leslie than any of the others, ardent and stirring though they had been.

Leslie, however, did not let herself be carried away. Though she warmed to Stephen's embrace and took full measure of his kiss, she knew what she wanted, and when they drew apart she had in her hand the box of matches he had tucked in his pocket. More than that, though she had never climbed a second-story ladder and quailed at the thought, she had one foot on the bottom rung. Stephen would be so feeble climbing the ladder she could not bear to let him try. "Dearest," she said, "let me lead the way."

"Lead the way where?"

Leslie rose to the first rung and climbed to the second, escaping Stephen's grip. "I'll go up to the room first and you follow."

He was startled. "It's dark. You can't—"

"I've got matches!" Leslie showed him the box and tucked it in her pocket as she climbed higher.

"You vixen." Stephen tried to come after, but his leg buckled and he almost fell.

Leslie moved farther up the ladder. She had not climbed so high before. Women never did *anything*, she thought in frustration. Boys climbed trees, jumped fences, swam, threw balls, got themselves conditioned to a life of action. Girls stayed home and played with dolls, learned to sew and cook, and never lifted anything heavier than a bag of groceries, or ran for anything more than a departing horsecar. If she had been climbing ladders since she was ten, she would think nothing of being this high off the ground.

She held on tight and fought back panic. She made herself look at the window above and mechanically move toward it, and she did not look down again until she had reached the ledge. When she did, it was with relief and to concern herself with Stephen's situation. He was way below. It was doubtful that he had risen another rung.

She turned to the window before her. There was a twelve-inch gap between sash and sill, letting in the winter air. The door was locked, and so, she was certain, were the other windows. The room had been sealed off from the rest of the world except for this one, inexplicable opening. It was the one entrance no one expected would be used.

Leslie put her gloved hands under the sash and the window raised easily. She pushed it to the top and looked inside. The dark beyond was like a wall, but Leslie was not daunted. Perhaps there would be forgotten oil lamps her matches could light.

Without thinking further, she climbed over the sill and, in a moment, was safely inside, leaning out to wave down at Stephen below. Then she turned to face the room itself.

The darkness that surrounded her was far different from the night outside. There, she had enjoyed the dim glow of the post light. Here, it was Stygian and there was nothing at all to see.

She stayed for a moment, just inside the window, trying to sense her surroundings. It was a frozen room and nothing could live in it; yet, as she stood there, she began to sense an aura around her, something that frightened her. Queenie had said a man had been murdered in that room, that the walls were stained with blood. Stephen said it was not so, that no one had been murdered at all. Then, what was there about the room that made her afraid to grope her way one step from the window? What made her want to get back on the ladder again?

Staying close to the window, Leslie pulled out matches, selected one of the sturdy, phosphorus-tipped sticks, struck it and held its flame high.

There was a cold, empty fireplace, a table with a couple of chairs close at hand. Off to the left, the rest of the room faded into a dark blur, but Leslie had seen what she needed. A kerosene lamp was on the table.

She struck a second match to light it, then held it aloft to look around. Still the shadows were deep and dark, moving as she moved, like mounting terrors on the wall.

A larger lamp stood on a nearby bureau which had two drawers missing and which stood like an empty relic. Leslie lighted that lamp as well and now could see quite clearly.

She turned with growing boldness to assess her surroundings. What she saw, however, so filled her with horror that she gasped and nearly dropped her lamp.

The walls, as Queenie had warned, were covered with blood. Great stains splashed the furniture and large pools lay on the floor and rugs. Blood had soaked into the scattered papers that had become stuck to an open desk. Hardly a thing had escaped the ugly telltale splotches. The room had been the scene of a most hideous crime, and Leslie trembled in its middle.

Slowly, holding herself under tight control, she advanced farther. A large double bed protruded from the far wall supporting a bulky, shapeless mass which lay on the mattress under a large white bedspread. It looked to be a collection of objects heaped on the bed with a covering over them to keep out dust. The bloodstained papers on the desk promised the best clues to the mystery surrounding the Barrett family, but the pile on the bed drew Leslie's attention more strongly.

She went to the bedside and held the lamp high as she raised the corner of the spread. First she uncovered a wooden drawer from the bureau that contained a tumble of men's shirts. There was, on the other side of the bed, a drawer of underclothes and, between them, a dark, flowery pillow lying on top of something else. Leslie folded back the spread, leaving the drawers half exposed and leaned forward to see what was under the pillow. She lifted it away and found herself staring into the sightless eyes and ashen face of a gray-haired corpse.

Leslie screamed!

CHAPTER FIFTY-TWO

Long after the echoes of her scream had died away, Leslie remained in frozen horror, the lamp shaking in her hand. She had never seen a dead man before and the shock and terror of the experience left her flesh acrawl and her heart in her throat.

Her first urge was to flee the frightening room, and her feet had carried her to the window before she had a chance to think a second time. She paused, however, upon reaching the sill. Should she run like a frightened child because she had seen a body? What would Stephen think? She had climbed into the room in his place. He would not flee in terror, so neither could she. Below, on the ladder, he was struggling slowly, but he had more than half the distance to go. If she would help him, she must put aside her fears.

Leslie forced herself back to the bed to look again at the dead man's face, wincing at first, then making herself approach closer. It was the face of a rugged man, seamed and strong. It was obvious that this room had seen him murdered, but the injuries that had killed him were hidden under the bedspread and other pillows that had been placed over the body.

Leslie wondered who the man was and how long he had been dead. There was no way to tell, for the open window kept the room at outside temperature and the body had long been frozen solid. For all Leslie knew, it had lain there since winter began, stretched on a bed in a freezing room, covered with pillows, flanked by drawers to disguise its shape, the whole thing covered with a bedspread and left there, behind a locked door. And it could remain like that without change until the spring thaws.

And Uncle Walter, Queenie, and George knew it was there. They had, in all certainty, put it there. They had killed the man, probably with a shotgun because of all the blood, laid him out and locked the door—and then what?

What about the servants? How did one keep such secrets from servants? And then Leslie knew why the whole staff was new. Sometime before Christmas, Queenie had dismissed every servant they'd had and hired all new help. And it wasn't because there was a thief in the house at all. It was because Queenie and George and Uncle Walter had committed a murder.

Who was the victim? What was he doing in the house? Leslie began to get a very scary feeling about the answer. A thought was starting to grow, but she didn't want it to, for it frightened her too much.

She left the bedside and went to the desk and its bloodstained papers. She set her lamp beside them and unstuck their bloody pages. The papers were few and scattered and in Uncle Walter's handwriting. The top two sheets were of parchment and had an impressive, legal look. It was to these that Leslie devoted her attention. There were bloodstains on them both, but they did not blot out the writing.

The first paper was a will, drawn up by the Chicago legal firm of Bentley and Mason and at the bottom it bore the bold, heavy signature of her Uncle Walter. The date at the top was December 5, 1876, and it brought forth to Leslie the unbidden recollection that it was the following night that her mother had died, and the day after that that she had sent him the news.

The will itself was handwritten in careful, legible script and started in the customary way: "I, Walter Barrett, being of sound mind and body—" What came next, however, caused Leslie to gasp. "—having caught my wife, Queenie," it went on, "with one Leonard James, a lover of long standing, do hereby draw up the following will and testament, which supersedes all other wills and testaments."

Leonard James! So that was where the name came from? And Queenie? Long-time lovers, and Uncle Walter had found them out? Leslie returned to the will. Uncle Walter went through various legal phrases or, rather, his lawyer did, specifying that Queenie and all her heirs and assignees were cut out of the will and were in no way to share in the proceeds of Walter Barrett's estate. After cutting Queenie out, the will then said in unmistakable fashion: "Therefore, I do will and bequeath all my worldly goods to my sister, Mary Barrett Marsh, and her heirs and assignees." The will went on to stress once more that, under no circumstances was Queenie Barrett or her son, George Trowbridge, to receive a penny from the estate. Everything went to Mary, and Mary's heirs.

Which, Leslie thought, frowning over the document, now meant that everything Uncle Walter owned went to her, or would go to her upon his death.

And Uncle Walter *was* dead. Leslie knew it with sudden certainty. It was Uncle Walter's body that lay frozen on the bed, waiting to be thawed and "discovered" as "recently killed" at some propitious future time. And who had been her pseudo-Uncle Walter, the Uncle Walter who worked at a desk filled with the business papers of a Leonard James? The answer was frighteningly obvious.

Leslie snatched up the other legal document. It bore the same December 5 date and had been drawn up at the same time. It was brief and blunt. Walter Barrett was giving Queenie Barrett and her son, George Trowbridge, until December 12, 1876, to pack their belongings and get out. When Walter Barrett returned to the house on December 13, he expected it to be empty of all save his dog, Blenham, who should be left well watered and fed. If the conditions of the ultimatum were properly met, Walter Barrett would pay, through his attorneys, Richard Bentley and Robert

Mason, the sum of ten thousand dollars. This sum would be payable upon word from Walter Barrett to the firm that the conditions had been met. If the conditions had not been met, no monies would be forthcoming.

Leslie did not have to skim the rest of the document to know the conditions had not been met. George and Queenie—and Leonard James—had not moved out, bag and baggage. They had got rid of the servants, but they had waited, themselves, for Uncle Walter's return.

Despite the new will that cut them off, and despite the offer of ten thousand dollars to speed them on their way, Queenie and George and Leonard had stayed behind. They had given up the ten thousand dollars to lie in wait and kill Uncle Walter.

And they tried to kill his dog! Suddenly Leslie knew why a crippled animal came back as soon as it was able and howled in the night.

She shuddered in horror. She had come into the clutches of beasts far worse than the one whose howling they feared. But why had they not taken the ten thousand dollars and been grateful for Uncle Walter's generosity? Why did they stay and kill him instead?

And why on earth did they write and summon her to Fletcher after they had killed him? Why did they forge his signature to a letter, luring her into this trap?

And then, because she was not used to the fact, the answer only slowly dawned upon her. Everything he owned had been left, not to them, but to *her*.

And it was at that moment of realization, when she looked up in shock and turned around, that she saw she was not alone. Standing near the bed, blocking her from the doorway, dressed in nightclothes ill-fitted for the freezing room, stood a very solemn George, Queenie and Leonard. And George had Stephen's gun.

CHAPTER FIFTY-THREE

Leslie, at sight of the frightening trio, let out a startled shriek. She had been so engrossed in her discoveries she had never heard the key in the lock of the far-off door, had not heard the three murderers enter near the bed. Now she was trapped in the front part of the room at the desk by the open window. They faced her like horsemen of the Apocalypse, filling the gap between the foot of the bed and the corner that hid the door, and Leslie knew she could expect no mercy.

It was Queenie who spoke. "You're quite a shrieker," she said. "You shriek when you see us, but it's nothing like the scream that woke us. Pray, what did you see then?"

Leslie did not have to answer. She knew Queenie had already observed the drawn-back coverlet and the dead face it exposed. An attempt to dissemble was useless. There was nothing she could do to save herself.

Her thoughts went to Stephen, struggling on the ladder outside. They did not know about him. If he, in innocence, reached the sill, he would be seen and seized and there would be two new bodies to lay beside Uncle Walter's instead of one. If she could not save herself, perhaps she could save him. Leslie, facing the trio, tried to speak clearly from near the open window so that Stephen would be sure to hear.

"Yes, Queenie," she said, "I will tell you what made me scream before. It was the body lying on the bed beside you. That's my real Uncle Walter, isn't it?"

"That's—?" Queenie replied, finding herself at a loss.

"That man you've told me is Uncle Walter is really Leonard James. That's his name, isn't it, Queenie? Leonard James, your lover. And you killed my uncle when he found you out, didn't you?"

Queenie swallowed and tried to collect her thoughts.

Leslie didn't wait for an answer. "Here's Uncle Walter's new will," she said, indicating the paper on the desk. "It cuts you out because you cheated on my uncle. And here's the other paper my uncle signed." She indicated the one she still held. "It says he'll

246

pay you ten thousand dollars to be off his property and out of his life by last December twelfth. But you aren't off his property, because you killed him. You and George and Leonard James, the three of you, all standing there, and George has Stephen Crawford's gun. George thinks he's going to shoot more people. He shot Uncle Walter, didn't he? And he tried to kill Uncle Walter's dog. Except he only wounded him and the dog came back. And then he took Stephen's gun and tried to kill Stephen with it—"

George leaned forward, his face contorted. "How do you know that?"

It was a slip and Queenie's pounce was almost as fast. "Yes, how did you know that? Where is Stephen?"

Leslie tried to put them off. "You did want to kill him! I knew it," she said. "You didn't want to kill a dog last night, George, you wanted to kill Stephen. Why? What did you think he knew?"

"He was a spy," George snarled, defensively. "That's all we had to know."

But Queenie homed in. "And you know where he is," she said menacingly.

"What were you afraid he would find out?" Leslie said, desperately stalling for time. "Was it that you killed Uncle Walter? Or was it that you'd brought me out here to marry George?"

"Dearie," Queenie said, "we didn't bring you out here for that. We—"

"Of course you did. Uncle Walter cut you out of his will and threw you out, Queenie, because he caught you with Leonard. That's what happened, isn't it? He went away on a trip, but he came home unexpectedly, and Leonard was here. Wasn't he?"

Queenie's eyes were red coals, and the man Leslie pointed her finger at blanched. George said defensively, "It was his own fault. He wasn't supposed to come home till the thirteenth."

Queenie said to him, "Shut your fat mouth. Let her talk."

Leslie kept talking. It kept them from acting. "He stopped by unexpectedly. It would have been December fourth. And Leonard was here. And he saw a lawyer on the fifth and changed his will and gave you till the twelfth to get out. Then he went away on business again.

"He'd give you ten thousand dollars if you were gone when he got back. But you didn't go. You waited for him and killed him instead. Why? That's what I don't understand. Why didn't you take the money? You couldn't touch anything else he had, except the cash he had on hand or jewelry you could sell."

"It's not like that," George said. "We didn't want to hurt him."

Queenie's flashing eyes abated. She smiled. "You have it wrong, dearie. I mean, you're right about Leonard. But Leonard and I—" She patted the man's arm. "We've been close for many years. Since shortly after I was widowed."

"He's a house-to-house salesman?"

Queenie nodded. "That's how we met. I was in a house. A long time ago."

"And he didn't go to Colorado last month. He went selling!"

"He's got to keep in touch with his customers."

"And George?"

"He was not yet a man when it started, but we taught him a few things." Queenie even smiled. "I wasn't cheating on your Uncle Walter. Not really. Leonard was my beau long before I met your uncle. And your Uncle Walter was a fine man, Leslie. I had a lot of admiration for him. But he was not meant to be a husband. He was a promoter, developer, adventurer, but not a lover. He could have had me completely had he been something else. But if he had been something else, he would not have had the money and I could not have afforded to marry him any more than I could afford to marry Leonard. It's a complex world, Leslie, far more complex than you have yet learned." Her smile was becoming unctuous. "But let us forget about this room and about your Uncle Walter. He died, but we did not kill him."

"You didn't kill him?"

Queenie shook her head. "It was his heart. He returned and collapsed and we put him here—"

Leslie could not believe what she was hearing. "Queenie, you lie! His blood is all over the walls."

248

"That's not *his* blood, dearie. I told you another man was murdered here. Why would we want to harm your uncle? To do that would be to lose the ten thousand dollars he was going to pay us."

Leslie wished she could believe. She wished she could learn that the people before her were not guilty of such a crime. But the truth came through to her, unbidden, and she had to speak it. "Oh, no," she said. "That's the way it started, but not the way it ended. You packed to leave and you fired the servants. You were going to take the ten thousand and make the best of it. But then you got my telegram saying that my mother had died. And then you realized that my mother was no longer the heiress to his estate. *I* was.

"And it occurred to you that if George married me, you could have Uncle Walter's whole estate and not just a paltry ten thousand dollars. So you killed him and brought me here to marry George. And once that happened, then Uncle Walter's body would come to light somewhere, and only *I* would know that there had been an imposter. Only *I* could testify against you, but a wife can't testify against her husband—and maybe the wife wouldn't be alive to testify against anyone. I would be gone and Uncle Walter would be gone, and you three would have his whole estate."

George said, "It only started like that, Leslie. But you came here and I didn't just pretend. I really fell in love with you."

Queenie said, "It's too bad you had to come into this room. It could have worked out very well."

George said, "It still can. Leslie can still marry me—"

"It's too late, you fool," Queenie snapped.

"But she can't testify against her husband." He turned. "Leslie, if you'll marry me—"

"Be quiet," Queenie said and turned to Leslie. "If you had behaved, we would have let you live. Originally, we would have been satisfied with the marriage and seen to it that you did not return from your honeymoon, and that your uncle's body was found in between. However, in deference to George's inexplicable craving for you, we would have let you live, had you been willing to co-operate."

"She still can," George said. "Tell them you'll co-operate, Leslie."

"Forget it," Queenie said. "It's all over."

"But we can't get any money without Leslie," George protested.

"It's all over, I said," Queenie reiterated bitterly. "We had big hopes but they've been blown to pieces. Now it's only a matter of survival. We've got to cut and run; the gold mine has run out. We'll have to pack it in and look for another." She said to Leslie, "But when you leave a lode, you make sure nobody else can get any good out of it. You make sure nothing you leave behind can hurt you. And I'm talking about *you*, Leslie."

"Yes, but—" Leslie's knees began to quake inside her boots. Conversation had run its course and the time had come for action. "Look," she said, "if you want me to marry George—"

Leslie thought she saw a widening glint of hope in George's eye, but Queenie said, with finality, "It's too late for that." She signaled the young man holding the gun. "All right, George."

CHAPTER FIFTY-FOUR

Leslie shrank against the desk, her eyes wide. The gun George held rose up and aimed at her dead center, and the distance was no more than seven feet.

She wanted to cry, to beg, to plead. She wanted to fall on her knees in supplication, but she could not move. So she stared and trembled and looked into the muzzle of the near-pointed gun, waiting for the explosion that would end her life.

The moments dragged and it did not come. It was as if George were relishing the torment, as if he wanted her to scream some more. "For God's sake," she cried in anguish, "what are you waiting for? Shoot!"

The muzzle wavered and she looked at the face above the gun. It was wretched and tormented and turning toward its mother. "Ma," he said, nearly as distraught as Leslie, "we can still get married."

"Stop it, you fool," Queenie snapped. "Can't you see she knows too much?"

"We can take her with us. If we're married, she can't testify against me—"

"Give me that gun," Queenie ordered, seizing it from his hand. "If you're afraid—"

"No, Ma." He tried to get it back again. They wrestled.

Queenie said, "Give it to me!"

"Ma, please don't kill her."

"I said, give it to me!"

At that moment, Stephen Crawford threw himself over the windowsill and into the room beside Leslie. His momentum scattered the table and chairs by the fireplace and, as he rolled over on the floor, Leslie saw that he was holding a small black gun.

Queenie, still struggling with George, saw it too. She screamed and her own gun roared. She freed it from George's grip and fired point-blank at Leslie. She would have turned it next on Stephen, but he was on his knees with his own weapon pointed. "Drop it, Queenie," he ordered, "or I'll kill you."

The impact of Queenie's bullet hit Leslie in the chest so hard it knocked her to the floor and she lay there stunned and stricken, only dimly aware that Queenie, at Stephen's order, had dropped her gun. It lay on the rug beside George, who had sunk to his knees.

"Kick the gun over here," Stephen said, and Leslie saw Leonard's foot give it a shove. Leslie raised her eyes then to Queenie's face. The orange-haired woman did not wear a gloating expression. She was ashen and her mouth was sagging.

Leslie felt a heavy, throbbing pain in her chest and she wondered if she were dying. Beside her, Stephen snatched up the gun

Queenie had used and dropped the other. It clattered beside her and she saw that it wasn't a real gun at all. It had been whittled out of wood and darkened with lampblack from the lantern in the barn.

Then Stephen had her in his arms, his gun keeping the others at bay. "My darling," he whispered, "where are you hurt? Where did she hit you?" He was looking for a telltale stain of blood.

"My chest," she said, wondering that he could not tell.

"My God!" He saw the hole in her blouse, grabbed the material and ripped it wide open. "My God," he said again and Leslie looked. The bullet had not touched her. Instead, its silvery metal form lay half buried in the gold nugget that her dead Uncle Walter had given her, while around the nugget an ugly purple bruise had formed.

"Thank the Lord," Stephen said and clutched her close with his free hand while, across from them, Leonard and Queenie stood staring.

Then George fell onto his side and a bright-red stain was spreading across the front of his robe.

Queenie's face contorted at the sight. "George!" she screamed and knelt beside him. "Oh, no, George."

Leslie, her own pain forgotten, sat up in dismay. "Oh, George." No matter what he had done, she could not wish him this. She moved quickly beside him too. "Let me see."

George shook his head and clutched the edges of his robe together. "It's all right," he said. "It doesn't hurt."

"No, but—" Leslie turned to Stephen, who with the help of a chair was struggling to his feet.

"Get Swift," Stephen said huskily. "Tell him to hitch Dandy fast. We've got to get him to the doctor. Then get blankets—"

"No," George said. "Don't go. It's no use." He reached for Leslie's hand with his own bloodied one. "Leslie."

"Yes, George."

"I really—did—love you. I was—to—marry you—for the money. But then—I—fell in love."

"Yes, George."

"I—wanted you— to know—that."

"I did, George. I could tell."

His voice was very weak. "I—wouldn't—have let—them—kill you."

"I know you wouldn't, George."

His eyes were closed now. He took a breath and stopped. The stain on his robe was enormous and blood was soaking into the carpet. Leslie bent over him and wept. Queenie shook him once and leaned closer. "George," she cried at him, "you can't die! You can't die!"

Leslie rose slowly, leaving George to his mother's tears. Leonard stood like a marble statue by the bed and Stephen was erect by the bureau, his gun held firmly. "Get Swift," he said to Leslie again. "Tell him to hitch the sleigh. We've got to take these two to the sheriff."

Leslie nodded obediently and went around the corner, out the door.

As she started for the stairs, Queenie was shrieking, "I did it for you, George. It was all for you!" And Leonard was saying, "She did it. It was all her idea! I didn't want any part of it. She made me. She made all of us."

CHAPTER FIFTY-FIVE

It was three o'clock in the morning by the time Queenie and Leonard were safely delivered to a sleepy-eyed sheriff who grew rapidly awake at the tale he heard. Queenie was stunned and numb with shock, but Leonard was voluble and could not stop talking until he had answered all questions, volunteered what he was not asked, and bared his soul, all the while protesting he had never wanted to play the role of Leslie's uncle, that he knew it would never work.

For a moment, while the sheriff was putting the couple into a pair of jail cells at the rear of his house, Leslie and Stephen were alone on the couch in his parlor. She leaned a head against his shoulder in fatigue while he put an arm around her and kissed her hair. He hugged her tighter and said, "Ouch."

Leslie lifted her head quickly. "Your leg! Your poor leg. We've got to get you to the doctor's as soon as we can."

"After the sheriff lets us go, but it's feeling better all the time. You're the one I'm worried about. You're exhausted. You've climbed ladders, you were shot at; you were only saved by a miracle—by a golden nugget."

"I think Uncle Walter worked it that way," she said. "He wasn't going to let Queenie do to me what she'd done to him."

Stephen smiled. "You think he put that nugget in the way of the bullet?"

"It's *his* nugget. I think he did. And I think he tried to tell me he was in that room. For no reason I kept having nightmares about it."

"And I suppose you're going to tell me he made the dog howl?"

"You don't believe in such things?"

Stephen shrugged. "I don't know about such things. I wouldn't even try to guess."

"But the dog did call to me and lead me to you. He did save your life." She sat up. "Stephen, we've got to rescue that dog."

"We will," he assured her. "He's coming to trust me. We'll lure him home."

"You know something, when he got into the barn with Brindle, I think she reared in joy, not fear. The nail that caught her was up at the front of the stall, not the back."

"It will all be taken care of, don't you worry. You need to rest."

"I'm all right," Leslie said. "I'm just sad. I feel sorry for everybody—for Uncle Walter, for George, even for Queenie and Leonard. And it's all because my mother died and I sent

Uncle Walter a telegram he never got. They got it instead and decided to kill him. I wish it had never happened." She looked at Stephen quickly. "Except for you. I'd never have found you."

"Nor I, you." He kissed her lips tenderly. Then he told her his plans. They and Swift would go to an inn for the rest of the night, see the doctor in the morning, and return to the house. The sheriff and funeral directors would come and take care of the contents of the locked room. Then, in the afternoon, a minister would appear and they would be married.

Leslie gasped. "You can't be serious. Tomorrow—today?"

Stephen laughed and lifted her hands for a kiss. "My dearest, think of you alone in that house unchaperoned—the male servants—!"

"Oh, that house. I wish I didn't ever have to go back."

"You have to. You can't leave the dog, you know. Besides, it's yours now. It's your responsibility, and so are the servants. You're a very rich young woman if you haven't come to realize it."

"I don't feel rich," Leslie sighed. "I don't even have money to pay for the inn."

Stephen laughed. "I have money. Remember, valeting isn't my true occupation. We get married today, we spend the weekend at the house, then we go to Chicago and see your uncle's lawyers about the will, and I explain things to my family, and after that we'll take a long honeymoon. Have you ever seen Niagara Falls?"

Leslie shook her sleepy head and laid it, smiling, back against Stephen's shoulder. "No, dearest, but I'd love to—if it's with you."